M000209773

GRAY AFTER
DARK

NOELLE W. IHLI

Published 2024 by Dynamite Books

www.dynamitebookspublishing.com

© Noelle West Ihli

All rights reserved. No part of this publication may be reproduced, distributed, or transmitted in any form or by any means, including photocopying, recording, or other electronic or mechanical methods, without the prior written permission of Dynamite Books, except in the case of brief quotations embodied in critical reviews and certain other noncommercial uses permitted by copyright law. For permission requests, write to the publisher, addressed "Attention: Permissions Coordinator," at info@dynamitebookspublishing.com

Any references to historical events, real people, or real places are used fictitiously. Names, characters, and places are products of the author's imagination.

ISBN: 979-8-9878455-7-8

First printing, March 2024

Cover design by Lisa Amoroso
Cover images: cabin © Larry Lynch/iStock; mountain landscape © Roksana Bashyrova/iStock; fog © Balakleypb/iStock

PRAISE FOR GRAY AFTER DARK

"Noelle W. Ihli has established herself as queen of the survival thriller. Every one of her novels delivers heart-thumping suspense, nonstop action, and heroines you root for—and *Gray After Dark* is her best work yet."
-Faith Gardner, author of *The Prediction*

"*Gray After Dark* is impossible to put down. It's thrilling, twisty, and utterly addictive, with characters I was immediately invested in."
-Steph Nelson, author of *The Final Scene*

Gray After Dark is a no-holds-barred, gut punch of a book that had me gritting my teeth as I read. With a crackling plot, an epic setting, and characters who are both compelling and brutal, this remarkable tale of survival is one I won't soon forget.
-Caleb Stephens, award-winning author of *The Girls in the Cabin*

"*Gray After Dark* cements Ihli as a master of the suspenseful thriller, once again showcasing her ability to navigate heartstopping suspense and heartbreaking emotion in equal measure. The vast Frank Church wilderness, as much a character as the complex cast, provides a perfect setting for this gripping tale of resilience and determination. You won't be able to put this one down and, even if you survive the soul-stirring finale, the story will never let you go.
-Brett Mitchell Kent, author of *Whispers of Apple Blossoms*

"Hands down, my new favorite Noelle W. Ihli book. It had me biting my nails from start to finish in the best kind of way."
-SavvyyReads

Content advisory: This book includes references to pregnancy loss, infertility, domestic abuse, sexual violence, and gun violence.

For Kari and Alan.

MILEY

I pressed my body tighter against the trunk of the big Douglas fir and listened.

The lodgepole pines surrounding the cabin creaked in the chilly breeze, whispering a warning. The underbrush rustled, hinting at creatures seen and unseen. Some hunters. Some prey. Some both.

No footsteps. No voices.

What was taking so long?

The sky had settled into early dusk the color of a bruised plum. Still milky indigo at the edges, but shriveling fast. I had maybe an hour until it was fully dark. Already, the round moon peeping into view above the treeline felt like a spotlight, daring me to step into the open. Take my chances and run before they realized what was happening.

Not yet. This was my last shot. I knew that in my bones.

If I wasted it, we all died tonight.

I shivered hard in the thin, long-sleeved dress that rustled whenever I moved an inch. The stiff, ugly fabric should have at least kept me warm. Instead, it seemed to absorb the chill, drawing it close to my skin. The mountain air turned crisp the minute the sun slipped behind the nearest ridge. In a few hours, it would dip near freezing.

By then, I'd be gone.

Either tearing through the forest at a dead run—or just plain dead.

It took everything in me not to sink down beside the enormous tree. Close my eyes, just for a minute. But if I did that, my leg muscles would cool too much, making it so I couldn't run when it was time.

I couldn't let that happen.

This was the closest I'd been to escape since they'd brought me here. I'd imagined this moment so many times. The adrenaline, the dizzy desperation, the terror. Never the raw hesitation rooting my stocking feet to the forest floor.

I stared at the tree trunk, eyes blurring in and out of focus as I traced the pattern of the bark. *Just breathe,* I reminded myself. *Just listen. Just wait. Then run.*

In, two, three, four ... I tucked my face into the neck of my dress to hide the warm exhale, a white cloud that might easily announce my location to scanning eyes. *Out, two, three, four.*

Where were the men? What the hell was taking so long?

I squeezed my eyes shut and focused on counting my breaths to calm my pounding heart. Just a little longer.

Bam.

My eyes flew open at the sound of the cabin door, followed by footsteps.

"Ruthie Sue!" Hamish bellowed. His angry voice was distant, and I imagined him standing on the front porch. I shouldn't look. If he was staring in my direction across the clearing, he'd see the movement.

If Fred had the scope out, he'd definitely see me.

I forced down the adrenaline begging me to tear through the treeline. I breathed into my shoulder again, trying to hide that white cloud.

Fred's voice cut through the silence, a little lower, a little meaner. "Ruthie Sue!" he yelled alongside Hamish like I was a dog that would come running. "Told you she weren't tamed," he spat.

"We'll find her," Hamish said calmly.

I knew that tone. And it scared me more than if he'd raged.

Pine needles crunched beneath heavy footfalls. They were crossing the clearing, heading my way now.

I fought to keep my breaths steady and even, even as terror wrapped its hands tighter around my throat, turning the blood in my veins to ice water.

"Ruthie Sue," Fred crooned, switching tactics. "You'll die out here if you run," he added, just as sweetly.

I gritted my teeth. I'd been their pet for months, but they didn't know a thing about me.

I carefully leaned forward a few inches so I could get eyes on them. I had to know exactly where they were.

The quick glance showed familiar, unkempt beards. Heavy coats. Thick boots. Shotguns at their sides. They were maybe fifty yards away, moving fast in my direction.

If either of them looked directly at the Douglas fir, they'd see me, too.

The thinner shadow, Hamish, stopped near the water pump and whispered something I couldn't hear.

I took a step out from behind the tree.

It was now or never.

PART 1

THREE MONTHS EARLIER

1

MILEY

My feet pounded hardpack dirt on the old logging road.

I tried to focus on their cadence, on the dense forest whirring past, on the sour taste in my mouth from the morning's coffee.

But I couldn't help it. I was thinking about my shoulder. It throbbed with every footfall.

"It's all in your head," I hissed between breaths. That's what Sara, my sports psychologist, had said. More or less, anyway. She couched it in medical lingo like *non-pathological, guilt complex,* and *trauma.* What it boiled down to was that my central nervous system was lying to me. Shooting phantom pain where my shoulder had been dislocated and my arm broken in the accident years ago. It felt pretty damn real, though. Sara had referred me to a therapist in Boise, but I still hadn't called him.

I didn't need to dredge up old memories. What I needed was to reach the podium at the Milano Cortino Olympics in 2026. I had three and a half years to get back on track. Make my body the finely tuned machine it had been before.

Make all the pain worth it.

To be fair, I'd come a long way. My run times were still abysmal, but my stamina was improving. If it wasn't for my damn shoulder, I'd feel pretty confident that I could whip my body into shape—eventually.

It'll pass, I told myself when the pain got bad, pretending I hadn't been repeating the same song for years. But if the pain wasn't real, I reasoned, it had to go away at some point.

My long braid swung faster, slapping my back as I picked up the pace on a flat stretch where the tall pines gave way to an open meadow. The blinding morning sun was a welcome change from the still-cool shadows. The late-spring days were hot here, but the mornings and nights were still chilly enough for a coat.

It was my first time in the Frank Church Wilderness, even though I'd been born and raised in Idaho. At over two million acres, it was the largest forest system in the US—although these early morning runs were the only time I'd get a chance to experience its majesty. Once the first guests arrived at Hidden Springs next week, I'd be spending most of my waking hours in the kitchen.

I was fine with that. The posh summer lodge and its bougie guests weren't really my speed. I was here to earn money and cross-train. Hidden Springs Resort had a short season, just four months from the end of June to October. But the dirty dishes and long days came with endless trails to run, so I'd be ready to hit full-time training hard in the fall. I wasn't going to be the weak link at the Italy Olympics, phantom pain be damned.

A bird sang brightly from behind where I'd left a thick snatch of pine trees. My shoulder throbbed harder, unwilling to be distracted.

Work with the pain, not against it, Sara had said so many times the meaning barely registered anymore. I tried. Swear to God I did, but on days like today, it felt like the pain just got worse.

The trail spooled back into the darkness of the tight pines, then rose sharply in an incline. I pushed myself faster, refusing to give in to the daggers spearing my rotator cuff. I'd mapped out this run the morning I arrived at Hidden Springs, after unloading my belongings in one of the tiny women's staff cabins at the resort. I'd hoped to take advantage of the "dead week" with some extra endurance runs. Instead, the owner had given me the longest tour on the planet. Jennifer had introduced me to what felt like every warm body within a ten-mile radius then dumped me right into kitchen training. I hadn't anticipated that there would be so much to learn about working behind the scenes. As far as I understood, I wouldn't be interacting with any of the guests directly. But there was a reason the guest lodge was rated so highly. Each task—including washing dishes—had rigorous protocols.

I glanced up at the mountain peaks still dotted with snow, thinking about how good an ice bath would feel on my tired muscles. I could hear the sound of gurgling water above my steady breaths and footfalls, but the river itself was still hidden from view in the thick forest.

According to the topographical map I'd scoured in the dark this morning, the river led to a small alpine lake just beyond the midpoint of my six-mile run. I hoped so, because I was dying to strip down and swim in the icy water. If I just pushed a little farther, that swim would be my reward for the punishing pace. I wouldn't have to worry about crossing paths with backpackers yet. The ground was still too spongy for camping after the spring snowmelt. So for now, I had the wilderness all to myself.

The trail took a sharp left into a crowded copse of aspens. As I came onto the straightaway, I saw a flurry of movement out of the corner of my eye.

An enormous great horned owl burst into flight right in front of me, shooting out of the brush to my left in a soundless flurry of wide gray wings.

I skidded to a stop just in time to avoid a collision, heart beating faster.

It landed on a branch barely ten feet away then swiveled its head to face me, making a low, throaty noise and puffing its feathers.

"Hi," I murmured, shoulder momentarily forgotten. "You're beautiful."

As I studied the magnificent bird, the smile slowly died on my lips. The first person I wanted to tell—the one person I couldn't tell —was Mom.

No matter how many deer or foxes or owls we came across hiking or skiing, she always got the same look on her face. Pure awe. Pure joy. Every single animal. Every single time. *Look, Miley,* she'd whisper. *Just look.*

I always teased her about it, even though it was one of my favorite things about her.

The fact that I'd never see that look again—and the fact that it was my fault—was an ache I knew would never go away.

My shoulder, which I'd almost forgotten about, pulsed poker hot, and I picked up my feet to continue the run. My patterned breathing had a new hitch to it, but it would disappear if I kept pushing through. It always did.

As I pushed forward, a strange sound made me stop in my tracks. A thin, soft cry that caused the sweaty baby hairs on the back of my neck to prickle.

It was coming from the brush the owl had just burst from.

The shadows among the blades of grass moved, and I recoiled.

A tiny rabbit, eyes half-open, fur matted red, lay stretched on its side.

Bile rose in my throat, and I cut my eyes back to the owl.

It sat perfectly still, eyes trained on me—and on the rabbit I'd forced it to abandon to a fate more gruesome than one more quick swipe of that razor-sharp, black beak.

"I'm sorry," I whispered, torn between the need to put the rabbit out of its misery and rushing away to leave the owl to its meal. If I scared the owl away, the bunny's death would be on my shoulders.

I already knew I couldn't handle that weight.

In, one, two, three, four. Out, one, two, three, four. I forced the awful image out of my mind, refusing to look back.

If I kept moving forward long enough, kept breathing in and out, the sick feeling in my stomach would pass.

When I reached the midpoint of the run, I pushed myself to continue instead of stopping to stretch. The alpine lake was just a quarter mile away, and I needed the icy shock of the water more than ever.

As I settled into the final stretch, I started working on my breath again, slowing my heart rate. It was the exact opposite of what my body wanted to do.

In a biathlon, this part of the race was called the cut. Instead of tennis shoes, I'd be wearing cross-country skis. And instead of a water flask strapped to my back, it'd be a rifle. If you didn't slow your heart rate enough before you reached each shooting checkpoint, your hands would be too jittery to get a clean shot.

It was almost impossible. *Almost.*

My event was the four-by-six kilometer mixed medley. You skied one leg of the course, dropped your poles, loaded your rifle, took position, aimed, shot, rebolted. Then rinse and repeat until you either made all five shots, or you ran out of ammo. If you waited to slow your breath until it was time to shoot, it was too late. And if you missed your shot, you got hit with a penalty lap.

Nobody thought I'd come back after the accident. Including me. When I announced I was training for Beijing just a few months after the accident—just a few weeks after missing my chance to compete at PyeongChang—there was no champagne and smiles. Just incredulous looks and plenty of "Are you sures" and "Good for yous." Deep down, I doubted myself, too. If it hadn't been for Brent, I probably would have tucked my tail between my legs and sunk back into the pain.

Not that the Beijing Olympics had been any kind of redemption trip. They were a total bust. But it was enough to make me mad. Made me determined. And that fire burned away the fog just enough for me to see what was still possible.

Keeping my running pace steady, I shifted into come-down mode. Instinctively, I surveyed the pine branches to see which way the wind was moving. *East.* If I had my rifle, I'd be calculating the adjustments I needed to make to my sight in order to accommodate the conditions.

When I reached the edge of the frigid lake, I came to a full stop and stood completely still, forcing my breath to comply with my demands. *In, one, two, three, four. Out, one, two, three, four. Slower. Slower.*

The lake itself was long and narrow, crowded by jagged peaks and boulder-strewn hillsides. It looked like a piece of cut glass, sharp and blinding in the light. The air here smelled like fresh pine needles and the musk of leaves ground into the mud and gritty sand at the shoreline. The forest was silent, except for the breeze moving through the trees and the burble of the river in the distance, where it met the lake.

I stayed where I was for a full twenty seconds.

Then, instead of picking up my imaginary weapon, I undressed and dove into the frigid water.

2

MILEY

BEIJING OLYMPICS

February, 2022

"An extra seven seconds to load your rifle and slow your breathing is nothing compared to a twenty-second penalty lap for missing your shot!" Brent barked. White gusts of air exploded out of his mouth with each exclamation. Tiny ice crystals had formed around his nose and mouth. He was still out of breath from his own race.

"I know," I muttered. "You don't have to say it. I already feel like shit." My shoulder was throbbing like hell, but I wouldn't make it my excuse. The pain was nothing compared to the way my insides had seized when I earned that penalty lap.

"It's not enough to feel like shit, Miles." He rubbed his chin with a white-and-blue gloved hand, brushing away a few of the ice crystals clinging to stubble.

I set my jaw. I'd expected a "Well, you tried," not a shakedown of my performance on the range. I couldn't believe he was coming at me like this. Like I was the same person I'd been before the accident.

It wasn't completely my fault we didn't place. But mostly.

Brent's bright green eyes, usually half-lidded, sparked with frustration. I always thought those eyes looked like emeralds against the snow, set next to his pale, wind-burned cheeks. His dark brown hair, which usually curled from under the trucker hat he wore like a second skin, clung to his forehead in sweat-slick strands that stuck out from beneath his black ski cap.

"You're the best shot I know, but you turned that whole race on its head because you wouldn't take the time to get clean shots off." He raised his thick eyebrows and bent down a little to lean his face nearer to mine, like whatever he was about to say was for my ears only. His rifle, still strapped to his back, moved with him like an extension of his body.

Instead of feeling comforted by the intimate gesture, fresh anger rose up in me. Brent was my teammate—and my best friend—but not my coach.

"Fine. Let's talk about your race for a hot second," I snapped, taking a step back from him. "You're the fastest skier on the team. You hit your shots. The race was a gimme—until those three guys passed you in the final stretch. All because you got emotional. Thought you had it in the bag, then you lost your shit and fell apart when it didn't happen that way."

Brent narrowed his eyes, but his face softened. Instantly, I felt bad for what I'd said. He just wanted to help me. I just wanted to hurt him. To take the pain in my chest—and my shoulder—and spread it around. "I don't want to argue," he said softly. "Yeah, I'm frustrated, but only because I know you're better than that. Just slow down for once in your life."

"You could speed up for once in *your* life," I shot back, but the ice in my voice had melted.

"Who's full of shit now?" he challenged with a raised eyebrow and a half-smile. "You just said I'm the fastest skier on the team."

I smiled back and pushed him away gently. "Not today, you weren't." His criticism still stung, but not like an injury. It hurt like a hard workout if you skipped too many days ... or weeks. Knowing he thought I could take the heat felt weirdly good. Like he knew I was still strong enough, beneath all the scar tissue. And I loved him for it.

Ever since the accident, everybody else had walked on eggshells around me. Like I'd fully shatter into a million pieces if they asked too much of me or said the wrong thing. It just made me shrink deeper into myself.

I held his gaze for a few long seconds until he grabbed my arm and pulled me toward the team cabin, past the finish area.

I didn't shrug away this time. I needed him on my team. Needed him to mourn this loss with me. We both felt terrible. We'd just lost our chance at the podium, and there wouldn't be another one for four years. It was my first Olympics, Brent's second. I knew how much he'd wanted to place today. Every bit as much as I had. He always raced the very last leg in our mixed-medley team. Our last hope when everything else went sideways—like it had today.

Biathlon was so volatile that an early lead could get shot to hell —literally—by teammates who missed too many shots on the range. Teammates like me.

The cross-country skiing portion of the race was important. You needed endurance, technique, and speed. But that's not where you won, or lost, a biathlon. The shooting portion of the sport had the potential to completely upend everything else, make it anyone's game.

I always ran the second leg in our medley. As much as I hated to admit it, Brent was right about my performance. I'd missed way too many shots. I rushed them—then got hit with a penalty lap that even Brent couldn't compensate for.

We settled into silence as we skied toward the team cabin. Despite the crowds and the media vans parked everywhere, the snow muted the sounds of cheering and controlled chaos as the other teams waited for the race results. I knew we should have stayed with the rest of the team at the finish area, but I couldn't be there right now. Not when I was the weak link. The one who had cost us our shot at victory.

I tried to focus on the fat snowflakes clinging to my eyelashes. The feeling of Brent's arm tucked tight into mine. The fierce, biting cold that numbed my cheeks. The enormous Wukesong Sports Center that looked like a winter wonderland. It was the kind of place you saw on holiday postcards with "Season's Greetings" emblazoned on the front.

We'd only made it a few yards toward the cabin when chaos erupted behind us, breaking the silence in a volley of whoops and cheers. We both startled and looked back at the finish area. That was the sound of Norway exploding in celebration over their big win.

"Damn Norway," I muttered, turning to face Brent and letting out a tiny smile.

"Damn Norway," Brent repeated, smiling wider.

As I shifted my weight, intending to continue toward the team cabin and lockers, his arm slipped down to my waist for a fraction of a second. I froze. This was new.

He pulled me closer to him, jostling my shoulder a little. It throbbed in time with my heart as it sped up by a few beats.

I looked down at his hand, then back up at those half-lidded green eyes and cocked my head. This gesture wasn't the kind of intimacy you got from a teammate—or a friend.

"Kinda feely for having just lost the Olympics," I joked, grasping for solid ground.

He pulled his arm away like I'd burned him, hurt flashing in his eyes. Before I could open my mouth to tell him that I was only kidding, but that my shoulder hurt like hell, he skied away. I stared at his retreating form shrouded in snow, then shook my head and followed him. Feelings ran high after any race. Especially a career-breaker like that.

I left him alone until we'd both showered and dressed. I didn't bother taking ibuprofen for my shoulder, knowing it wouldn't help. When I came up behind Brent in the lobby, waiting for the bus that would take us back to our hotel, he was staring out the window. He wore a solemn expression, and I knew without asking that he was replaying our race. Same as me.

"You okay?" I wove my arm through his and hip-checked him gently.

He blinked and shook his head. "Yeah. You?"

I nodded. "Sorry I rushed my shots. I'll work on it."

"Sorry I lost my shit at the finish line. I'll work on it." He cracked a smile, then held my gaze for a beat too long.

I looked away. Brent had always treated me like a sister, a buddy. But over the last few months, something had shifted between us —despite my persistent efforts to dig my heels into "just friends."

"You want to come up to my room for a nightcap later? An un-celebration?" he asked hopefully.

Usually, I'd say yes without any hesitation. For all I knew, he was inviting the rest of the team, too. But the way he said the words told me otherwise. The invitation felt weighty. Like he was asking about the possibility of more than a nightcap.

I looked over my shoulder as if I were trying to find someone. Anything to cut the sudden intensity between us. Anything to buy myself a few more seconds. A spark of the irritation I'd felt earlier bubbled to the surface, needling my gut like a pincushion. Why was he pushing this right now?

I didn't want things to change between us. I wasn't ready.

I shoved the annoyance down, telling myself he was just being sweet to make up for our fight. Making the most of the time we had together before I went back to Idaho and he went back to Denver. Then we'd meet up again in November to start training like usual. I just had to keep pretending everything was normal until then.

"What kind of nightcap?" I hedged. The words came out bouncier, more flirtatious than I'd meant them to. *Dammit.*

He shrugged. "Whiskey. That's what you always drink after you lose."

"After *we* lose," I clarified with a smirk, meeting his gaze again. "Don't you just want to hop in bed though?"

His eyebrows shot up to his hairline, and I could almost hear my words echoing in his head, twisting to a meaning much different than I'd intended.

My cheeks burned. "I mean, I want to go to *my* room and go to sleep. My shoulder is killing me." I patted him high on the shoulder, deciding it was a safe zone of touch. A silent nudge right back into the friend zone.

I picked up my gear and led the way toward the bus that had just pulled up, hoping he hadn't noticed the fact that my face was on fire.

I loved Brent. And I was honest enough with myself to know that I'd sleep with him in a heartbeat if he were just another pretty face. I didn't need a boyfriend, though.

Opening up your heart is messy—and risky. But keeping your heart locked is risky, too.

I sighed. That's what Mom told me once in high school. I knew why she said it. Her own marriage had ended in divorce two months before I was even born. She insisted she didn't regret a thing, because she got me out of the deal.

Her words sounded wise right up to the moment I learned that it didn't actually matter whether you kept your heart open or locked. Twisted metal and broken glass sliced through it either way. So did loss.

My heart was already a mess.

That was all I deserved.

3

MILEY

By the time I pulled my Wrangler into Hidden Spring's staff parking lot after my run, my legs felt like tubes of jelly. Part of it was the higher altitude, but I couldn't blame the mountains completely. I'd let my training regimen slip a little during the few short weeks I'd spent in Boise, getting ready to put Mom's house on the market.

The house had been sitting empty for way too long. As much as I hated to sell it, I couldn't take care of it properly with my training schedule. A family of skunks had moved in under the porch during my months-long absence for training, and the lawn was so crowded with spring dandelions that I actually gasped when I pulled into the driveway.

It was done, though. The house was sold, and I was here. That was what mattered.

I swung my legs out of the Jeep and headed for the staff cabins. To my surprise, the grassy field that separated the staff cabins from the main guest lodge was a hive of activity. Not what I imagined "dead week" would look like. Staffers darted back and forth carrying trays from the kitchen and setting up tables. Nobody had even been awake when I left for my run, and I'd only been gone a couple of hours. I frowned, wondering what I'd missed.

Wes Something—the only person I actually remembered from the previous day's introductions—spotted me and jogged over. He was wearing his green-and-white staff polo and name tag, which looked ridiculously buttoned-up paired with the shaggy blonde hair he wore flopped over in a deep side part. He wore wire-rimmed, aviator-style glasses that made his wide blue eyes look enormous. It was hard to tell how old he was—twenty-one, maybe? Definitely a couple of years younger than me. Probably still in college, like most of the other staffers here.

"Coming to the orientation breakfast?" he asked skeptically, looking me up and down. Not checking me out, at least I didn't think so. More like trying to understand why I was in a sports bra and running shorts. Why my hair was wet.

I made a face. "What? No. The schedule said ten."

He sighed and pushed up his glasses. "It *starts* at ten. But guess who gets to prep the breakfast?" He flashed a goofy grin and gestured to the other staffers. "You should probably put a shirt on, then report to Jennifer. And fast. She always acts like this staff breakfast is the event of the year."

I winced. Jennifer was the owner, and we'd hit it off when I applied to work in the kitchen back in February. But apparently Zoom-interview Miley didn't quite measure up to Actual Miley, and I was already on her bad side. Maybe it was the fact that I'd arrived wearing a crop top and running shorts instead of my staff uniform, but she'd been a ball of nerves and snappy comments ever since.

I hurried toward the staff cabins, and Wes fell into step beside me. "She'll calm down once the guests settle in," he said with a shrug. "Always does."

A staff member carrying an armful of white folding chairs struggled past us, huffing and puffing. I made a face. "We really have to set up our own welcome breakfast?"

Wes laughed good-naturedly. "I've never thought about it that way. But yeah, I guess so." He had a runner's long, lanky frame—but none of the sinewy muscle. In contrast to his bleach-blonde hair, his skin was a deep golden brown, like he'd spent his whole life outside, studying the world through those aviators.

"So ... you're the athlete?" he asked casually, and I forced myself not to react.

"Yep," I replied, not wanting to get into it. He wasn't the only person here who seemed to know who I was from the second I arrived. The attention used to flatter me, but now the recognition usually came with a look of pity that said, *I know all about what happened to you.*

"I played rec soccer in elementary school," he revealed unprompted. "But that's the last time I did anything remotely athletic. I love the outdoors. I'm kind of a plant nerd. But don't ask me to run a mile."

I laughed. "Don't worry, I won't ask." People always felt compelled to confess their lack of sportiness to me. Like it was a sin they needed absolution for.

He lingered near the women's cabins while I threw on my staff polo and wrinkled khaki shorts then hurried back outside.

"You didn't have to wait," I said. "You're going to get in trouble now, too."

He shrugged. "If we hurry, Jennifer won't even know we were late."

The smell of sizzling bacon and pancakes got stronger the closer we got to the lawn, making my stomach rumble—and making me wonder if I should have been helping the cook instead.

Too late now.

When we reached the nearest fold-up table lying on its side, we hefted it upright and opened the legs. "Were you on a run?" Wes asked, glancing at my shoes.

"Yeah, I found a trail I really like."

His eyes got big and he raised an eyebrow.

"What?" I asked, moving to the next table. Wes moved with me, pulled it off the ground so it teetered on its side, and wrenched the legs out from their clip. I did the same.

"Bears, that's what."

I gave him a look. "No bears in the Frank Church," I shot back, thinking I had one on him. Idaho had seen an influx of new blood in the past few years, many of them city dwellers who arrived thinking that every stand of trees in the gem state had a bear behind it. "I thought you said you'd been here before," I teased him. Mom and I hiked all the time when I was growing up. Exploring the Idaho mountains was good summer cross-training and "cheap entertainment," Mom always said. A win for both of us, given the fact that any spare money tended to go toward new gear, new opportunities for me to train. I'd only ever seen a bear once in my life. It wasn't interested in me—at all. And that was in Yellowstone.

Wes tilted his head to one side. "Maybe there weren't bears in the Frank Church before, but in the past few years they've moved in. Good habitat here. Frank Church has all their favorites—Buffalo berries, chokecherries, huckleberries." He rattled off the plants like he was naming friends.

I shrugged. Maybe he was right, maybe he wasn't, but I didn't want to argue with the one person whose name I remembered. Besides, he'd just helped me avoid earning more negative points with Jennifer. And I'd promised myself that I'd step out of my comfort zone this summer and make a few friends. Training for the Olympics didn't leave a lot of wiggle room in my social schedule. In high school, while my peers were sneaking out of windows to attend sketchy parties, I spent my free time with Mom. Being at home, going for a hike with her, felt like a treat. During the winter training season, I spent my free time with Brent. That was enough for me.

"You don't believe me, do you?" he asked with a half-smile.

I smirked at him. "The only thing I'm afraid of in this wilderness is Jennifer."

Wes opened his mouth to reply, then clamped it shut. His blue eyes went wide, but he wasn't looking at me. He was looking over my shoulder.

Shit.

"Nice of you to join us, Miley." Jennifer's tone was sweet, but there was no mistaking the reprimand. I cringed, wondering if she'd heard what I just said. From Wes's expression, she had.

I whirled around, wishing I'd taken the time to run a brush through my damp hair. "Sorry, Jennifer. I won't let it happen again."

She glanced between Wes and me, like she was reevaluating how much she liked him now that I'd befriended him. "Wes is more than capable of setting up the tables by himself. Get that stack of tablecloths and start spreading them out," she said, motioning to my left. Then she walked away.

I hurried toward the tablecloths without missing a beat, not wanting her to see me dawdle.

"Miley?" Wes called, then waited for me to turn around and acknowledge him. "Take bear spray with you next time you go for a run, okay? Just in case," he added.

I held up my hands. "I don't have any. I'll grab some next time I drive into town."

"The resort has some. I'll show you when we're done here."

I rolled my eyes and laughed, shaking my head. "The huge cans by the landline? I can't wear a backpack while I run." *Especially not with my shoulder*, I added silently. The dull ache took any opportunity to flare into a sharp, stabbing pain. "I'll be okay until I can get to town and find a keychain," I insisted, picking up the first tablecloth. "I've spent plenty of time in the woods."

"Not these woods," Wes said solemnly, then ducked his head and turned away.

4

MILEY

Compared to my seven-mile morning run, the welcome breakfast was an absolute slog. The rubbery pancakes, overcooked sausage, and weak coffee were a far cry from the five-star ratings I'd read online about the food at Hidden Springs, but then again, we weren't guests. We were staff.

Speaker after speaker stood up in the shaded gazebo that would be used for live music once guests arrived, waxing on and on about the guest lodge, its proud history, and the famous people who had stayed here. By the time we finally made it to the closing icebreaker activity called "My Legacy at Hidden Springs," the sun was high in the sky and tipping westward. And I wasn't even trying to hide the fact that I was tapping my feet under the table.

I was a hard worker. I knew how to buckle down and get things done. But not because some guy in a polo shirt helped me embrace "My Legacy at Hidden Springs." I was glad to be here for the trails and the extra cash, but the gig itself was just another reminder of my stalled dreams. Most of my coworkers were still obsessing over dorm room decor, toga parties, and first jobs. At twenty-four, I was only a few years older than most of them, but I didn't feel it. Most of the time, all I felt was a gnawing sense that time was slipping away. I'd be twenty-eight by the time the Milano Cortina Olympics arrived. It felt like my last chance to prove that my life hadn't been a waste of time. Sure, I could keep competing every four years until I was thirty two, then thirty six, then forty. But I knew better than anybody that most biathletes were in their mid twenties. Give me a few more years, and I might as well be a relic.

The payoff for everything I'd sacrificed—everything Mom had sacrificed—wasn't supposed to take this long. The feeling that it was slipping through my fingers with every passing day made me itchy in my own skin.

When the last speaker finally dismissed us, I made a beeline for my cabin. I needed to take a shower and report to kitchen training in twenty minutes, but all I could think about was getting through the day, going to bed early, and going on another run—and swim. The isolated alpine lake felt like my new private oasis, and I'd already decided that I would make it my reward for each training session.

Wes fell in step beside me as I hustled away. He held a ginormous can in his hand. Before I could protest, he pushed it into my arms.

The can was about seven inches long, and it was covered in warning labels. A fierce silhouette of a roaring bear was plastered on the front next to the bright orange safety clip.

I rolled my eyes. "Wes …"

He grinned. "Kidding, kidding." Then he pulled a much smaller black tube from his pocket. A silver key ring dangled from the end. "Take this instead."

I studied the tiny spray bottle labeled simply MACE.

"The big can is better, but this thing still packs a mean punch," he insisted. "A few years ago, one of the staffers—"

"Thank you. This is great." I tried not to roll my eyes again and accepted the keychain. He was just trying to be thoughtful. I appreciated the concern, but I didn't need a babysitter. What I needed right now was a shower, not a rendition of whatever urban legend he was about to launch into to prove his point about bear spray.

I pocketed the tiny canister and pasted on a smile. "I'll take it with me when I run, okay? I need to get ready for my shift, though. I stink."

His blue eyes softened, like he was genuinely relieved I wasn't going to fight him. "Good. I'll see you there."

I hadn't realized Wes worked in the kitchen with me. I found myself smiling as I hurried away. He seemed like friend material.

Inside my cabin, I found a handwritten message on top of my sleeping bag.

Miley, call Brent. 303-876-0098.

My stomach flip-flopped. It had only been a few days since I last talked to Brent, but already it felt like a lifetime. We'd spoken on the phone the night before I left for Hidden Springs—and he'd said a hell of a lot more than I was ready to hear.

Even so, the thought of hearing his voice was enough to kick my ass into double-speed. Despite the way our last conversation had ended, I missed him fiercely. And talking to him was the closest thing I'd get to calling home.

I sped through my shower, not even bothering to let the water dribbling from the rusty, tiny spout get warm first. Then I wove my long, blonde, still-dripping hair into a quick braid and threw on the same polo I'd worn to the staff breakfast.

The sound of snapping twigs and female voices drifted past my cracked bathroom window as I grabbed my fitness tracker to check the time. Still ten minutes until my training shift started. Not too shabby.

I was about to pull on my shoes and race out the door when I heard, "Pretty sure she was the one driving the car. Do you think she dopes up?" one of the voices was saying.

A giggle in response. "Probably. They all do, right? God, that would suck to live with."

The towel I'd been holding slipped out of my hands and onto the spongy beige tile. My bad shoulder went rigid. Tears pressed at the back of my eyes, hot and angry.

For a moment, I considered staying in the cabin until they tramped past. But that would cut into my time on the phone with Brent. So instead, I marched outside, letting the cabin door slam shut hard behind me.

The two girls stopped short when they saw me, their faces pale with shock, then red with embarrassment. Clearly, they hadn't realized that this was my cabin—or that my window was cracked open.

"FYI, doping makes you shaky," I told them, focusing on my breath like I was in the final stretch of a race. Yeah, the accident was my fault. But not because I'd been doping. "If you dope up for a biathlon, you'll miss your shots."

Guilt tried to force my pulse faster while I fought for control. *In, one, two, three, four. Out, one, two, three, four.* My heart rate responded in kind, turning steely and steady.

"Sorry ..." one of the girls began weakly.

Without waiting to hear her out, I turned and marched toward the kitchen, feeling grateful for the tiny, individual staff cabins—instead of a bunkhouse.

When I arrived in the kitchen with five minutes to spare, I made a beeline for the landline phone in the corner of the kitchen. The guest lodge was so remote, I hadn't even bothered to recharge my cell phone yet from when it died on the first day. Guests had access to landline phones in their rooms, of course. And each main section of the lodge—including the kitchen—had a landline phone for staff use. There was a weak Wi-Fi signal in the main lodge, but even that was spotty.

When I was steps away from the phone, Jennifer appeared around the corner.

She saw me and smiled brightly, her mouth making a little O of surprise, like she hadn't expected me to be such an overachiever and show up early for my shift.

"Glad to see you making up for this morning," she chirped. Then, glancing at my polo, she added, "Do you remember where we keep the aprons?"

She'd shown me less than twenty-four hours ago. But I just smiled, nodded, and walked over to the pantry to get one without a snarky response. I'd have to call Brent later.

Jennifer's eyes stayed on me while I walked. "That's right," she called after me, like I had just passed another impromptu test. I looked back at her and waved, hoping she'd leave. Jennifer wasn't my direct supervisor, thank God. But she had a way of popping in to look over my shoulder with frustrating regularity.

Jennifer was one of those women who would call you honey in the same breath she told you to go to hell—all without breaking a smile. Sweet, but prickly. Efficient, but mostly because of her white-knuckle grip on micromanagement. She was in her mid-forties, teensy wrinkles just appearing around her eyes from years of smiling. She had shoulder-length dark hair that sported a few shimmering silver strands. She was pretty, and she carried herself like she was comfortable being in charge. Maybe a little too comfortable. Because in the five or so interactions I'd had with her, it was like she thought I was twelve instead of twenty-four.

Wes walked into the kitchen just as I finished tying the apron behind my back. He had a bagel hanging out of his mouth, and he was carrying a stack of industrial-sized cookie sheets.

When he saw me, his eyes lit up and he set down the stack of cookie sheets. He took the bagel out of his mouth, but not before pulling off a big bite and waving a greeting.

"How are you hungry again? We just ate a ton of food," I teased.

Wes swallowed and slapped his thighs. "You see this hot-ass, bean-pole physique? I'm hungry all the time."

"Hot-ass, bean-pole physique?" I laughed. "I like your confidence. What are those for?" I motioned to the stack of cookie sheets.

Wes grinned. "I'm on chocolate chip cookie duty today. Enough dough to freeze for a month, for the afternoon lounge hour. So like … a thousand cookies. You?"

"I'm not sure, I—"

"Equipment training." Jennifer suddenly appeared beside Wes, leaning in close to his ear as if she'd been waiting for the opportunity to interrupt. Then she walked away again.

I shrugged. "Equipment training, I guess."

"Marco doesn't get here until tomorrow," Wes called after Jennifer.

"Who's Marco—" I started, before Jennifer cut me off, her voice testy like Marco's absence was somehow my fault.

"Fine, then help Wes with the cookies. He'll show you what to do. When you're done, I'll show you the ropes in stocking and inventory," she called in an irritated singsong as she walked into the other room.

I exchanged a look with Wes as if to say, *Jennifer scares me way more than any bear.*

He shrugged, and I bit my tongue to keep from blurting the words out loud. Based on recent history, Jennifer could probably overhear anything I said. I had no doubt she was keeping an ear on our conversation. Instead, I repeated my question. "Who's Marco?"

"He's the only one who really knows how to work the fancy espresso machine and dishwasher," Wes explained. Then he lowered his voice. "Jennifer tried to show a staffer herself last year and got … flustered. She actually broke it."

I swallowed back a laugh and in a mock-serious tone whispered, "Her legacy at Hidden Springs?"

Wes's face broke into a delighted grin. "Yep. She's actually an okay boss. Just gets stressed easily and takes it out on everyone," he added in a whisper. "This is my fourth year here. I've kind of figured out how to stay out of her line of fire. Kitchen duty is pretty chill for the first week since, well, no guests. But don't get used to it. It'll get crazy soon enough."

"Good to know," I said. "So, the cookies. Is there a recipe, or …?"

"There is, but we don't need it." He tapped a finger on his head with the same hand holding what was left of the bagel. "It's all in here. Grab all the eggs in the fridge. I'll get the flour and sugar."

I nodded and moved toward the industrial refrigerator, casting a last longing look at the phone in the corner.

The thought of bears didn't make my pulse rise. But trying to guess what Brent wanted to talk about after our last conversation made my heart beat so fast I could feel it thump against the stack of egg cartons against my chest.

5

MILEY

By the time I finally got the chance to pick up the landline in the kitchen to call Brent, all I wanted to do was lie down.

Making cookies with Wes had sounded fun at first, but the endless cycle of mixing, shaping, baking, and storing the cookies en-masse was overwhelming. My shoulders and arms ached from scooping dough, and my calves burned from standing in one place for so long. I'd have to spend extra time stretching tonight, to make sure I wasn't a disaster on the trail tomorrow.

I'd hoped I might get to know Wes better while we worked side by side, but I'd quickly learned that wouldn't be happening. Each batch's ingredients had to be triple checked for accuracy and exact measurements, bake times, and cookie size. A single mistake could mean a ruined batch—according to Jennifer Standards anyway—and I was not about to let that happen. By the end of the day, I was actually looking forward to learning the inner workings of the dishwasher with Marco.

I decided I would call Brent back, but then I was heading straight back to my cabin and crashing hard. I hadn't expected it to be quite so ... peopley ... at the guest lodge. There was a reason I'd applied to work in the kitchen instead of a guest-facing position. I wasn't a hermit or anything, but I craved my space.

The empty, semi-dark kitchen was a welcome change from the clanging, bustling space it had been an hour before. For the first time since my run, I felt like I could relax without counting each breath.

Leaning against the wall in the now-quiet kitchen, I dialed Brent's number. He picked up on the second ring, and I immediately wondered if he'd been waiting for my call.

My heart thudded faster, right on cue.

"Hey," he said.

"Hey," I replied softly.

There was a blip of awkward silence that neither of us tried to fill. There was no ignoring how our last conversation had ended—with him confessing his love in that sweet, dogged way and me spinning out, unable to say anything coherent in response.

I did the only thing I could after he finished talking that night. I got off the phone as quickly as possible. Because despite the way his words landed in the pit of my stomach, true and sweet, the only emotion that bubbled to the surface was anger. The same inexplicable anger I felt when he tried to put his arm around my waist after our Beijing race.

It didn't make sense, but it didn't have to make sense to be real. I wasn't ready for this, and he'd barreled forward anyway. And now there was no going back to what we'd been before. We'd exited the friend zone whether I wanted it or not, and for once, a small part of me was grateful to be hundreds of miles away from him. The space between us was all that was keeping me from lashing out with words I didn't mean, fueled by white-hot feelings I couldn't touch without getting burned.

So far, I'd successfully avoided thinking about his confession—until now. I shoved it down to the same place the phantom pain in my shoulder came from. At least, that's how I imagined it. The dark, festering spot where I pushed everything that threatened to pull me under. I only hoped that the strangeness between us would dissolve, bit by bit, over the summer until we returned to training in the fall.

"What's up?" I finally said, desperate to end our silent game of chicken.

"Just wanted to check in."

I squeezed my eyes shut. *Just breathe.* "Things are going okay. The owner is kind of … uptight." I lowered my voice, just in case Jennifer was still lurking over my shoulder somewhere. "Besides that, it's great out here. Beautiful. How's Colorado?" I asked.

"Things are good," he replied slowly, and I could imagine his body shifting subtly, relaxing. I closed my eyes and pictured him leaning closer to the phone, his favorite ratty blue trucker hat hiding his messy brown hair. My heart hurt when I imagined him. So did my damn shoulder, for no reason at all.

"I'm at the range every day," he told me. "My run times are good. I've been lifting weights a lot. Jed emailed me a new routine to follow that should help with my tight traps."

Jed was our coach. Like the rest of us, he spent the spring and summer off-season working a day job, gearing up to drop everything for winter training.

"Your damn traps," I said, a smile playing on my lips. People always thought that shooting came down to the biceps and triceps in the arms, but the muscles in the upper back and shoulders were key to keeping the rifle butt stable against the shoulder for a clean shot. Brent was obsessed with his traps.

He laughed softly, and for a second it felt like everything was okay again. Like maybe our last conversation really would dissolve into the ether if we ignored it long enough. God knew I was game to try.

"I wish I could lift out here," I told him. "Or shoot. You should see the staff cabins. They're basically tiny houses. I'll make up for the range practice in the fall."

I waited for him to respond, but there was that heavy silence again.

I closed my eyes and sighed. "What's up, Brent? I know you didn't call just to talk about training."

He waited a beat longer, then said softly, "I don't know. I missed hearing your voice, I guess."

Dammit. The honest thing to reply would be that I missed his voice too. Missed it so deeply it felt like a muscle cramp. But I still wasn't ready to go there. Everything felt loaded and complicated between us, and that made me angry all over again. I needed more time to sort through my feelings.

Before I could put the jumble of thoughts into words, he cleared his throat. "How's your shoulder?"

I sank down against the wall in relief, letting the phone cord trail with me. The kitchen floor was sparkling, thanks to another poor kitchen staffer's work earlier today. "It's the same as always. Hurts, but I'm not letting it hold me back."

"Have you called the therapist Sara recommended?"

I shook my head, annoyed again. Talking about my shoulder didn't bring up the same panic that talking about my feelings for him did, but it was a close second. "I don't need to see another therapist. I just need to get stronger. I can do that on my own. If it's phantom pain, that means it's not real," I repeated for what felt like the millionth time.

"Nobody said it's not real—" he started softly.

I sighed again. "Did you call to start an argument about my shoulder?"

"No, of course not," Brent replied quickly. "You're just on my mind, that's all."

A wave of exhaustion washed over me. I wished I could let him in. But the wall I'd built wouldn't let me.

"I'm fine," I said, the words sounding brittle even to my own ears. "Really. I'm just tired. It's been a long day. When Wes first told me we were going to bake a thousand cookies, I thought he was exaggerating. But honestly, I think we made way more." I shifted into a split-squat stance to stretch out my aching legs.

There was a brief silence on the other end of the line. "Wes?"

"My coworker," I clarified. "In the kitchen. He's like, twenty. And he can't stop talking about bears. He's Idaho Dwight Schrute."

Brent made a surprised sound. "Back up. Bears? Miles, if there are bears—"

I laughed. "I'd be lucky to see a bear. And if I did, it'd be a black bear," I told him. According to Wes, most of the—rare—bear sightings in the Frank Church were mild-mannered black bears, but the occasional grizzly did show up. "Besides, I took the damn bear spray," I told him. "He gave me a keychain that I can clip to my shorts."

"Good," he said, sounding relieved. "Just ... be careful, okay? Stay close to the lodge."

I leaned into a side stretch, cradling the phone to my ear. "I know, I know. I promise I'll be safe." I didn't make any promises about staying close to the lodge. The icy alpine lake I'd found was too beautiful. And, despite Wes's warnings, I actually had done my own research on the Frank Church before I arrived. The Fish and Game message boards and blog posts were filled with novice campers asking questions about predators—and plenty of reassurance from veteran backpackers.

Finally, Brent said, "It sounds like you had a long day. I'll let you get some rest. Take care of yourself, though, okay? It won't help anything if you train too hard and reinjure that shoulder."

I stiffened. The injury had happened five years ago. If I hadn't healed by now, when would I?

"Don't worry, I won't let the team down," I mumbled, cringing as I remembered my botched shots in Beijing.

"The team?" His voice went tight. "Screw the team. I care about *you,* Miles. More than anything."

I could just imagine him raking a hand through his dark hair in frustration, pushing back the faded blue trucker hat. This conversation was getting way too serious, teetering on heavy. So I did what I always did to weasel out of it. I cracked a joke. "Fine, I guess I'll ditch my training and eat cookies with Dwight ... I mean Wes ... if you don't care about winning. Screw the team. Screw the podium finish."

Brent finally laughed. I loved that sound. Deep and warm, like a blanket I could wrap myself up in. "Don't do that. Let's win, but not at your expense."

"I'll think about it."

Then the silence was back. "Hey, I gotta go. If I want to be up early to see the bears—I mean, go for a run."

He laughed again, softer this time. "Yeah, of course."

The words *I miss you* hung silent in the air, but it felt impossible to say them out loud.

"Hey, Miles?"

I hesitated, afraid he was going to try to take the conversation deeper than I could swim again.

"I really have to get going ..." I hedged, trying to end the call. Terrified I might find the words *I love you* floating into my ear.

When he spoke, the ache in his voice was obvious. "Okay, never mind. Get some rest. Talk to you soon."

"Bye, Brent."

"Bye, Miles."

The line clicked dead, and I was left alone in the silent kitchen.

6

BRENT

As soon as Miley hung up, I groaned and laid my head on the table. My trucker hat slid off, but I didn't try to push it back into place.

I was a damn idiot.

What did I think would happen tonight? That she'd get on the phone and tell me she'd thought things over and realized she loved me too? That she suddenly wanted to build a life together?

I'd pushed her too hard, and now I had to live with the consequences.

I'd always hoped that, deep down, she was just waiting for me to make the move. Waiting for me to be the one to strip naked—emotionally—and tell her exactly how I felt. Because deep down, I thought she felt the same way.

We'd been friends—and only friends—for years, but there was a good reason for that. And not all of it had to do with me gathering the courage to tell her how I felt. I had fully intended to confess just before the accident five years ago, right down to writing her a letter like an old-fashioned dope.

I still had it in my sock drawer.

It wasn't hard to back-burner my own feelings while Miley counted her losses. In a lot of ways, we'd gotten even closer over the past five years. But she needed a friend more than she needed a boyfriend. Especially since there were no guarantees that she wanted *me* as a boyfriend.

I knew she still blamed herself for what happened. The newspaper articles and social media clickbait that sensationalized the horrible accident didn't help anything. Headlines like, "Olympic Hopeful's Fateful Decision: What Really Happened the Night of the Crash?" or "From Gold Medals to Grim Reality: An In-depth Look at the Crash that Shocked the Nation." Even bullshit like, "Behind the Wheel: Was Star Athlete Responsible for Horrific Accident?"

There was no getting around the fact that each Olympic cycle sank fresh barbs into a wound that was still so tender.

It tore me up. I could only imagine how much it hurt Miley.

I stood up from the table and got a whiff of how badly I stunk after a day of running and lifting in the already-hot Colorado summer. I'd been planning to grab something to eat at home, then hit the shooting range. But it was later than I'd realized, and now I just want a shower and a good night's rest. I also wanted an off-switch for the frustration and longing churning in my gut, but sleep was the best I could do.

I knew I was grasping at straws, but I told myself there was still a chance with her. That "processing" wasn't code for, "I can't bear to tell you outright that I don't feel the same way."

Either way, wallowing wasn't going to help. I needed to calm down and give her time—like she'd asked. Wasn't I the one always telling her to slow down a little before taking her shot on the race course? And wasn't she the one always telling me not to lose my head and get too emotional?

It was uncanny how closely life mirrored the course. You raced the way you lived. Unlike me, Miley never got lost in her feelings, on the course or off. The opposite, actually. It was like she kept her emotions in a little lockbox where they couldn't pop out and surprise her—ever. The woman was born confident. From what I could tell, the injury to her shoulder was the first time she'd ever doubted her ability to muscle her way through any situation, and even then, she refused to back down from the challenge. She kept insisting the phantom pain wasn't real, as if everyone around her thought she was being dramatic, but it was the opposite. Just once, I wanted her to tell me how much it hurt. The only time I'd ever seen her cry was in the hospital, so pumped full of painkillers and grief that it all poured out. Never again.

I turned on the shower and waited for the water to warm up. Miley's confidence was one of the first things I noticed about her when we met as teens. It shone through as bright as her big smile and that tangle of long, blonde hair in the sunlight. Her lean body had always been the perfect height for her head to rest against my shoulder when we hugged.

I stepped into the still-cold, stinging water to shut the memory down. I needed to accept the real possibility that we'd stay friends and teammates. Nothing more. But that thought was even more unbearable than daydreaming about how beautiful she was.

When we were teens, I took great pleasure in the fact that she devoted so much energy into trying to catch me—on the course, anyway. No matter how hard she tried, she couldn't beat my ski times, though. So she shifted her focus to shooting. It was a perfect fit for that steely confidence.

We ended up on a team together pretty quickly. The mixed relay biathlon event was introduced at Sochi in 2014, and our coach was set on bringing up the next crop of U.S. biathletes to compete at that level. Over the years, our team of four was a revolving door. But Miley and I stayed put, competing together every chance we got in addition to our individual races. We made a good team. There was no denying that.

When I realized I was shampooing my hair for the second time, I groaned out loud, then rinsed and turned off the water, not bothering to shave the day-old stubble that was already shaping up to be a beard.

The bathroom mirror was fogged up, so I swiped it with a hand towel and stared back at the stranger in the mirror. I didn't look the same to myself since I'd told Miley how I felt. The weight of my confession hung heavy, changing my posture, my expression.

"Stop being a dope," I chastised my reflection. Then I headed for the bedroom, my footsteps echoing in the sparsely furnished apartment I was renting for the summer. I didn't bother with clothes immediately. Instead, my gaze went to the unframed photo I'd pinned to the wall by my bedside. It was from one of our competitions in high school. Miley and I were in full racing gear with snow-capped peaks behind us. Silver medals—not an Olympic currency, but still—hung around our necks. Both of us had sweat-drenched hair and wide grins.

I'd never quite noticed the way she was looking at me in the photo. There was a glow in her eyes, a fierce intensity. We were surrounded by our teammates and the chaos of the post-race bustle. But in that photo, it looked like she only had eyes for me.

My heart twinged. I didn't have to study my own expression in the photo to know that I was giving her the very same look.

7

MILEY

FRANK CHURCH WILDERNESS, IDAHO

I followed the narrow, wooded trail that led from the main lodge to the cluster of women's cabins, letting the cool night air wash over me like water.

I focused on the feel of it in my lungs, cooling the flush in my skin. I couldn't put off sorting through my feelings about Brent forever, but it definitely wasn't going to happen tonight.

Crickets chirped so loudly they nearly drowned out the laughter in the distance, where the staff campfire was in full swing. Thank God it was optional.

The silhouette of my cabin's steep A-frame roof came into view just as heavy footfalls crunched through dry leaves to my right.

I stopped walking and listened for the sound to come again. The crickets stopped chirping. A handful of twigs snapped, the sound accompanied by a loud grunt.

Not a bear, I reassured myself, annoyed at how quickly the thought leaped to the front of my mind. Wild animals didn't make that kind of clatter when they moved through the forest. They moved like the owl: silent and often deadly.

Even so, my spine tingled, and I moved into a slight crouch, ready to run or stand my ground, depending on who—or what—barreled through the tree line.

My mouth twisted up in a smile as the shadowy figure emerged through the trees, revealing a lanky frame, aviator glasses, and blonde hair.

Wes.

"Aren't you coming to the campfire?" he asked, like he already knew the answer. Apparently, catching me slacking on training was his thing.

Despite my exhaustion, I was glad to see his easy smile.

"You're ditching, aren't you?" he said, nodding toward my cabin.

"You bet I am," I told him firmly. "It's not mandatory."

"Yeah, right." He gave me a look that I knew well even though I still didn't totally know Wes. It was the you're-going-to-piss-Jennifer-off look.

My heart dropped. "But the schedule said—"

Wes laughed. "It's up to you, but I've learned to take the word 'optional' very lightly around here.

I groaned and slapped a mosquito. How many team-building exercises could Jennifer cram into one training day?

"Fine, I'll be there in a few minutes. I just need to grab a sweatshirt," I grumbled, already calculating that I would show my face at the campfire then slip into the darkness and head back to the cabin—making way less noise than Wes just had.

"I'll hoard a Hershey's for your s'more," he promised. "They disappear quick."

I laughed. "Thanks. My hero."

The comment was supposed to be playful, but when I met his gaze, I recognized the look on his face. Pretty damn similar to how Brent had been looking at me lately.

I broke eye contact immediately and turned toward my cabin door.

"See you soon!" Wes called to my back.

I waved but didn't turn around. The last thing I needed was anybody else catching feelings. I hadn't dated anybody, even casually, since the accident.

I threw on a sweatshirt and headed to the fire pit. There would be plenty of time to sort through how I felt—later.

Loud cackles and snippets of conversation filtered through the air, along with the crack and pop of what I could see was a huge fire. Forget campfire—that thing was a bonfire.

I made my way past the outer ring of polo-clad staffers, smiling at people I barely recognized in the daylight, let alone in the dramatic shadows the flames cast. The event seemed like it had barely gotten started. People were still chatting, milling around.

Jennifer stood out like a sore thumb in the center of the fancy outdoor amphitheater, looking like a queen bee with a bob.

The enormous fire pit was encircled by a ring of boulders and had stone benches on all sides. It was much fancier than your average summer camp. Case in point: There was a fully-plumbed bathroom complete with lavender potpourri just a stone's throw away. Everything about Hidden Springs screamed, "Welcome to the wilderness, but don't worry, we know you like things bougie!"

The smell of charred wood and burnt marshmallows mixed with the smell of pine needles, and I breathed in deep. This was what summer in the mountains was supposed to feel like.

Wes sat on one of the stone benches right next to the fire, focused on a marshmallow at the end of a long roasting stick that he held directly over the open flame. I watched his serious expression as he yanked the smoking marshmallow out of the bonfire just before it erupted in flame. This was very much not a marshmallow-roasting fire, and with the size of that blaze, it might not get down to coals before the sun rose.

There was an open spot beside him on the bench, so I plopped down and immediately pulled off my sweatshirt. It was downright toasty.

He grinned at me and held out a full-size Hershey's bar. "Last one. You're welcome."

Our fingers brushed as I took it from him, and I pulled back like I'd been burned. *Easy, trigger,* I told myself, glad for the firelight that hid the blush on my cheeks.

Wes didn't bother hiding his smile. "This fire is total garbage for roasting marshmallows, but I think I've got this one just right. I always use birch branches because—" As if to spite him, the smoking marshmallow at the end of his stick burst into flames a second time.

"Crap." He blew on it furiously.

I was about to crack a joke about the blackened puck at the end of his stick when Jennifer put her hands in the air and clapped to get everyone's attention. "Okay, everyone. I think we're all here now." She scanned the crowd quickly, as if ticking through her mental list. "Find a seat. We're going to start. Who wants to open?"

"Like … open with a prayer?" I whispered to Wes in mock horror. The joke came out before I could vet it, and not nearly as quietly as I thought, because Jennifer shot me a look.

"Miley. Why don't you start? Share what you've learned about yourself in the first few days at the resort."

I glanced around the circle. All fifty-some-odd people were now staring at me expectantly. I suspected they were just glad it was me and not them.

I cleared my throat. "Okay … I'm glad to be here," I said honestly. "It's beautiful. During my off-hours, I've been exploring trails. Cross-training." I made brief eye contact with one of the girls I'd caught gossiping outside my cabin earlier. She quickly looked away, and I continued. "And … I'm learning a lot in the kitchen. I've never seen so many cookies in my life. Let alone baked them."

Jennifer gave a flat smile. "Great. But what have you learned about *yourself?*"

I tried not to roll my eyes. At least she hadn't asked about my "legacy" at Hidden Springs. I looked down and shuffled the dirt with a Chaco-clad foot. I could feel everyone's eyes on me. Heat rose to my face, but I honestly couldn't think of anything to say.

"Miley is learning that she's stubborn as hell," Wes announced, nudging me in the side and earning a few laughs.

I gave him a look, and my mouth opened in a little O. My first reaction was to defend myself, but he wasn't wrong. "Whatever," I retorted, nudging him back. It was probably better than the answer that might have tumbled out of my mouth.

"Tell us more about that," Jennifer prodded, cocking her head to the side like she was a therapist instead of a CEO.

I held back a sigh. I hadn't signed up for this. But Jennifer wasn't going to relent. I just had to get through it so she'd find someone else to pick on.

"Wes gave me a lecture about bringing bear spray on my morning runs. I can't run with a pack, so I told him no at first."

A few gasps and a collective murmur ran through the circle surrounding the bonfire. *Shit.* Not only had I completely failed in taking the attention off myself, but I'd apparently stepped right into a hornet's nest. The orange glow and the heat from the fire felt like a hot seat in more ways than one. I shifted uncomfortably on the bench, my brain scrambling for a way to backpedal. "He gave me a keychain version," I added loudly. "It's fine." What the hell was everyone's fascination with bears out here?

Jennifer looked at Wes. "Did you tell her about Rayna?"

"Who's Rayna?" I asked, glancing between Jennifer and Wes when the silence stretched too long, not sure who I was asking.

A prickle of warning ran down my spine, and my stomach tightened. The other staffers had gone so quiet that the only sound was the hiss of flames licking the pile of wood in the deep iron fire pit.

Jennifer's face looked pinched in the firelight, like she'd taken a sip of something sour. For a few seconds, she kept her gaze zeroed in on Wes, who just stared back.

"Rayna was a staff member here. Years ago," Jennifer finally began. "She went missing," she added stiffly. "Her body was never recovered."

8

MILEY

"What happened to her?" I asked, not sure I wanted to hear the answer.

Jennifer looked around at the group. None of the other staffers had even flinched when she revealed that a woman had gone missing years ago. Did they all know this?

"Bear attack. It was all over the news at the time." Jennifer's frown deepened, and she added, "You're an adult. I can't tell you what to do in your free time. But this wilderness isn't a joke, and there's a good reason we keep bear spray in the lodge for staffers to use."

Her words stung, but I clamped my mouth shut. It made sense now why everyone was so sensitive about bears.

"Rayna Carposa was only nineteen," Jennifer started. All eyes were fixed on her. Her frown had softened, and she lifted her hands while she spoke, like she had decided to fully embody this teaching moment. "Sweet girl. *Smart* girl. It was her first summer after graduating high school, and she was planning to go to Yale in the fall," Jennifer continued. Her eyes flashed gold in the firelight as she got into the story, and the whole vibe transported me right back to summer camp. Counselors telling scary stories, trying to terrify us into staying in our cabins instead of sneaking out for late-night pranks.

Jennifer didn't lower her voice for effect, but she may as well have because dread pricked the hairs at the back of my neck. She raised an eyebrow and fixed me with a look. "Rayna was a runner too—"

"I'm not a runner," I blurted. Like that mattered.

Jennifer looked away, clearly annoyed with the interruption, but she didn't grace it with an answer. She went on. "She had a cross-country scholarship at Yale in the fall. She ran all summer long when she wasn't working. Just like you."

I squirmed in my seat, wondering for a moment if this was some kind of new staff hazing. It seemed like a major coincidence that the missing girl had been running in the woods, just like me. I made a mental note to look up the story the next time I connected to Wi-Fi in the main lodge.

Still, there was no mistaking the sadness in Jennifer's voice. If she was making the story up to scare me, I would have expected a few giggles from staffers who couldn't hold a poker face. But the snapping of the fire was the only sound.

Jennifer let the silence linger. I was sure she'd continue, but I couldn't handle the suspense.

"How do you know it was a bear?"

Jennifer bristled, like she hadn't planned on sharing this detail. Finally she said, "They found blood. A lot of it. And shreds of her bloody clothes."

Just like that, her demeanor completely changed. She peered into the crowd of staffers. "Chad, can you break down these logs a bit so we can actually roast marshmallows sometime tonight?" she asked, moving toward the edge of the circle.

I blinked, stunned by the sudden shift. Staff members went back to chatting, laughing. Some were making their way to the s'mores station off to the side, where rows of graham crackers and marshmallows had been spread across platters for the taking.

I swallowed hard and looked at Wes, silently asking for confirmation that the story was true.

He nodded. "Yeah, it actually happened that way. Four years ago. My first summer here," he said.

"Why didn't you tell me?"

He gave me a look. "I tried. You didn't want to hear it."

I shrugged. Fair enough. And deep down, I wasn't planning to ask for more details. I'd heard enough. It was a horrible story, but the world was full of horrible stories.

If I took my cues from every bad thing that happened, I'd never get into a car again, either.

I was here to train. To get stronger. And that meant running—without a giant metal can flapping against my ass.

I bit the inside of my cheek. The sadness in his eyes made me wonder if this was more than just a cautionary tale. "Did you know her?" I asked hesitantly.

"A little." Wes winced. "She was really nice. Quiet. Liked plants, too. We only talked a few times, but when she disappeared … it messed everybody up."

He moved closer, and it felt like he might try to touch my hand. Instead, he tossed the burnt marshmallow he'd pried off his roasting stick and chucked it into the flames. It landed with a quiet sizzle.

"Just bring the keychain with you when you run, okay?"

I nodded and stood, eager to shift topics like Jennifer had done. "I promise. I'm going to get a marshmallow. Want anything?"

What I really wanted to say was that approximately 43,000 people die in car wrecks every single year—a stat I knew from the last article I'd read about what happened to me five years ago.

There had been *one* bear attack in all of Hidden Springs's storied history.

I'd take those odds.

9

MILEY

Training week at the lodge ended on Saturday, which left my Sunday morning wide open.

I'd already turned down an invitation from Wes to hit the pickleball court later that afternoon. My shoulder ached like hell, which meant that the last thing I wanted to do was smile and hold a racket. Besides, the first week's guests would be arriving bright and early Monday morning, and I intended to take full advantage of every second of silence at the lake before that happened.

"Go to hell," I murmured to the phantom pain when I reached the lake shore, kicked off my shoes, and counted my breaths. After a week of learning everything there was to know about food prep, dishes, and other heavy labor in the kitchen, even my good arm was sore. My bad arm—as Sara had specifically warned me *not* to call it —was a total mess. As it turned out, I'd be lifting plenty this summer, in the form of bulk ingredients, produce cartons, and endless bins of clean and dirty dishes that had to be loaded and unloaded into the dishwasher that I'd finally mastered with Marco's help.

I bit my lip to hold in a whimper as I tried to peel off my sports bra. Sharp pain sliced into my rotator cuff, and all I could imagine were broken shards of bone grinding against each other.

They weren't. I'd seen the X-rays. But that knowledge did nothing to stop the white-hot agony. No way I'd be able to get my sports bra off to get in the water.

I closed my eyes and refocused my breath, the one thing that always saved me from spiraling into despair. "It's not real," I reminded myself—another phrase Sara had specifically asked me not to use. But it was the only thing that comforted me.

My early morning training run times had improved every day over the past week—even with the obnoxious mace canister flopping against my hip, where I'd looped the keychain through the drawstring of my shorts. To my surprise, the run to the alpine lake had been a breeze this morning, and my shoulder hadn't even hurt—until now. I'd need to map out a longer trail soon. Or at least one that was more difficult.

I had to push myself harder. I wouldn't be the weak link this time. Wouldn't throw away my last shot to make it all matter.

Giving up on removing the sports bra, I peeled off my running shorts with the opposite hand, leaving my underwear in place. Then I waded into the icy water that was so clear I could count every pebble. The water shocked and soothed my tired calves at the same time, and I sighed with pleasure. This kind of pain, the burn in my exhausted muscles, was the type I craved.

When the water hit my thighs, I wrapped my long French braid into a sloppy bun and tucked the end underneath my hairband. Then I eased myself into the water, creating the only ripple across the entire expanse of smooth, sparkling blue.

I swam tentatively at first, moving my legs in a frog kick and testing my shoulder. Immersed in the cold water, the burning pain withdrew as quickly as it had flared up. I let out a sigh of relief, glad it was gone but knowing it wouldn't stay away for long.

When I was partway across the lake, I flipped over and floated on my back. The blue sky felt endless, an extension of the lake beneath me.

Like it had so often over the past few days, my brain pulled me back to thoughts of Brent.

Think about something else. Think about Wes, I demanded, bringing to mind an image of his wide smile and blue eyes. We'd become fast friends in the kitchen, but I already knew that the banter was mostly a distraction from my feelings about Brent. Not any kind of spark. He'd hugged me once—after walking me back to my cabin in the dark after a staff safety training on the resort's emergency generator system. I tried to lean into his embrace, but deep down I just missed Brent. Afterward, I'd sat alone on my bed, in the dark cabin, trying to peel back the layers of confusion and doubt holding my heart in a vise.

I'd stopped returning Brent's calls. Not because I didn't want to hear his voice, but because I knew I wasn't a single step closer to finding the words he needed to hear.

It was like my brain shut off when I tried to probe its tender parts. I'd barely scratched the surface of my own feelings, and Brent deserved more than that. That was for damn sure.

When I thought about him, my heart seized up. I knew he was my person. I couldn't bear to imagine life without him. I'd thought about kissing him more than a few times, if I was being totally honest.

So, do you love him?

My brain answered the question with a question every time. *Do you deserve love?*

The answer came all too easily. *Not anymore.*

A commotion, loud even to my ears beneath the water, jarred me out of my thoughts.

I jolted upright to tread water, scanning the thick brush and steep, lichen-draped boulders that surrounded the lake on nearly every side.

The sound came again, rapid fire and closer than I'd expected. A flurry of branches breaking.

Something was careening through the dense forest, but no matter how much I craned my neck, I couldn't see anything yet.

A bear, came my first thought, which I quickly shoved away. A quick deep-dive on the lodge's hit-or-miss Wi-Fi had confirmed the story Jennifer told at the bonfire about the staffer who had been killed by a bear. Yes, a grizzly had been shot in the aftermath—but it was one of *three* who lived in the nearly three-million-acre wilderness.

Even so, a chill that had nothing to do with the cold lake water crept down my spine as the crashing sounds drew closer. The canister of mace was far out of reach on shore, still attached to my running shorts.

My gaze stayed locked onto the tree line.

You're fine, I reprimanded myself.

A cluster of skinny pines shuddered and bent. I couldn't see what it was, but there was no doubt something big was crashing toward the lake.

I swallowed. *Rare* wasn't impossible. What the hell was I going to do if a bear did burst through the treeline and caught sight of me in the lake, looking like a dumpling?

But a bear wasn't what came charging out of the woods.

Instead, a massive bull moose with towering, velvety antlers plowed through the foliage toward the lake's edge, its eyes wide with terror.

I couldn't stop the audible gasp that tore from my lungs.

The massive rack of antlers were nearly as tall as the moose itself. He was magnificent.

Relief zipped through me. I could almost hear Mom's voice in my head. *Look, Miley. Just look.*

The wonder was short-lived, though. The big bull didn't hesitate at the water's edge. Instead, he locked his gaze on me, nostrils flaring.

Then he charged directly into the water.

Shit. For a few seconds, I flailed in the water, thinking the moose was headed straight for me. Bulls had a reputation for being aggressive, but I'd never heard of one acting like this before.

Just as quickly though, my panic subsided.

The moose was swimming away from me, toward the treeline on the other side of the lake.

I cracked a slight smile, already dying to tell Brent and Wes about my "bear" encounter.

I shivered in the chilly water and drew in a steadying breath. It was time to head back to shore and finish my run.

I turned and swam freestyle toward the speck of sandy shoreline where I'd left my clothes. My shoulder obliged, still letting me take clean, pain-free strokes. I closed my eyes and let myself imagine what it would feel like to have this full range of motion back all the time.

I jolted as a single, loud bang cut through the soft, rhythmic splash of my strokes.

My throat closed. I knew that sound.

A gunshot.

Before I could process what was happening, I heard a deep, guttural bellow behind me. This sound was quieter than the gunshot, but it ripped louder through my chest with more force. I spun in the water.

The bull moose, maybe eighty yards behind me in the water, moaned and thrashed in agony.

I watched in horror as the placid lake frothed red, churning with the frantic splashing of his hooves.

He managed to keep his head above the surface for only a few seconds before he sank beneath the water.

It's not hunting season, my brain whispered, buzzing with fresh horror.

I whirled around in a circle, trying to see where the shot had come from. Who would fire at an animal in a lake? Even a poacher had no reason to shoot the bull, knowing he'd only sink to the bottom a hundred feet down.

My eyes landed on the shoreline I'd been aiming for just seconds before.

My stomach coiled like a spring.

The spit of sand wasn't empty anymore.

Two men had emerged from the treeline, standing right next to my pile of clothes. There was about a third of the lake between me and them. Maybe two hundred yards.

One of the men whooped, slinging his rifle over his back. The spring in my stomach tensed tighter, harder. Even at this distance, his clothes looked strange. Old-fashioned. The man standing next to him looked older but nearly identical.

Both men wore packs. Both had long, untrimmed beards that made their faces look fuzzy. One gray, the other a strawberry blonde color that matched his shaggy hair.

The younger man with the rifle tore the cowboy hat off his head and swung it like a rodeo clown. "Hell yeah, told you I could make that shot." His voice, grating and deep, carried through the sudden silence.

The older man didn't acknowledge him. Just removed his own rifle slung across his shoulder and stared across the lake.

Right at me.

An involuntary chatter clacked my teeth together.

"Get out of that water now, honey," Gray Beard called, nestling the rifle butt against his shoulder. He wasn't pointing it at me, not directly, but that could change in a heartbeat.

I choked back the panic fizzing through my veins. I couldn't see his face clearly, but I didn't need to. Every part of my body flared like a neon sign blinking *danger*. The only thing I knew for sure was that I didn't want to be out here alone with these two men.

The lake was maybe four hundred yards wide in total, but the tiny crescent of shoreline was the only easy exit I could see. Slick boulders and thick forest flanked the deep water on all sides, except for the grassy meadow beyond the sandy shore.

I could probably find another slip of shoreline amid the boulders and trees if I swam all the way around the lake, but I wouldn't get far shoeless and basically naked.

Of course, that was assuming they wouldn't shoot me the second I tried to swim away from them.

The guy with the cowboy hat had hit that moose with one shot. Nearly three hundred yards. I knew better than most that it wasn't a feat most people could pull off. He was a damn good shot.

Gray Beard shifted his stance and repositioned the rifle. This time, there was no question he was aiming it at me.

I gasped. My teeth chattered so hard I wondered, distantly, if they'd break. If I ducked underwater, I'd be a tougher target to hit— until the second my head surfaced so I could take a breath.

I imagined myself sinking beneath the depths, the water frothing red as I clawed for air like the moose.

"Ain't gonna ask again, woman," he called.

The steel in his voice told me he wasn't bluffing.

Clear as the water that swirled beneath my tired legs, two truths crystalized in my mind.

If I swam for the opposite shore, they would shoot me rather than let me get away.

But if I swam toward them, I might wish they had.

10

MILEY

Cowboy Hat made a guttural sound in the back of his throat that might have been a snicker.

"We just wanna talk to ya, sweetie," Gray Beard said.

His words did nothing to ease the cold dread making my limbs feel like lead, pulling me down in the already freezing water.

The seconds were adding up. I had to act. And I couldn't just do what they asked and swim toward them.

Before I could second-guess my decision, I gulped for breath and dove beneath the water, eyes open, legs frog-kicking desperately.

I could hold my breath for at least a minute. How far could I get in sixty seconds?

Boom.

The sound of the bullet cracked loud in my ears. Louder than I would have thought possible beneath the water.

I swam harder.

Boom, boom.

My lungs screamed for air. When would they hit me?

Boom.

I had to come up for air.

When my head broke the water, I gulped in a lungful. There wasn't time to look around. I arced my body to dive again.

Before I could blink, a bullet winged by me, hitting the water mere inches from my face with a violent splash.

I screamed as loudly as if the bullet had pierced my skin.

It almost had.

"Last chance, honey," the old man called.

I stayed where I was, treading water, unable to convince my body to move toward the men but just as terrified to dive again.

Gray Beard cocked his head to the side, shifted his pack, and raised the rifle.

Cowboy Hat didn't try to hide his guffaw this time. It rang through the quiet forest and rattled through my brain, loud as the gunshot's echo.

"No need for all that fuss," Gray Beard called. "You seen my aim? If I wanted you dead, you'd be a sinker right now. I'm still willing to be reasonable if you'll just swim on over here."

"Aw, come on," Cowboy Hat chimed in loudly, still laughing. "Just do as he says. We ain't gonna hurt you."

No, no, no,

When I lifted my arm to swim for shore, my shoulder screamed at me to stop.

As if I had a choice.

I pushed through the pain and took a stroke, then another, swimming as slowly as I could while my brain spun faster, trying to come up with a plan.

As I drew in a gasp of air and lifted my arm past my face, a flash of orange caught my eye.

My fitness tracker.

The sight of it made me want to cry. I had no idea if someone could use it to find me. Doubtful. I was pretty sure it had to ping off a cell phone tower—and there were none of those anywhere near the Frank Church. But it was the first sliver of hope I'd found since the two men shot the moose.

If they saw the tracker on my wrist, they'd take it. But how the hell was I going to get it off without them noticing, and where was I going to hide it?

I fought for composure and whipped my legs harder in the water, trying to propel my body forward while I brought both arms to my chest beneath the lake's surface. I couldn't let them see what I was doing, but I had to keep swimming toward them.

The plastic watch strap was slick in my clumsy fingers, but the buckle gave way in seconds. I clutched it tight in my right hand, knowing that if I let go, it would be lost to the lake in a split second.

"She sure is taking her time," Cowboy Hat piped up, just loud enough that I could make out the words. "Want me to speed her up?"

I gritted my teeth and shoved the tiny fitness tracker under the band of my sports bra, right between my breasts. "I hurt my shoulder," I called, hating that I was revealing anything about myself but desperate not to give them an excuse to fire off another shot.

I was maybe fifty yards from shore now.

Shit, shit, shit. This couldn't be happening.

It was, though. And it was about to get worse.

When I wiped water from my eyes with my next stroke, the details of the men's faces sharpened, adding new depth to my terror.

Gray Beard's face was nearly obscured by sparse, shaggy whiskers the color of soot. His eyes were set deep in his skull, and the weathered tan skin across his cheeks was covered in liver-colored age-spots. Wrinkles creased his forehead, but there was nothing feeble about his grip on the rifle.

Cowboy Hat smiled with yellow teeth that jutted from his mouth at an angle that made me think he'd never seen a dentist. If it weren't for the raw-red skin around his rheumy eyes and the pockmarks covering his cheeks, I might have mistaken him for handsome—with his mouth closed.

The two men shared an uncanny resemblance in the shape of their long, straight noses and identically hunched shoulders, and dirty brown packs. I shuddered. Were they related? Father and son? What was in those packs?

My eyes darted past them to the meadow trail, bathed in sunlight that contrasted sharply with the deep woods surrounding the lake. Was there any way I could sprint past the men and into the trees, fast enough that I wouldn't feel a bullet between my shoulderblades? A moving target was difficult to hit, but not at close range.

If I gave them a clear shot, they would take it. I felt sure of that.

A squirrel chattered from the top of a nearby lodgepole pine, furious at the scene unfolding below her.

Help me, I begged the universe, willing some camper or hiker or Hidden Springs staffer to appear at the edge of the meadow.

I knew that wouldn't happen. It was too early in the season. I was the only one stupid enough to be out here.

"Don't be shy," Cowboy Hat cooed, then nodded at my pathetic pile of rumpled clothing. "We'll let you have your clothes back ... if you're real sweet."

Could I uncap the mace keychain and spray them before they realized what was happening?

I needed those clothes back.

Gray Beard smirked. His eyes roved over me, sending prickles of dread down my spine. I didn't want them to see me without my clothes on. But that's exactly what was about to happen.

I found the rhythm of my breath despite the panic as the lake's sandy bottom drew closer and closer. I would be able to touch the bottom soon.

What were they planning to do to me?

What did they want?

I pushed the horrifying answers away. They'd only freeze me up.

If I could just break through the treeline and run serpentine through the forest, I'd have the advantage of built-in cover from the big pines. Even shoeless, there was no way the men could beat me in a sprint.

I didn't care if my feet were bloody stumps by the time I got back to the lodge. I would run myself down to the bone to get away from them.

I just needed the element of surprise to get a head start.

The men fanned out, one guarding my pile of clothes, the other blocking the opening to the meadow trail.

Shit.

There was no way I could make a dive for the bear spray.

When my feet brushed the bottom of the lake, I stood up, hating how exposed every inch of me now was.

I shivered harder, unable to control the chattering of my teeth. I wasn't cold. Just terrified.

I wrapped my arms around my body and waded a few steps toward shore. "Please, put the gun down," I said, trying to hide the tremble in my voice. "It's scaring me." *I just need a few seconds to make it to the treeline.*

"You don't gotta be scared, honey." The rifle stayed trained on my face.

The way he said the word *honey* made my skin crawl.

Taking slow steps, I calculated the distance between them. Ten feet, maybe.

If I threaded the needle and ran between the two men, they'd hesitate before they fired their rifles, not wanting to shoot each other in the crossfire.

At least, that's what I was banking on. That moment of hesitation, that confusion might give me just enough time to dart into the trees before they could shoot me at point-blank range.

Eyes open, Miles, a voice that sounded like Mom's whispered, and the warning sent adrenaline streaking down into my legs as I got ready to run.

This might be my only chance.

When the cold water rimmed the tops of my feet, I stopped walking. Just one more step would put me on hardpack. "Please," I begged. "You said you just wanted to talk. Stop pointing the gun at me."

They both stared at my body, naked except for the sports bra and underwear clinging to my wet skin.

"C'mon Dad. Ease up. You ain't gonna shoot her," Cowboy Hat drawled.

Dad. They were father and son, I cataloged distantly.

The old man grunted but didn't contradict him.

I watched the barrel of the rifle as if it were moving in slow motion, making its way from pointing at my face to tilting skyward. He was now hugging the butt next to his torso, apparently satisfied that I was within easy reach.

But I was already in motion.

Run.

11

MILEY

As I darted between them, the father lunged at me.

I gasped, shocked at how spry he was.

Bright pain exploded at my bicep, but not from his grip.

A stream of red liquid ran down my wet arm.

Blood.

He'd cut me. I never even saw the knife come out.

I kept running, but the hesitation was my downfall. The son scrambled toward me, away from my pile of discarded clothing, and grabbed my other arm.

His breath was ragged and hot as he pulled me to his chest. It smelled like meat left in the fridge too long.

I screamed as loud as I could.

He grunted and shook me so hard my teeth rattled in my head.

As I tried—and failed—to wrench out of his grip, I could feel his eyes move over my body. His hunger, his desire for something— Violence? Sex? Both?—oozed from him.

The father flanked my other side as I thrashed to break free from the son's grip.

It was no use.

They were both too strong.

I'd lost my chance.

My bad shoulder throbbed in time with the stab wound, even though it hadn't been cut. The long slash in my arm burned hot, spilling red liquid across the dirt each time I jerked my body.

It was more blood than I'd expected to see.

My stomach flipped, and my eyes blurred at the sight of it.

I stopped thrashing and went still.

I couldn't pass out. I couldn't lose control. Not now.

The father snorted. "Giving up that easy?" He still wore a smirk behind the whiskers that curled past his upper lip. "Hamish here thought you'd put up more of a fight. I knew better."

He shot a self-satisfied look at his son—*Hamish.*

When I kept silent, he laughed softly. "That's right, honey. Settle down and let it happen. These are our mountains. The sooner you learn that, the better." He leaned close enough that there was no escaping the rank smell of his breath. "If you try to run—or scream—again, I will put a bullet directly in the back of that pretty blonde head," he whispered.

I believed him.

The memory of the sound the moose made right before it went under the water echoed through my brain, merging with the scream begging for release in my own throat.

I closed my eyes and swallowed the scream. When I opened my eyes, Hamish was staring me in the face, like I was some kind of rare animal he was seeing up close for the first time.

"Get her clothes. I'll hold her," he said to his father.

The old man shot him an incredulous look. Clearly, he was the one who usually gave the demands.

Hamish shrugged. "Last thing I need is you seeing her like this, getting ideas."

I felt the color drain from my face.

The father broke a smile and laughed. "Come on, now. You think I'm gonna horn in on your prize?" He bent over and slapped his knee in laughter. "I got my own pussy."

I recoiled at the words.

Hamish didn't reply. Just stared his father down until the old man finally stepped away to get my clothes.

Don't find the mace, I prayed. *Just grab the clothes in a pile and give them to me.*

"Don't mean nothin'," Hamish whispered to himself.

The old man was back at my side in an instant.

To my horror, he examined the pieces of clothing one at a time instead of handing them to me.

My heart dropped when the keychain fell from my shorts, dangling by its latch. The old man laughed. "Worried about bears, honey?"

I stayed silent.

He smiled to himself. Then, instead of handing me my clothes, he balled them up and used them to wipe the steady flow of blood dribbling down my arm.

When I tried to pull away, Hamish grabbed hold of my bad shoulder. I bit my lip to keep from crying out.

I couldn't let myself panic.

They would get distracted at some point. Then I'd have another chance to run—or grab that mace.

The old man took a step closer, keeping my clothing out of reach. "Might as well take a peek at the whole package while I'm at it," he said dryly, and before I could react, he'd pulled up my sports bra, exposing one of my breasts.

I recoiled and pulled my bra down—but not before the bright orange fitness tracker fell to the ground at my feet.

Hamish saw it, too.

He grabbed hold of my wet bun like a handle. Before I could reach down to snatch the tracker, Hamish pulled my head to the side so roughly I almost fell over.

He shoved his father. "The hell you doin'?" he yelled. Then he ripped the shorts away and handed them to me—but not before tearing the keychain off.

I fumbled with the stretchy material, my fingers numb from the shock of the old man's fingers on my skin.

Nobody had ever touched me like that before.

I wanted to cry from a place so deep down the tears wouldn't reach.

The old man rose up to his full height, sunken eyes flashing deep in his skull. Without a word, he snatched the shorts away before I could put them on.

For a moment, Hamish drew back but kept his fingers tight on my hair.

I shrank into myself, desperate not to let them take my last shreds of clothing. My mind spun as I tried to follow the old man's line of thinking.

White spots swam in front of my eyes but I fought to stay present, to keep looking for another chance to run.

I edged my toes toward the fitness tracker, but it was too far. Hamish's grip on my hair was too tight.

What were they going to do with me?

"Give her the shorts at least," Hamish said. "You're not gonna walk behind her, drooling like a dog all the way back home cause she's in her birthday suit. Not if I got a say."

Drooling like a dog. All the way back home. Vomit pressed at the base of my throat.

"You don't. Never did," the old man muttered, tucking my shorts under his arm. He held my bloodied tank top at the shoulder seam and tore into it with his knife. The ripping sounds made me recoil.

When he was finished, he threw the tank top to the ground next to the dark splotches of blood. Then he held up my shorts and sniffed them like a dog. I tried to back away from him, but Hamish held me steady.

"What the hell?" Hamish muttered, sounding more annoyed than outraged this time. He looked away from his father and pulled me back toward the fitness tracker, so he could reach down and grab it.

He handed it to his father, holding it by the strap like it might be dangerous. I got the distinct feeling he'd never seen one before. That thought scared me almost as much as the weapons they carried. Who were these people?

"You won't be needing this anymore, honey," the old man said, then tossed the tracker into the lake. It landed with a soft splash then sank beneath the surface.

I stared at the glinting water.

No, no, no.

The old man turned to Hamish. "Now hold her down. Do as I say."

Bile rose in my throat. Were they going to assault me right here, on the beach, beneath the blazing sun.

My knees went weak.

I opened my mouth to beg for mercy.

Instead, the old man picked up my ripped clothing and rubbed it against the thick trail of fresh blood oozing from my arm until it was fully saturated. "Just for good measure," he said with satisfaction.

Then he tossed the stained clothes on shore and kicked the mace keychain toward the water's edge.

I stared at the bloody pile in mute disbelief.

Hamish silently ran his fingers along my braid until he got to the end, then pulled out the rubber band. I stayed perfectly still, afraid of what would happen if I resisted. His huge hand covered the back of my head as he used his other fingers to pull the braided bun loose in careful tugs.

"Her hair is really pretty," Hamish whispered as he rubbed my head so that the braid uncoiled fully.

I bit back a sob. The old man was staring at us now, eyes fixed on his son's hands in my hair.

"Real pretty," Hamish repeated, petting my head.

I kept myself still as a statue, despite the gooseflesh prickling my skin. Not because I wanted to, but because a steely voice in the back of my head whispered that for now, at least, doing what they demanded was my best chance of surviving whatever came next.

12

MILEY

"Leave her shoes by the clothing," the old man barked at Hamish when he dragged me toward the sneakers lying in the sand.

"But her feet will get all cut up," Hamish protested.

I got the impression he wasn't worried about any pain I might feel. Just the idea of his new prize getting scuffed up.

"Then she'll be less likely to run, won't she?" his father barked.

Hamish shrugged, grabbing my bicep like a leash and tugging me toward the treeline—the opposite direction from the lodge. "Fine. Then let's get going. Long walk ahead of us."

Panic bubbled up in my chest. I couldn't let them take me deeper into the forest. I was already so far away from help I might as well have been on a different planet. But the idea of letting them drag me farther into the woods felt unthinkable.

"My name's Miley," I blurted, saying the words as they popped into my head. Anything to stall, anything to humanize myself.

I locked my gaze on the old man and kept talking, the words spilling out fast and acrid like vomit. "Will you tell me your name? I'm working at the—"

He put a hand up to silence me, and I stopped talking out of surprise.

"You can call me Fred, but I don't care what your name is, honey. Your name'll be whatever we say it is. Hamish will decide."

I gaped at him. *Hamish* would decide? Fear and anger churned like a sick stew in my stomach.

Hamish laughed softly and scratched his long sideburns. A lopsided, dopey smile parted his red beard, chilling me more than any scowl.

He studied me intently, curiously, like he was examining a new pet.

I stared back, wide-eyed and bracing.

With their uneven beards, old-fashioned packs, dirty clothing, and body odor strong enough to peel paint, the two men would have fit right in with the Clampett family, but there was none of the goofy bumbling from the *Beverly Hillbillies*. The sharp, mean glint in their eyes warned me that if I underestimated them, I'd pay the price.

Up close, I could see that their clothes and packs were covered in a mottled black coating that looked like charcoal. Or maybe that was just what clothes look like when you never, ever washed them. Fred had to be in his sixties, at least, but Hamish seemed much younger. Early twenties, if I had to guess.

"What do you want from me?" I asked, forcing my voice to come out clear and strong even as the tender skin on the sole of my foot hit a sharp rock. "Where are you taking me?"

They laughed.

Hamish tugged on my arm, forcing me to walk another few steps.

"We ain't gonna violate you if that's what you're thinkin,'" Fred said.

My cheeks burned, and I glared daggers at him. If this wasn't a violation, the word clearly meant something very different to him.

Fred smirked. "You're gonna be trouble, ain't you?" He rummaged through his pack then lifted his eyes to Hamish. You sure 'bout her, Hame?" He flicked his eyes toward me and smirked. "We could still get rid of her. Take the next one we find."

Bile rose in my throat again.

I lifted my eyes to look at Hamish. He held my gaze for a moment. Then his eyes trailed down my body, stopping at my chest, which was still heaving with panic. The tip of his tongue snaked out and ran across his chapped bottom lip. Then he slowly nodded. "I'm certain. She's gonna be worth it."

My skin crawled. I couldn't stop the scream itching in my lungs from leaking out in a high-pitched whimper.

"Now that's an ugly sound," Fred tutted. "Even Hame here won't put up with that for long."

The sound died on my lips as he pulled a huge chain out of the backpack, then a carabiner. Before I could process what was happening, he had the chain wrapped around my bare waist, using the carabiner to clip two links together. "If you're gonna act like a dog, I'm gonna have to treat you like one," he said matter-of-factly.

Hamish snorted and held my wrists as his father slipped zip ties around them, then anchored the ties to the chain.

The world blurred with fresh, hot tears.

There was no hope of running anymore.

I swallowed my tears and clenched my jaw shut so hard my molars creaked.

My hair fell around my shoulders and grazed my waist, getting caught in the zipties and in the metal links. Fred handed the loose end of the chain to Hamish and brushed his hands together. "All yours."

Hamish yanked the chain, like he was testing it. I stumbled forward, losing my balance. The slack disappeared as I fell, and the taut chain snapped across my lower back, sending a ripple of pain through my body.

"Atta boy," Fred murmured and led the way into the trees.

I struggled to get up, failing and landing hard on my bad shoulder. Sharp pain shot up my spine, but it was nothing compared to the terror slicing through me.

How long would it be until someone realized I was missing? Not until tomorrow, at the very earliest, when I didn't show up for my shift in the kitchen.

Jennifer would be furious.

Please, God, let her be furious.

I could only hope she'd march straight to my cabin door and barge inside, but would she think I was just sluffing off work? When would she—or Wes—start to worry about my safety? Even then, how long would it take before anyone started searching for me? Where would they even start looking? Nobody knew where I was.

Despair pushed the searing pain in my shoulder to a fever pitch as I struggled to stand, tangling myself further in the chain as it looped around my body and bit into my skin.

Hamish watched passively until I finally pulled myself upright.

His goofy smile had twisted into a leering grin.

And those baby blue eyes looked black as death.

13

MILEY

At first, I dragged my heels with each step, trying to tear up the ground as much as possible to create a trail. Surely, someone would come looking for me, I thought. And when they did, maybe they'd see the evidence I'd left of a struggle.

But each time I looked behind me at the vastness of the forest, despair curdled the hope. What were the odds someone would even know to look here? This wasn't a real trail we were following through the dense trees. Barely more than a game trail. All I was doing was cutting up my feet more and more.

By the time Fred and Hamish stopped walking to rest, the sun had dipped past its meridian, hovering just above the tallest trees. And my feet were screaming in agony.

We hadn't actually traveled that far. A few miles, if I was gauging the distance correctly. But a few miles of walking barefoot through dense forest was far worse than I'd imagined. My soles were stuck through with splinters and pine needles like pincushions. Not enough to make them bleed. Just enough to send pain screaming through me with every step.

I wobbled where I stood, and Fred snickered. Each time he noticed me dragging my feet, he slapped the back of my head and told me to knock it off.

The first time he did it, I yelped. Hamish whipped around with the chain in his hand and glared at his father. "Give her an inch, she'll take a mile," Fred called. Then, for good measure, he slapped me again.

Hamish glared at both of us then turned around, muttering something I couldn't hear.

After a couple of hours, the dragging walk I was trying to pull off was no longer an act. When Fred slapped me for what felt like the hundredth time, I yanked back hard on the chain and whirled around to face him. I nodded at my bare feet, holding one up so they could see the sole.

"How the hell am I supposed to walk? You wouldn't let me wear my shoes," I spat, lifting up the sole of one foot so he could see the mess of pine needles and angry scratches. The sight of it made me want to vomit. The pockets of skin I could see were broken and swollen, oozing a yellowish liquid.

"Wouldn't be so torn up if you'd walked right in the first place," Fred said matter-of-factly. "Besides, those things barely counted as shoes. You'll need work boots—when you've earned them." He laughed, then reached out a hand as if to touch my long hair. I recoiled instinctively, and his eyes flashed. In an instant, his hand shot out, tearing a handful of hair strands from their roots. I couldn't help the scream that ripped through me.

"Don't touch my woman!" Hamish barked, finally finding his voice.

Fred glared at Hamish then darted toward him.

Hamish was head and shoulders taller than his dad, but he cowered like a child.

"You don't know jack shit about taming a woman. First lesson: *You* break *them*. Not the other way around."

Hamish furrowed his brows, clearly confused. But I wasn't. Despite the horrifying words, I grabbed hold of the idea that maybe there was some mercy in Hamish that I could manipulate. A crack I could work to break him open. He wasn't on my side. Not by a long shot. But still, a flicker of hope lit up inside my chest.

Then a fist connected with my cheekbone, and I went down hard.

Heavy chains crashed against my legs, and the pain searing my cheek, legs, and feet made it feel like my whole body was on fire from head to toe.

Warm blood from my nose crawled down my upper lip. I wiped it against my shoulder then pulled myself up to sit, moving my hands to the ground in order to try and stand. I wouldn't cry. Or let them see how much pain I was in. I could control that much.

I locked eyes with Hamish first, trying to find some mercy in his expression.

He narrowed his gaze uneasily and held mine. This time, I didn't wipe the blood dripping down my upper lip. I wanted him to see it. To feel sorry for me.

Hamish looked away.

I finally turned and looked Fred in the face.

He laughed when he met my gaze. "I ain't so sure you can tame her at all, Hame. I might need to do it." Fred ran his eyes over my body, sports bra, exposed stomach, and underwear. I refused to shrink under his leering expression anymore, even though it felt like fire ants biting their way across my skin.

He took a step closer and grabbed the hair at the nape of my neck. He pulled my face close to his. "Would you like that, honey?"

I stared into his dead, shark eyes. Held my breath as long as I could so I wouldn't smell his stench.

"Her name's Ruth Suzanne. Ruthie Sue, for short," Hamish interrupted.

Fred loosened his grip and looked at Hamish in surprise. I seized on the distraction and scrambled back a few inches, which was as far as the chain would allow. Fred squinted at his son. "Sue?"

"You heard me. After my mama."

Fred was still so close, I could smell the mixture of his dirty clothes and body odor. His jaw rippled. "Your mama was a good for nothin' whore who left you before your balls dropped."

"You said she was mine to name." Hamish brandished the end of the chain in his hand, swinging it back and forth like a lazy whip.

Fred laughed. "Fine, then." He grabbed me by the chin and pulled my face close to his again. "That black eye's gonna be a shiner, Ruthie Sue."

I pulled my face out of his grip, but he grabbed my hair again. "Don't do that."

Fear overcame my anger. I lowered my eyes and held still.

He finally let go.

Hamish pulled the chain and I followed, my battered feet screaming for me to stop.

I ignored them, keeping my eyes on the blonde nest of hair Fred had pulled out. It was lying on the side of the trail, where he'd let it fall from his hands like a piece of trash.

It gave me an idea.

14

BRENT

AURORA, COLORADO

I adjusted my trucker hat in the reflection of the microwave and made a face.

Why did I wear it like a uniform, anyway? I probably looked like an idiot.

Same way I felt.

The knot of anxiety and dread in my stomach had pulled so tight over the past week that I could barely focus. I was used to Miley consuming my thoughts, but this was a whole new level.

Part of me still held on to the hope that she was doing what she promised—taking time to think through her feelings.

A growing part of me suspected she was pulling away. That I'd lost her altogether.

Even training, usually my mental escape, didn't offer relief. I knew Miley was busy. The distance between us wasn't all rooted in my confession. She was learning the ropes at the lodge, working a long shift as the first guests arrived. But she hadn't called since Saturday night.

And she hadn't returned the message I left on Sunday.

She always called me back.

The doubts circled my brain in the radio silence. Did she just need more space? Would I look like a moron if I called to leave another message so soon? Was she okay?

My phone, lying a few feet away on the kitchen table, buzzed to announce an incoming call.

My heart jumped when I saw the 208 area code.

Idaho.

It had to be her.

It had only been a day and a half since I'd last talked to Miley. But that day and a half had felt like a century, and I couldn't swipe the green answer button fast enough.

"Miley?"

The phone line crackled in response, and I strained to hear her voice.

"Hello? Miley?" I tried again. My voice held a note of desperation I couldn't mask.

More crackling noises. Then, finally, "I'm looking for Brent McGowen. Is this the right number?" a woman's voice said.

My heart sank. It wasn't Miley.

"That's me. I'm Brent," I said warily.

She cleared her throat. "This is Jennifer Douglas. I own Hidden Springs Resort where Miley Petrowski is working this summer. She has you listed as her emergency contact."

"Okay?" I said slowly, my pulse racing, a thousand thoughts hitting my brain. "Is everything all right? I left a message for her on Sunday evening, but she hasn't called me back."

Silence.

Shit. What was going on? My temper rose. "Are you there? Is Miley okay?"

"Miley is missing. Nobody has seen her since Sunday morning."

A wrecking ball slammed against my chest. For a few seconds, I couldn't breathe. Today was Tuesday. How the hell was I just learning about this? I couldn't form the questions.

Jennifer cleared her throat again, like she was having a hard time bringing the words to the surface, too. "She went for a run. That's what we think, anyway. She didn't tell anyone where she was going, but based on what we know ..." She trailed off.

"Hold on. Why didn't somebody let me know sooner? What the hell?" I exploded. This couldn't be happening.

"When she didn't show up for work on Monday and I saw that her car was gone, we—I—thought she was playing hooky," Jennifer said, her voice measured. "Running the trails. She wasn't exactly ... our most enthusiastic staffer. But when she wasn't back by this afternoon, I called the police immediately," she rushed to add. "We've got a search team fanning out, doing their best, but the Frank Church is huge and ..." She stopped talking.

"And what?"

"We don't know which trail she might have taken. There are hundreds. It's difficult to narrow a search area."

"She didn't tell anyone her route?" Anger flashed bright in my veins, this time directed at Miley—and myself. Why hadn't she told anybody where she was running? Why hadn't I asked? She was in the goddamn wilderness. Why hadn't anybody realized she was gone sooner?

"Who saw her last?" I demanded.

Jennifer let out an audible breath. "Her kitchen coworker, Wes. He talked to her Sunday morning. Invited her to some staff get-togethers. She made it clear she wanted the day to herself," she added with just a touch of defensiveness. "He let me know right away when she didn't report for work this morning."

Wes. I had no reason to hate him. If anything, I owed him my thanks. But I hated him anyway.

I raked my hands through my hair, tipping my hat onto the floor in the process. It landed on my apartment floor with a hollow *thunk,* next to the running shoes I'd been about to put on.

"I'm so sorry," Jennifer was saying. "I want you to know we're doing everything we can—"

I didn't hear whatever she said next. My thoughts spiraled, colliding with each other as I tried to grasp the gravity of what she was saying. All my half-baked worries about Miley avoiding me felt ridiculously small now that they'd been replaced with a deep, primal fear for her safety. "Her fitness tracker," I blurted. "She always wears it. Has anybody—"

Jennifer cut me off. "Yes. The police were able to get the data. The last time it pinged was in the main lodge, on Saturday night. There's no cell towers out here. It's … it's not useful."

The hope shriveled into dread. "We have to find her," I said through clenched teeth, more to myself than to the stranger on the other end of the line.

"I know. We're trying," she said softly. "Everybody within twenty miles is out here looking for Miley."

"Tell me more," I barked. The Frank Church was more than four thousand miles of dense wilderness. Twenty miles basically meant the local police and Hidden Springs Lodge.

"The sheriff's office is leading the search efforts. We've got ATVs. Even a chopper, but the canopy is so dense…" She trailed off. "Is there anybody else I should call? Parents, siblings, or—"

"No," I cut her off. We were wasting time. I sat down at the kitchen table and started lacing up my shoes, suddenly sure of what I was going to do next. "I'll be there late tomorrow morning," I said, glancing at the clock on my microwave and mentally calculating the distance and whether it was any use looking at flights. I shook my head. Driving would be faster. About ten hours if I drove through the night.

"I'm not sure that would—"

"I'll be there tomorrow morning," I repeated, not caring one bit about whatever she was about to say in protest. "You don't have to put me up at the lodge. I'll bring my gear. Sleep outside if I have to." Then I hung up the phone and stuffed everything into the car so fast you'd think it was a race.

As far as I was concerned, it was.

Every second that ticked by might mean the difference between seeing her again—or an alternative I couldn't let myself imagine.

* * *

The drive was pure torture.

All I could imagine were worst-case scenarios. As I barreled through the dark, rural roads to reach the Frank Church, the lack of sleep only made my mind spin faster, my thoughts bend more irrationally.

By the time I crossed the border of Utah into Southern Idaho, I was a total mess. Too much caffeine, not enough sleep, no relief in sight. I still had about a hundred and fifty miles to go, and I was running on pure adrenaline. My fingers clenched the wheel so hard they ached.

I didn't release my grip until I finally skidded into a gas station for another fill-up.

What if she hurt herself and couldn't make it back to the lodge?

What if she really did run into a bear?

What if she got lost? How long could she survive?

I tried the number Jennifer had called me from when I got cell service back.

It went straight to voicemail. I hoped that was because she was using every second she could to find Miley, but the silence drove me to distraction. There was every possibility she'd tried to call me back while I drove through pocket after pocket of dead cell coverage zones, but that didn't stop me from letting the silence seep into my bones like poison.

No news was bad news. No news meant they still hadn't found her.

My brain sifted through the horrifying possibilities on an endless loop. I felt completely helpless, stuck in a car, going over the speed limit but never fast enough to reach the last place anybody had seen her.

I refused to think of life without Miley.

No, I told myself forcefully.

She was alive. If she were dead, I'd know it somehow. The same way that feeling of dread punched me in the gut when I picked up the call from the hospital the night of the accident, right before I heard the nurse's voice.

I would find her.

I didn't care what it took. I'd find her.

* * *

After two more hours, I sped down a narrow dirt road and into a parking lot with a huge, ornate wooden sign that read "Hidden Springs Resort."

A shiny metallic leafing had been inlaid in the rustic, carved letters. They glowed in the light of the four spotlights that illuminated the sign, impossible to miss. My throat closed as I tried to swallow.

This was supposed to be one of the most upscale resorts in the country.

It was supposed to be safe.

The clock on my Nissan Altima read six fifty-two a.m. I hadn't slept in twenty-four hours, and I was dead on my feet. But still, I parked my car in the lot and made a beeline for the resort office.

The windows were dark.

Even the lodge itself looked like it had shut down. I turned in a circle, looking at the parking lot for the first time. It was mostly empty, aside from a smattering of vehicles that must have been staff, two Lemhi County Sheriff SUVs, and a truck with the Idaho Fish and Game logo emblazoned across the side. Had they sent the lodge guests home? Where was everybody?

Out looking for Miley, I hoped to God.

"Can I help you?"

I spun around to see a tall, blonde guy hurrying toward me along one of the lit walkways that led to the main office.

I didn't waste time with small talk. "I'm Brent. Miley's friend. I'm here to help look for her. Where's Jennifer?"

The guy stiffened and fiddled with his glasses like I'd given the wrong answer. He looked me up and down before he answered. "She's out there searching with the sheriff. I came back to fill up the water jug." He held up an old-school orange Igloo water cooler.

"Can you take me to them?" I pressed when he didn't offer.

He shook his head, like his mind was elsewhere. "Yeah, yeah, of course." When I squinted at his face through the darkness, I could see the dark circles beneath his eyes. My irritation softened. He must have been out there with them looking all night, too.

I fell into step beside him and took one handle of the heavy Igloo cooler. "Do you know her?" I asked.

He nodded, eyes on the ground. "Yeah. I worked with her in the kitchen."

I shot him a sideways glance. "What's your name?" I asked, pretty sure I already knew the answer.

"Wes," he confirmed, not meeting my eyes. *Idaho Dwight Schrute.*

"I thought it was strange when she didn't show up for her shift, but then Jennifer made it sound like she'd flaked to go on a long run …"

I swallowed the anger rising in my chest. Miley wasn't the type to brown-nose someone like Jennifer. But she wasn't a flake. If anything, she was too stubborn to quit anything she'd ever put her mind to. She'd never just ditch a shift without giving notice.

"That's not like Miles," I muttered. "And she didn't tell you anything about her running route? Not even a general area?"

He shook his head. "No. I knew she was running trails, but that's it. She seemed like a kinda private person."

"Tell me about it," I muttered.

"How do you know her again?" Wes asked, and I bristled. *Miley didn't mention me?* The question burned on my lips, but I refused to voice it.

"I'm her teammate. And her best friend," I added, like I had to justify the reason I was here. It physically hurt to say the words. I was so much more than both of those things, but that was all I had to work with right now.

"Oh," he said, then fell silent. I didn't want to read too much into that one word, but he seemed disappointed. If I had to guess, he had a crush on Miley, which didn't surprise me. Over the years, lots of guys had.

None of that mattered, though.

All that mattered was finding her.

15

MILEY

FRANK CHURCH WILDERNESS, IDAHO

When we finally made camp on the first night, they chained me to the base of a tree.

The men pulled thin bedrolls out of their packs and laid them around a flickering campfire a few yards away. Just far enough that I couldn't feel its warmth.

Hamish offered me some kind of jerky that I ate without complaint, even though it was dry and gamey. I hadn't eaten anything for twenty-four hours. I always did my morning run on an empty stomach.

It was nearly impossible to tell how far we'd walked. Every step felt like a tour de force with my battered feet. If I had to guess, we'd traveled maybe six miles, winding through the trees in a way that told me they were trying to get me lost.

It was working.

I had no idea where I was.

All I knew was that I was deeply, completely alone with two of the most terrifying people I'd ever met.

The second day passed in a blurry repeat of the first day, ending the same way.

Numb. Maybe three more miles covered. Blisters on blisters. Feet that felt like raw hamburger. Chained to the base of a tree.

I could barely walk anymore—something I'd never, ever experienced. Not even after the accident. For once, a new kind of pain took center stage in my body, screaming through my legs so loudly I barely registered the throb in my shoulder.

I almost missed the phantom pain.

My head lolled forward in the dark, the edges of my vision dissolving into blackness as delirium threatened to pull me under. Still, I refused to fall asleep for the second night in a row. The cold metal chain dug into my chafed skin, anchoring me to the coarse bark that bit into my back. Every few minutes, tiny insects skittered across my skin, breaking through the numbness. I couldn't let myself think about what they were.

I tried to cover my torn-up feet beneath the small, dirty blanket Hamish had tossed me, almost like an afterthought, before falling asleep next to Fred around the tiny campfire that had long since died to coals.

Fred snored like a freight train. Hamish thrashed around in his sleep, twitching in the dirt every few minutes like he was running in his dreams.

Thinking about how much farther we might walk terrified me.

At what point would my feet simply give out?

Equally terrifying was the thought that we'd eventually arrive at our destination.

I still had no idea where they were taking me.

I watched the dark figures lying near the campfire through bleary eyes, feeling as numb as the bare skin on my stomach, shoulders, and thighs. The air temperature was probably fifty degrees and falling fast. Not freezing. Not enough that I'd die of exposure—with the blanket, anyway. But so painfully cold that my skin was pure gooseflesh.

I had no way of knowing how much time had passed since the sun sank. All I knew was that the night was so dark, all I could see were the last of those glowing embers a few yards away.

At first, I'd been terrified that Fred might come after me once Hamish fell asleep, but he'd barely looked at me before hunkering down next to the fire.

My mind demanded a plan, insisting there had to be some way out of this. Something else to try. But after a while, my thoughts just spun into static like a record running off its tracks. Had anyone at the resort even noticed I was missing yet? Surely they'd come looking soon. Would they at least find my car?

Probably not for a while.

Nobody knew where I'd been running. Nobody had any idea where I'd parked the Jeep.

Stupid. So stupid.

I was on my own.

I closed my eyes and tried to focus on the last sliver of hope I had left. The one act of defiance I'd managed to keep up since this nightmare began.

When Fred had pulled out those strands of my hair yesterday, it had sparked an idea. Every few feet, I'd started discreetly pulling little clumps from my own long, blonde hair. It hung so far down my back, I could easily grab a handful of strands, even with the zip ties.

The sting as the hair ripped from my roots was nothing compared to the tiny spark of satisfaction as I brushed my hands against waist-high leaves and brush while we walked deeper into the forest. I tried to get the strands tangled into the weeds without being obvious. Hoping that some of them would stay put, little golden breadcrumbs that the wind wouldn't carry off.

It had worked. At least, in the sense that Fred and Hamish hadn't noticed.

There was no guarantee anyone would ever see the evidence of my abduction that I'd left behind.

As the night wore on, the thick, rough bark that bit into my back was almost as painful as the chain. I could feel sores developing from the constant chafing of metal and rough wood. I felt like if I could just scoot a little lower, maybe I could get some relief from a sharp chunk of wood that dug deeper into my spine each time I shifted.

I leaned to the side and tried to shimmy down a little.

When I moved, a chunk of bark gave way, falling off the tree behind me with a quiet ripping noise.

I froze. My eyes cut to the two dark figures sleeping just a few yards away.

I stayed still and waited.

They didn't stir.

I drew in a breath, and my chest expanded in relief. Holy hell, there was a fraction of give in the chain now that the piece of bark had fallen. Not much, but the chain was definitely looser around my waist.

A new possibility sprouted in my foggy brain.

Pulling up the edge of the disgusting little blanket, I tried to wedge it between the chain and my bare stomach. My zip-tied hands fumbled clumsily with the material as I tried to work it between the cold metal and my skin. I was chained so tightly, it was still a tight fit. I just needed to maneuver the fabric so the chain wouldn't cut directly into my skin as I worked.

There. Finally, the blanket lay wedged beneath the chain.

I gripped the chain with one hand at an awkward angle and started moving it in a sawing motion, side to side. After a few seconds, another piece of bark fell off the tree and the blanket slipped down to my legs from the new slack that had been created. It was next to nothing, but it was *something.*

If I could rub the bark off around the circumference of the thick tree trunk, maybe it would create enough slack for me to slip out of the chain.

It wasn't a great plan. I'd have to somehow pull the chain down over my hips without the use of both hands. I didn't have the classic female athlete's body. I had hips. They weren't wide, but they were wide enough. I groped along my pelvic bones to see how much give I'd need in the chain. Then I lay my head back against the tree and closed my eyes in frustration. I wasn't sure there'd be enough bark on this tree to create the sort of space I'd need to get out of this.

I'd try my damndest, though. I'd try anything to get out of this nightmare.

Careful to make as little noise as possible, I slid the chain back and forth, trying to keep it in the same spot so that I wasn't wasting my efforts stripping bark up and down the tree. I needed the bark to come off all the way around the trunk in a full circle to create more slack.

Those first two swaths of bark had come right off, but the rest wasn't so easy. I didn't feel anything happening for a few minutes. Couldn't hear it ripping from the tree, didn't notice any more slack in the chain.

I worked for another two hours before I felt another tiny piece of bark fall away. I nearly cried from frustration but kept going, rubbing the skin on my wrists raw even as gray light filtered through the trees announcing dawn.

Keep going. The men were still asleep. This was my last chance.

I rubbed the chain against the tree with everything in me.

Another scabby piece of bark fell to my right. The chain slackened another inch. The men stirred gently.

I pulled the chain down, shimmying my body up so that the cold metal links sat at the top of my protruding pelvic bones.

A hacking cough cut through the forest sounds. I froze and locked my gaze on the sleeping men.

Fred was waking up.

I wrenched the chain down with more force and worked my body upward, pushing on the ground with my battered feet, but there wasn't enough room. I pushed harder, frantic and determined to get the metal over bone, even if something bled or broke.

At that moment, Hamish stood up lazily, his back to me. He stretched his arms into the sky.

I pulled harder, desperately, wanting to scream from the way the soldered links of the chain tore the skin on my hips. Instead, I bit down and counted my breaths to distract me from the fresh waves of pain.

In, one, two, three, four. Out, one, two, three, four.

I got the chain around one of my hips. *Yes.* But now the chain dug into the flesh above my other hip even tighter. It wouldn't budge.

Hamish turned around. "Ruthie Sue, stop that!" He marched over and got a grip on my wrist in seconds. Then he pulled the chain back around my waist roughly, tearing up my skin all over again.

I rationed my breaths, staring at him with a blank expression. Every inch of me screamed for relief from the pain in my torso, but I knew better than to think any would come.

In my peripheral vision, I could see Fred watching. A smile ticked at his lips.

Hamish, seeming to sense his father's approval, gripped my chin and held it in front of his face. "The quicker you learn your place, the quicker those chains come off, Ruthie Sue. You're only gonna hurt yourself more if you keep this up."

I spat in his face, unable to stop myself. "My name is Miley."

Hamish stared at me for a moment. Then, without even bothering to wipe the spittle away, he slapped me hard. The sound it made seemed to echo in the now-quiet forest. Even the birds had stopped their morning warbling.

"Your name is Ruthie Sue. That other girl's gone."

Fred was up now, standing a few yards behind Hamish. He laughed. "Atta boy. Maybe you can tame her after all."

Hamish kept his icy blue eyes fixed on mine. "I ain't gonna tell him what you were doin'," he whispered. "He'd lose his shit, and you need to heal up before he has another go at you."

I stumbled to my feet as he yanked the chain away from the tree and refastened it around my stomach, tighter than ever. He looked down at my bedraggled feet and stomach, then wrinkled his face in disgust. "Sure hope you ain't too far gone to make yourself pretty again."

The floaty, fuzzy feeling came back as my feet tried to find a way to stand without pain.

I would have cried tears of joy to trade the past two days for a chance to face off with a bear instead of these two monsters.

16

MILEY

Inch by inch, foot by foot, hour by hour, we moved deeper into the forest.

We walked until the parts of me that weren't numb were completely raw, including my scalp. It was hard to believe I had any hair left after the number of strands I'd pulled out as we walked, but somehow it still hung long and thick around my arms.

I was too tired to fight against the chain anymore. All I wanted was to stop the endless walking through the forest. To wash my dirty, oozing, bloodied, broken body and then curl up into myself and disappear until the misery was over.

"Almost there now," Fred said finally.

"Where?" I asked feebly, knowing that if I didn't acknowledge him, he'd step up and slap the back of my head again. Or worse.

"Home." He coughed and spit something into the dirt behind me. I cringed. "You don't know how lucky it is we found you. When SHTF, you'll be thanking us. We got enough supplies to ride out any disaster that's comin'," he said proudly.

"SHTF?" I asked dully. I knew I'd heard the acronym before, but I couldn't remember what it stood for. I didn't really care. But I'd learned that the more they talked, the less attention they paid me. It was like they got caught up in hearing the sound of their own voice for a few minutes.

"Shit hits the fan," Hamish said, readjusting his grip on the chain.

Another piece of the hellish puzzle clicked into place.

"You're preppers?" I asked, turning my head to look at Fred. The Frank Church Wilderness was a hell of a place to go off-grid. Miles and miles of backcountry that even the most experienced backpackers never touched.

Fred scoffed at my choice of words. "We ain't 'preppers.' We're real men. Nothing like those neutered sissies you know in the city. Last of a dying breed."

I turned away from him so he wouldn't register the disgusted look on my face—just in time to see a doe crash through the brush a few yards away.

She'd nearly disappeared when a gunshot discharged from behind me, so loud it felt like my eardrum had just been slapped.

I whirled around to see Fred with the butt of his rifle still tucked against his shoulder.

That bullet had whizzed right past me—and right past Hamish's head.

Ears ringing, I turned my head to look at the doe. She wobbled where she stood. One leg, bloody and shattered, hung at an unnatural angle. Then she regained her balance and disappeared through the trees.

Fred laughed. Hamish joined in.

My stomach heaved.

"Aren't you going after her? You hit her." My voice climbed in pitch with every word.

"Nah. Plenty of deer out here. It'll take too long to track her," Fred said. My heart sank with each word he said.

"We'll go hunting once we get home," he said to Hamish as if adding a gallon of milk to a grocery list. "While Ruthie Sue ... adjusts."

I didn't bother to ask what he meant. I didn't want to know. Pent-up rage boiled inside me and I stopped walking, swaying from my own injuries. The chain slack tightened, and Hamish tried to yank me along with him. It hurt like hell, but I turned to face Fred.

"Why did you shoot her then?"

The men laughed harder. Loud, cackling even. Fred went into a coughing fit, and while he was bent over, trying to breathe, Hamish said, "Already told you. This is our land. We do what we want. Take what we want." His eyes bored into mine.

"People will come looking for me," I said through gritted teeth.

And then, like a lightbulb had suddenly blinked on in his brain, Hamish asked, "You married?" His face twisted up, like he didn't really want to hear my answer.

"Yes," I lied without thinking.

This seemed to bother him, so I pounced on it. "My husband is back at the resort. He won't stop until he finds me."

"What's his name?" Fred asked, like he was quizzing me.

Brent. His name emerged through the haze in my mind so quickly I wanted to lie down and weep. I swallowed hard. "Brent," I finally said, when I'd wrangled my emotions into check.

"Brent, huh? Just spent five whole seconds tryin' to come up with his name. She ain't married."

Hamish grinned like he was pleased by the information Fred had ferreted out.

I didn't try to argue. Instead, I clung to the hope that Brent really would find me.

That he wouldn't stop until he did.

Tears stung my bleary eyes.

Hamish pulled the chain hard, and I stumbled forward.

Fred spat on the ground again, the wet sound making my skin crawl. "If anybody does come lookin' for ya, we'll shoot 'em."

It took everything in me not to respond. Even when his grubby fingers reached out to pet the back of my head, feeling their way through the strands of my long hair and wrapping around my locks, holding them in a ponytail.

A sly smile spread across his face as he glanced at the back of Hamish's head.

Hamish, oblivious to what was happening, jerked the chain to pull me forward again.

My sore head took another hard tug when Fred refused to let go of my hair.

"Ow!" I cried. Hamish stopped and turned around. His face darkened when he caught sight of Fred, whose hands were still snaked through my hair.

Panic bloomed in my veins.

I felt like a zebra pinned between two mangy lions.

Hamish's eyes narrowed. He chewed the inside of his cheek and then looked away, his cheeks burning crimson.

Fred took the opportunity to grab my face, forcing me to look at him. He ran his tongue across his bottom lip while he watched my mouth. Oh God, was he going to kiss me? I stiffened, trying to pull away.

After a long moment, he released his grip. "Like I said, won't be long before you're thankin' us for giving you a real life. Hamish'll teach you how to behave. And if he can't ..." He trailed off.

I took a few steps toward Hamish, even though he hadn't made a move to keep walking. Anything to get away from Fred by a few more inches.

He wasn't finished yet, though. "Whole world's gonna fall apart pretty soon. You'll be safe and snug here with us. If you think about it that way, we're your saviors." He smiled and moved toward me, leaning in so that his breath was hot on the nape of my neck. My scalp throbbed where I'd torn out bits of my own hair again and again. "And we're gonna teach you how to worship," he whispered.

* * *

We walked in silence for what felt like hours longer but couldn't have been.

I was losing track of time. The sun stayed high in the sky, trickling through the pines in fits and starts.

Just one more step, I told myself, not wanting to arrive wherever we were going but desperate not to collapse. If I couldn't walk, I couldn't run. And if I couldn't walk—or run—I couldn't escape.

That was unthinkable.

When we reached a wooden sign sticking out of the ground, my heart beat faster. This was the first indication of civilization I'd seen in days.

My stomach growled in torment as I tried to focus on the words, but my head felt so light and floaty that I could barely read them.

Protected by God and Guns. If you can read this, you are down range.

My knees threatened to buckle as my bleary eyes landed on an A-frame roof at the crest of a rolling hill, peeking through the trees in the distance. My heart sped up, clanging faster.

I blinked hard, trying to focus.

It was definitely a cabin.

As we got closer, I could see that it wasn't just any cabin, but a structure with windows, solar panels, and a propane tank.

A woman in a long, shapeless dress stood in the open doorway, holding a chicken. She waved furiously, moving her hand back and forth like a flag.

She was too far away for me to read the expression on her face, but her visible eye, the one not covered by her long brown hair, looked as black and sunken as Fred's.

Desperation burned at the back of my throat, leaking out in the form of hot tears. For reasons I couldn't explain, the sight of this woman made my insides hurt as much as my outsides.

"Home sweet home," Fred crowed. "That's my pussy cat, Mary."

"No cat about it. Just pussy," Hamish said, and they both laughed.

Fred leaned in close to my ear and whispered so Hamish couldn't hear. "Mary's all mine. But don't worry. Hame knows how to share."

17

MILEY

Mary stopped waving her arm when we got close enough to survey each other.

She had long, mouse-colored hair, and her visible eye was large and brown, like a doe's. Her skin looked weathered, like Fred's and Hamish's. I couldn't guess her age.

When she brushed the hair out of her face, I suddenly realized that she was wearing a crude eye patch over her left eye, stark black in contrast to her pale skin.

She frowned and scanned me from the top of my head to my bare feet. I offered a tentative smile, but she didn't return the gesture.

Instead, her mouth tightened into a wince, like my presence pained her.

I felt myself bristle. I didn't want to be here, either.

"Who's this, Freddy?" she asked, her voice soft and childlike in contrast to her haggard appearance. Mary pulled the chicken closer to the bodice of the long, pioneer-style dress she wore. It was cream colored with tiny brown flowers, and it hung from her bony frame like a potato sack.

The chicken she held, a black-and-white speckled hen, let out an annoyed cluck, like maybe she was squeezing it too hard.

"This is Hame's fiancée," Fred muttered in reply to Mary's question. Without any further explanation, he walked around the side of the cabin.

Hame's fiancée. The phrase made me want to vomit.

In stark contrast to the bile sloshing in my stomach, Mary looked relieved when she heard this news. She flicked her gaze toward me one more time and shooed the chicken away.

I tried for a smile again.

Her expression shriveled, just like it had when she'd first laid eyes on me.

Without offering a greeting to Mary, Hamish pulled me past her into the log cabin. Out of the corner of my eye, I caught her staring at my bare, bloody, mud-crusted feet in disgust.

I darted my eyes around the dim room, taking inventory of everything I could, hoping that something I saw would help me escape.

Just inside the door was a large main room with wood floors, a cast-iron stove, a threadbare couch, and some wooden chairs. On the far side of the room, the cabin opened up into a small kitchen with a sink, a round wood table, and cabinets. There was a large window near the front door that looked out over the forest and another window above the kitchen sink.

To my surprise, the cabin wasn't ramshackle. It was clean and almost quaint. Mary's doing, I suspected.

Hamish yanked me toward one side of the main room, adjacent to the kitchen. As I followed him, I saw a short hallway with two closed doors facing each other. Maybe bedrooms.

I shuddered.

Two chains, thicker than the ones that bit into the skin around my waist, hung from the wall above me. Huge metal shackles had been attached to the ends.

The whole thing looked straight out of a scene from a slasher movie.

I looked at Hamish, unable to hide my fresh panic. They were going to keep me here, chained up like a wild animal. I shook my head and tried to resist his order to sit down on the floor beneath the chains.

"If you buck and fight, this'll be your spot for as long as it takes for you to learn your place," Hamish instructed, sounding just like Fred. "If you're a good girl, it'll only be until the wedding," he added.

There wasn't a shred of comfort in anything he'd just said.

I sat in the chair obediently, knowing in my bones that I didn't have anything left to fight him with, even if I wanted to. I could barely stand up right now, let alone run.

Mary padded across the room quietly, coming to stand behind Hamish. She peered around his shoulder at me like a toddler in a game of peekaboo. For the first time I saw a touch of a smile on her lips as Hamish used a knife to cut the zip ties on my wrist, replacing them with shackles.

For the first time in as long as I could remember, my breath spiraled into hiccuping gulps. I couldn't get enough oxygen, couldn't suck the air down into my lungs fast enough. I was hyperventilating.

"Mary, she gonna black out. Get her some water," Hamish barked at the woman, who darted toward the kitchen.

Despite my agony, I looked up sharply at Mary's retreating form. Hamish was right. I was going to pass out if I didn't get control *now*.

I closed my eyes and pursed my lips, only allowing a little air in and out, slowing my breath until I could count four beats in and four beats out.

When I opened my eyes again, Hamish and Mary were standing above me, gawking. Mary held a tin mug in one hand.

Hamish took it from her and held it beneath my lips. I drank greedily, not caring that the water tasted so strongly of iron it reminded me of blood with each sip. It was cold, and I was way past dehydrated.

Hamish shot Mary a self-satisfied look, like the calm that had settled over me had something to do with him.

I ignored him and asked, "Please, can I clean my feet? If they get infected ..." I trailed off, unsure how to finish my sentence the way I really wanted to.

If they get infected, I won't be able to run when I get the chance.

Hamish looked at my feet, which had already made a mess of the cabin floor. He wrinkled up his nose, and I wanted to scream at him that if he'd just let me wear my shoes, they wouldn't be like that.

He looked like he was about to give Mary some kind of instructions, when Fred walked into the cabin.

When he saw me chained to the wall, he moved toward Hamish and clapped him on the shoulder. "Atta boy. I'll be surprised if she's tame by the wedding, but it's a start."

"When is the wedding?" I asked, trying to keep the tremble out of my voice. I'd aimed the question at Hamish, but Fred answered.

He tilted his head, like he was giving his response some thought. "That depends on you, honey. Hame wants to marry a proper wife, not a rabid dog." He nudged my briar-scratched, dirty leg with his foot. "We'll just have to see."

My silence prompted him to speak again. "I know Hame ain't much to look at, but you know what they say, 'All cats look gray after dark.' You'll get past his looks. Or lack of 'em." Fred laughed at his own joke then tramped out of the cabin.

Hamish shot his father a look, his cheeks tinged red, but said nothing until Fred had slammed the door shut behind him.

Hamish took a step closer and offered me another drink of water.

I accepted it, swallowing down the revulsion that made me want to kick and scratch him like the feral animal they all thought I was. "Can I use the bathroom? Please, I need to clean myself up," I asked with as much politeness as I could muster. Anything to get out of these chains. Anything to soothe the raw, weeping flesh on my soles.

As if on cue, Mary plopped down an orange Home Depot bucket and a roll of toilet paper within my reach.

I stared at them in fresh disbelief.

"The outhouse is a privilege for tame women," Hamish said. "And you ain't tame yet." He crouched down and petted my cheek with the back of one finger, as if testing to see whether I'd bite. His touch felt like sandpaper, but I didn't pull away.

Hamish smiled. "That's it." He turned his head to Mary. "When you think she's earned it, get her cleaned up," he ordered, staying crouched beside me. Mary nodded and scurried down the hallway without hesitation.

I closed my eyes, not wanting to look at him anymore.

Everything hurt, inside and out.

"We're goin' hunting tomorrow," he told me. "That'll give you time to ... adjust." He looked at my feet again and frowned disapprovingly. "Mary here will clean you up in due time. Find you something to wear. Teach you a thing or two."

I kept my eyes shut tight, refusing to acknowledge him. The only thing I could think about was the fact that he and Fred were leaving me here alone with Mary.

Were they really that stupid?

I wasn't about to question this development. With any luck, I'd be long gone by the time the men got back.

When I kept my eyes closed, refusing to acknowledge him, he finally stood. "Suit yourself." Then walked out of the room, leaving me alone until Mary's quiet footsteps told me she'd returned.

"It's a good life," she said abruptly when I opened my eyes to look up at her.

Her weathered face, crumpled on one side where the puckered skin met the eye patch, told a different story.

I lifted one arm to take the wet cloth she held out for me. The chains clanked softly against each other, and I stared at her incredulously. "A good life?"

She kneeled beside me, one side of her mouth finally perking up in a smile when she met my gaze. "It'll be hard for you at first, but you'll come around. Find love in your heart for him. They do so much for us here. You'll see," she said, dabbing another cloth into a tin pail filled with water and wiping my face roughly with a cold wash rag.

I jerked back at the sharp pain, but there was nowhere to go. She moved closer and gripped my chin in her hand, then scrubbed harder.

I couldn't hold the tears back any longer, even though the salt stung.

When Mary finally drew back the rag, it was stained dark red.

18

BRENT

"How long have you known Miley?" Wes asked me as we careened over washboard dirt roads. He was driving fast, and I kept one hand clamped on the dash to keep me from flying out of my bucket seat and through the open passenger window.

The beat-up blue truck, a Toyota whose back tailgate letters had been removed until it simply read "YO," looked like a throwback to the nineties, and my seat belt didn't work.

"Since we were kids," I said distractedly, scanning the trees whipping past. Looking for any sign that Miley had been this way. Had the search party already covered this section? My chest constricted. It was impossible to know. The forest was absolutely enormous.

Wes glanced over at me quickly and then back to the road. He gripped the steering wheel tight and leaned forward, hunching so his head didn't hit the roof of the little truck. He looked like a maniacal string bean.

"Really?" he called loudly over the wind rushing through the truck cab. "Like, little kids?"

"I grew up in Boise. We met in high school," I said impatiently, cutting my gaze back to the forest, combing my eyes back and forth for a flash of blonde hair, as if it would be that easy to find her. "We started training for the Olympics together freshman year." I didn't look at him again, hoping he'd take the hint and focus. "How long until we get there?"

It felt like we'd been driving forever, and the deeper we went into the forest, the worse the road got. Would Miley really wander this far to run a trail, when there were so many others closer to the lodge? The worry in the pit of my stomach grew with each minute that passed, but I refused to let it overtake the hope that I'd find her. Miley was a trailblazer in every sense of the word. She'd never been content to take the same path as everybody else. So yes, she absolutely might have followed these logging roads this deep into the forest in her Jeep.

"So you do that skiing and shooting thing, too?"

It took everything not to show my annoyance. Why were we making small talk right now? I didn't want to get to know this guy. He seemed nice enough, but all I wanted was to find Miley. "Biathlon, yeah. You didn't answer me, though. How much longer until we get there?"

Wes cleared his throat, like he'd finally picked up on the fact that I absolutely did not want to shoot the shit. "We know she was driving her Jeep when she left. This is the main logging road. It branches off into a few smaller roads we've already searched. I'm just trying to get us back to base camp. We move it farther down the logging road after we've searched each junction." He paused then added hopefully, "I think there's a good chance we'll find her soon."

"A good chance?" I couldn't keep the tightness out of my voice. There was no room in my mind for *chances*.

Wes nodded. "Yeah. If anybody can hang in there, it's Miley. She's a firecracker."

I couldn't help sending him an incredulous look. "You knew her for a week," I said, unable to keep the disdain from my voice.

He had the nerve to blush. "Yeah, I haven't known her as long as you, obviously. But we hit it off."

Hit it off.

I was trying to keep an even keel, but I was starting to absolutely hate this guy. "But it took you half a day to realize she was gone?"

Wes flinched, and he shot me a pained look. I turned away from him, keeping my eyes on the forest, wishing he'd do the same.

He cleared his throat. "Yeah, and I feel like crap about that. I got her to take the damn bear spray with her, though. At least she has that. No offense, but it's pretty obvious she does whatever she wants. You can't tell her anything."

I couldn't argue with that.

He finally stopped talking, but the silence was short-lived. My stomach unclenched a little just in time to hear him say, "Are you guys ...?"

"Are we what?" I growled. If this joker wasn't driving me to exactly where I wanted to go, I'd punch him in the face. When he didn't finish the question he'd started, I muttered, "Just keep your eyes on the road, all right?"

I lifted my hat and shoved my hair underneath so it would stop flopping into my eyes with every bump and jolt of the stupid truck.

Somehow, Wes managed to keep quiet until the logging road crested, revealing a handful of cars, a police cruiser, people in fluorescent yellow vests, and a few white canopies set up in the woods.

"Here's base camp. If you—" Wes said, pulling the truck into low weeds next to the other rigs.

I didn't even wait for him to finish. I jumped out and approached the first person I saw. "Where's Jennifer?"

The girl pointed to her left, where a woman with a salt-and-pepper bob was talking to a police officer.

"I'm Brent McGowen. Can one of you bring me up to speed?" I asked, not waiting for her to finish the conversation.

They both looked at me. "This is Miley's emergency contact," Jennifer told the police officer.

He nodded, reaching out a hand to shake mine.

I took it, desperate to be finished with formalities. I needed to do something. The idea of Miley spending another night alone in these woods was unthinkable. "What can I do?"

"Right now we're canvassing the area. We've got a good number of volunteers. Couple of dogs. Sixty people, give or take. We've been able to cover a lot of ground. Problem is, *the area* is millions of acres wide," the officer said.

"And nobody knows where she went running?" I asked for what felt like the hundredth time.

The officer's expression turned stony. "People don't usually go running out here. Hiking, yes. Backpacking, yes. But it's pretty early in the season for any of that."

"I tried to help Miley understand that—" Jennifer began.

"I'm sure she's learning her lesson now," I said sarcastically. Somewhere in the back of my mind, I knew I needed to rein in the fear and anger spilling out of me. Pissing these people off wouldn't bring Miley home faster. I took a deep breath. *Control.*

"That's not what I meant. I just ..." She shook her head. I noticed the dark circles under her eyes and realized she'd probably been awake since this nightmare started. "All that matters is finding Miley," Jennifer said, her voice softer. "We're doing everything possible."

I dropped my head, shook it. "I can see that. I'm sorry."

"We sent the first guests home as soon as they arrived on Monday. We're pushing back the resort's season opening until this situation is resolved. It'll cost me thousands and thousands of dollars. If I even get to open. It's such a short season," Jennifer said. Her eyebrows were up and there was a glisten in her brown eyes. Tears? "We're going to find her," she said, her voice taking on a determined edge. "I've got all the staff out here looking." She waved over a young woman who handed me a neon-yellow vest. "Put this on."

I did it without question. Before I could even buckle it, Wes was at my side, shoving an enormous can into my hands. "Bear spray. Just in case."

I took it without comment. "Still no sign of her Jeep?" I asked the officer, even though I suspected I knew the answer.

"Not yet," he confirmed.

The pit in my stomach grew.

Then a thought struck me like a bullet. "Are there any rivers or lakes nearby?" Last summer, Miley had built her runs around an alpine lake near Banks. She'd gone on and on about how good it felt to swim at the midpoint. Maybe that's how she'd plotted her route here, too.

The officer turned and walked away without a response. "Where are you going?" I called to his back.

"Need a map." He threw the words over his shoulder as I followed. "There are quite a few small alpine lakes in this area. Rivers, too. It's a long shot, but let's take a look."

19

MILEY

The smell of my own body odor was making me sick. Old blood, sweat, dirt, and something sickly sweet I was terrified might be the first signs of infection.

I needed more than dirty rags and a bucket of brown water. I needed antiseptic. Soap. Maybe antibiotics.

I wouldn't get them. Mary had made that clear. Like the men, she insisted that such things were privileges for "tame" women.

I'd never been this filthy. I'd never been in this much pain from head to toe. I'd never been this terrified. My feet and wrists screamed. My shoulder was killing me.

I'd counted three nights now that the men had been gone hunting, but not much had changed. I was still chained up. Still a prisoner. Still barely hanging on.

I spent the first two days trying to get Mary to let me go. I begged her to remove the chains and pleaded with her to bring me any kind of first-aid supplies so I could treat my feet.

Surely this woman would empathize with me. Surely, we could escape this hellhole together and find our way home. But in some ways, as the hours wore on and my words were met with stony silence from the strange, skinny woman with one eye, I started to feel even more terrified than I had in the forest. I still couldn't decide how old she was. The strange way she spoke, her weathered skin and matted hair, and the frumpy homemade dress made it difficult to guess.

"Hamish is a handsome boy," she said, like that would reassure me. "He'll be nice to you."

I shot her a sideways glance. At times, it seemed like she wished it was her marrying him. She never came out and said it, but I still picked up on it. I had to agree he was a catch compared to Fred, but that wasn't saying much.

This morning, when she walked out of the bedroom and into the living room, she smiled widely when she saw me. "Good morning, Ruthie Sue." She studied my face. "You're looking feverish."

"It's Miley," I said automatically. She was right, though. I felt alternately hot and cold. My body was breaking down from exhaustion and injury. If something didn't change—and soon—I wouldn't last much longer.

Mary ignored me, then went into the kitchen and put a cast-iron pan on a little camp stove, then lit the propane below it. "You'll learn," she said patiently. "The world is ending, and we're blessed to be here, off the grid."

I painfully changed positions on the hardwood floor. "Please, can I have something to put on my feet?"

I'd asked the same question at least a dozen times now. And, like before, she gave me the same answer.

"Not until you're tamed." She set the pan down and turned to look at me across the room. "Maybe that fever will burn up some of your pride." With a little shake of her head, she moved back toward the camp stove.

After an initial sponge bath, where she cleaned up the worst of the dirt and blood, all my requests for first aid had been met with encouragement to let go of my pride. Embrace this new life. Prepare myself for the men's return.

The thought made me sick all over again.

"How long have you been here?" I asked dully. If she wouldn't help me, maybe she'd give me some idea of how the hell she'd ended up here.

Mary snapped her face my way and narrowed her one eye. "I don't see why that matters." She turned back to the camp stove and cracked a few eggs into the pan. My mouth watered against my will. She'd been feeding me, at least, and her cooking was significantly better than the bits of jerky Hamish and Fred had tossed my way in the forest.

She hummed a tune to herself as she swayed in front of the camp stove. I couldn't place it until suddenly she sang the lyrics softly, "Run, rabbit, run, rabbit. Run! Run! Run!"

My stomach lurched. I swore I'd heard the song in a horror movie.

She repeated the words again and again while she cooked, sometimes seeming to get stuck on the word *run*.

She smiled when she took the pan off the camp stove and saw my expression. "Do you know that one? It's Freddy's favorite." Then she lowered her voice. "I don't really like how Fred looks at you."

I stared down at my feet.

BANG! BANG! BANG!

Mary hit the cast-iron pan against the wood countertop. When I startled, rattling the chains and gasping in terror, she stared back at me.

Some of the eggs had landed on the floor.

Mary looked at the eggs, then back at me. Then she kneeled, scooped the eggs back into the pan, and continued her song with a smile. "... goes the farmer's gun."

My mind whirled, and my stomach heaved. Had she always been this way? Or was this what being "married" to Fred had done to her?

Was that my future, too?

"When did you and Fred ... get married?" I stammered, trying to keep calm.

She shrugged one shoulder but didn't look at me. She ladled something onto the eggs. "Long time ago. Long enough."

"How did you meet?"

"He saved me."

I furrowed my brow. "Saved you? From what?"

"I was lost, and he found me. Gave me a home. I owe him everything. If only I could ..."

She shook her head hard. Then, without warning, she hit her temple with an open hand. It made a quiet *smack*.

Her story made no sense, but it was enough to make me feel sure that Mary hadn't always lived here in this cabin.

She wasn't wearing chains. She could walk out that door anytime and take me with her.

She wouldn't, though. I knew that now. But why? Suddenly, uncovering the answer to that question felt like as much of a priority as dealing with the brewing infection in my feet.

"Were you lost in the Frank Church?" I asked gently.

She went back to humming the awful song. "Yes. I was running. From myself. From who I was meant to be."

The feverish heat that had been pounding in my head suddenly dissolved into chills. As it did, little dots connected in my mind.

Four years ago, a staffer at Hidden Springs had gone missing. Killed by a bear, they thought. While on a run in the woods.

Only her bloody clothing had been found.

A hard shiver ran through my body, rattling the chains. Bloody clothing like what Fred and Hamish had left by the lake.

Mary gave me a strange look but went back to plating the grimy eggs. I stared at her. The girl who had gone missing would be about my age, but Mary looked older than me.

Was it possible? My eyes dropped to her hands. They were smooth, like mine. Not spotted with age or wrinkly. It was just her face that looked so worn.

I searched my brain for the name that Wes, then Jennifer, had told me. It was getting harder and harder to think straight. Would I even last until Fred and Hamish got back from their hunt?

"Rayna?" I finally whispered.

Mary startled like I had doused her with a bucket of ice water. She slowly set the plates down and glided toward me, her baggy, brown-and-cream flowered dress swishing against her ankles. She bent down, squatting so our faces were lined up. She was just inches away.

"Get that word out of your mouth," she hissed. Then she looked around as if the men would show up at any moment.

"You're her," I whispered, unable to stop the words from tumbling out. "You've been here for four years. Everyone thinks a bear killed you."

Mary's single eye flicked between my two, but she didn't say anything else. Her expression was empty, her gaze holding mine for what felt like minutes but was probably only seconds.

Then she smiled. Her teeth were a little yellow but not rotten. Not like Hamish and Fred's. Without another word, she turned back to the kitchen. "Run, run, run, rabbit. Run, run, run."

"You'd been accepted at Yale on a cross-country scholarship," I continued quietly. "You worked at Hidden Springs Resort that summer." I said the words fast, my voice rising in volume, knowing she might stop me at any second.

Mary strode toward me and dropped a plate of eggs at my feet.

It slammed against the ground with a loud *thud* but didn't shatter. The eggs flew onto the dirty floor for the second time that morning. "Run, rabbit, run, rabbit," she repeated louder, her eye wide and staring right at me.

I swallowed hard. "I'm sorry, Mary," I said finally.

When she walked away without responding, I reached out a shaking hand to pick up a bit of egg and shoved it into my mouth, swallowing it whole so I wouldn't have to chew the grit.

I didn't know what to do with the information I'd just uncovered. There was no doubt Mary had serious Stockholm syndrome. I could only imagine what she'd gone through during the past four years that had forced her to bond with these monsters. But was there a chance she might be able to find her way back to reality? Could she learn to trust me?

She terrified me, that was true, but she also made my heart hurt. Because regardless of the fact that she was intent on holding me prisoner here, there was no doubt in my mind that she was a prisoner too.

20

BRENT

There weren't just "quite a few" alpine lakes in the Frank Church.

There were a few *hundred*. Dozens and dozens of specks on the map.

To make things worse, the local news, then the state news, then the national news outlets had gotten wind of the fact that Miley was missing. The parking lot at Hidden Springs had turned into a circus overnight, filled with reporters waiting for a comment and updates from the sheriff at the end of the day. A few of the reporters had even been intrepid enough to drag their gear down the narrow, rutted logging trails to capture b-roll of the search in progress.

More than once, a reporter shoved a mic in my face, asking rapid-fire questions about the "promising young Olympian." I knew what kind of articles they were writing. First the car accident, now this. Tragedies made good news.

The media attention brought fresh volunteers, more ATVs, and fresh resources, including two choppers. But the forest canopy was so dense, the on-ground volunteers made the most headway. It was less like trying to find a needle in a haystack than trying to find a lost set of keys in New York City. Endless places to look. Endless ground to cover. Endless obstacles. Zero leads.

Memories of Miley played like a movie while I fanned out with the other volunteers, exploring increasingly remote areas on foot and with the ATVs.

Like a funeral slideshow, my brain whispered as the sun set, yet again, with zero sign of her.

I pushed the words away, but not the memories.

As my eyes combed game trails, I thought about the time we'd raced through fresh powder in McCall, the first ones on the cross-country trail. The sight of her braid swinging a few feet in front of me through the gray dawn, always out of reach. The way she flashed me a look of pure joy when the trail opened up to the frozen marsh, where a herd of deer had gathered to paw at the lilies.

As I scanned the endless treeline, I thought about the night we both skipped senior prom and went to IHOP in our sweatpants instead. We sat in a corner booth until midnight eating Belgian waffles, hip to hip. It was Miley's idea. I'd wanted to ask her to prom. Almost had, until she told me she wasn't going. The last thing she needed was a sparkly, expensive dress. Jane—her mom—had just surprised her with new gloves and ski bindings.

I wanted to tell her I'd buy one for her, but I knew how that would go. Besides, the idea of getting her to myself for the whole night was all I wanted anyway.

I still brought her a corsage. A spray of lavender daisies the other kids had overlooked in favor of roses, left over in the refrigerated section at Albertsons.

It made her laugh out loud. She wore it to IHOP, paired with her sweatpants.

That was the kind of girl she was.

The kind of girl she *still* was.

21

After I called her "Rayna," Mary stopped speaking to me.

For an entire day, she pretended like she couldn't see me, curled up on the dirty floor, a shivering ball of fever and pain. She approached only to drop a plate of food at my feet and empty my bathroom bucket, ignoring my pleas for help.

The chain was long enough that I fantasized about pretending to sleep, then leaping up and wrapping it around her neck when she got close enough.

I knew I wouldn't do it.

The idea of getting to my feet felt as impossible as choking another human being until she stopped breathing. Besides, I had no reason to believe the key was anywhere in the cabin. Hamish had probably hidden it or taken it with him. I'd only be in deeper shit when the men finally returned from hunting.

There was no question anymore that my feet were infected, and the smell was getting intolerable. Even Mary held her nose in the crook of her arm whenever she passed directly by me.

It wasn't until the second meal in a row that I barely touched the food she gave me for dinner that our stalemate broke.

She squatted down and nudged me with one hand. "Rayna is dead."

I stared at her listlessly, no longer caring what she said. Her shadowy silhouette seemed to ripple in the dark cabin.

"Rayna is dead," she hissed again, nudging me harder. Her bony fingers felt like sticks shoved into my skin.

I whimpered, distantly remembering that the only other time I'd felt this kind of despair was the night of the accident, in the hospital.

Mary made a frustrated noise, and I knew she was about to poke me again. Desperate for relief, I opened my eyes and stared at her. "Rayna is dead," I confirmed, my voice raspy.

I closed my eyes again, but I could feel her hovering in front of me for what felt like an eternity. The swish of her long dress swept the wood floor back and forth as she swayed on her heels in front of me.

Finally, she stamped her foot and walked away.

The bedroom door clanked shut and the room went quiet, filled only with the labored cadence of my breathing. Pain from my feet, my stomach, my wrists, my head, sent wave after wave of agony through my body.

I was losing touch with reality. My mind felt hazy and distant, like I was floating in a dream. Once, I felt sure I heard the sound of a helicopter whirring in the distance.

Then, out of the dark stillness, the familiar, grating sound of the bedroom door cut through the air. I kept my eyes closed as Mary's footsteps, hesitant but purposeful, moved toward me.

I forced my eyes open and blinked.

To my surprise, she held bandages, a pail of water glinting in the dim moonlight, and a small, misshapen bar of soap. Next to the pail was a small jar filled with a dark-green substance. When she pushed it toward me, I could smell it. Earthy and fresh, like crushed leaves after a rainstorm.

She set the water bucket and bar of soap next to the jar, her movements slow and deliberate. For a long moment, neither of us spoke.

Finally, she broke the silence, her voice low and gruff. "I made that salve. It'll take care of the infection."

I stared at the jar then back at her, searching for some ulterior motive, some sign that this was another tactic in the twisted game she and Hamish and Fred were playing. But all I saw in that wide brown eye was a glimmer of compassion.

"Thank you," I croaked, struggling to sit up.

Mary just gave a curt nod and stood up, eyeing me as I slopped some of the water onto a rag. Despite my efforts to be careful with the water, the bucket tipped dangerously. Gritting my teeth, I tried to prop myself up on my elbow to tend to the festering wounds on my feet first.

The world tilted. Each movement sent jolts of pain radiating up my spine, leaving my vision spotty and head spinning. My eyes welled with frustrated tears that I tried to hold back.

Gritting my teeth, I reached out for the water and soap that Mary had placed near me. But even that simple movement felt like a monumental effort. My hand trembled as I tried to grasp the bar of soap, and it slipped, clattering loudly on the wooden floor.

"Oh, for heaven's sake," Mary grumbled with an irritated sigh. Her steps were heavy and deliberate as she approached me once again, dress swishing with each step. I expected another rebuke, and for a moment I was worried she might take the supplies away, but instead, I felt her surprisingly gentle hands on my shoulders, steadying me.

"You're in no condition," she muttered, almost to herself.

Her fingers worked efficiently, damping a cloth with the water and applying the soap. The touch of the cloth was both agony and relief. She cleaned the cuts and dirt on my legs first, and though she tried to be gentle, I couldn't stop the hiss of pain that escaped every time she touched a tender spot.

"Stop your fussing," she snapped, but there was no real venom in her words.

When she reached my feet, Mary's usually stern face contorted in a brief expression of sympathy. She ignored my whimpers but took extra care as she cleaned the infected skin, using the salve she'd given me. It stung sharply at first, but soon a cooling sensation spread, easing some of the burning pain.

I studied her as she worked, tears pouring down my feverish cheeks. We didn't speak again. For what must have been an hour, the only sound in the room was her occasional grunt or sigh.

When she was done, she sat back, looking satisfied. Our eyes met. But when I tried to smile, the pleased expression on her face darkened, and she hurried to stand up like I'd caught her doing something wrong.

"Thank you," I slurred, delirious from pain and fever.

"Hush, Ruthie Sue," she muttered.

I knew better than to argue.

22

MILEY

The days melted together, punctuated by our strange new routine.

Each night, Mary left me chained to the living room wall. My feverish brain jolted me awake again and again at the sound of snapping twigs or shuffling steps outside the cabin. Once, I swore I heard a gunshot. My eyes darted to the window, then the front door, fully expecting to see Hamish and Fred. Mary refused to tell me how long they'd be gone, but from the cat-who-ate-the-canary look on her face when I asked, I suspected they were nearby.

Each morning, as the first light seeped into our makeshift prison, I would hear Mary rise and open the bedroom door. A few seconds later, she'd appear in the hallway, her shadow long and skeletal. Before gathering eggs to make breakfast, she'd pour a little water into a basin, methodically washing her face and hands. Then, she'd approach me, her steps silent, and begin the now-familiar, excruciating ritual of cleaning and dressing my wounds.

To my surprise, the damn salve actually worked.

As the fever left my body and my mind cleared, I sometimes flinched away from her touch, still half-expecting betrayal or cruelty. But as the days wore on, I started to lean into her care. The sting of the water, the rough scrubbing of the soap, even the sharp bite of the pungent salve on my raw skin, were daily reminders that I was still alive. Even if my muscles were shriveling at an alarming rate.

Once the immediate task of tending to my injuries was done, Mary would prepare the eggs for breakfast. Twice, she pulled out a Bible and read me page after page in a singsong voice until I pretended to fall asleep so she'd stop.

As my wounds began to heal, Mary let me apply the salve myself as often as I wanted. She left me alone in the cabin for longer blocks of time. I heard her moving around just outside the cabin, tending to the chickens and other chores, but I was out of her direct line of sight.

Each time she did, I took the small window of opportunity to test the limits of the chains and shackles. I inched my fingers along the cold metal links, feeling for any signs of wear that could be exploited. I had long since learned the length I could stretch the chain, the distance I could travel before it pulled taut. I could sit up and stand—when I could bear the pain from my feet. But I couldn't get the padlock to budge.

One day, with Mary humming a distant melody outside, I wedged my fingernail into the lock's mechanism, hoping it might catch on something, like a lock pick. My fingers ached as I pushed it hard into the lock, twisting until my nail chipped again and again. Sweat beaded on my brow as I strained, willing the lock to budge, even a millimeter.

Nothing.

Whenever I was alone, I gingerly shifted to a seated position and tried to strengthen my body. At first, just lifting myself an inch off the ground was an immense struggle. The chains clinked softly against the floor, reminding me of my limited range. My muscles screamed in protest, weakened from days of lying feverish in chains. If I had to run right now, I wouldn't get far. I'd never been this weak before.

I clung to the knowledge that with each bit of exercise, my muscles came back to life and my wounds healed. The only thing I couldn't do with the chains was get down on the floor for planks or push-ups. But if I could regain the strength in my legs and core, get my lungs back into shape, I might be strong enough to run away when I got the chance.

As my strength came back, I started doing the little workouts as soon as Mary retired to her bedroom at night. The chains made noise whenever I moved, so I went slowly, sticking with squats and lunges. I kept it up until I was out of breath in the early hours of the morning.

My shoulder throbbed dully no matter what I did. The stakes driving me to ignore it were higher than ever, though.

I watched the moon rise and dip through the window across the living room as I trained. Every time I lowered myself into a squat and then stood up, I pretended I'd see Brent's face through the glass. Imagining he'd found me.

Where was he right now? Were they still searching for me? Had they found my Jeep? The bloody clothing by the side of the lake? Each time my mind traveled down this path, I funneled the pain into my movements, trying for one more lunge, one more calf raise. The thoughts sent a dull ache of longing through me every time, but they were all I could think about.

The other thought pressing at the back of my mind each time I looked through the window was the mental image of Hamish and Fred appearing through the warped glass.

I knew they'd be back any time.

It had been a week, at most, since they'd disappeared. But even a week locked up in this cabin felt like an eternity. I couldn't let myself think about the fact that Mary had been here four entire years. No wonder she'd lost her mind.

Like I'd summoned her, Mary's door opened down the dark hallway. My eyes darted toward the sound, and I quickly moved to sitting, focused on slowing my breath down.

I tilted my head to the side, leaned against the wall, and closed my eyes like I'd been asleep the whole time. My heart still pounded from the squats, but I could bring it under control with just a few more seconds.

In, one, two, three, four. Out, one, two, three, four.

"I heard something. What are you doing?" Mary asked.

My eyes flashed open. She stood directly in front of me.

Without warning, she dropped to the floor beside me and reached for my forehead. "You're sweating again. Is the fever back?" She put the back of her hand against my forehead. "You're too warm."

"I'm fine," I said, mentally clocking my inhales and exhales. "I just had a bad dream. That's all."

Mary studied me intently and stood, her skinny frame blocking the moonlight streaming through the window. I thought she was going to walk away when she whispered, "They'll be back soon."

I swallowed hard. I knew it was inevitable, but the thought of the men returning sent waves of dread coursing through me. "What happens then?" I asked, my voice barely above a whisper.

She shifted her body toward the window but didn't answer my question.

"How long did it take you … to be tame?" I asked, trying to phrase the question carefully. Like I really wanted to learn the answer for myself.

She didn't respond right away. I wasn't sure she was going to at all until she said, "It was hard to shed my old skin. But that's all it was, Ruthie Sue. Dead weight." She took a step closer to the window, and the watery moonlight cast a stark shadow on her skin that ended abruptly in the dark eyepatch. When she continued in that Bible-reading, singsong voice of hers, it was almost like she'd forgotten I was in the room.

"This life is real. Close to the land. Close to nature. Close to what God intended for us all along. Fred and Hamish are the last real men."

The back of my neck prickled as the tiny hairs stood on end. What did that even mean? I bit my cheek to keep from saying something off the cuff. Mary stayed silent, and I debated whether I should press her for more information. The men would be back soon, though, she'd said. What if this time alone with Mary was my final chance to get her talking?

"The last real men?" I prodded. "I don't understand."

"The last men left who truly understand what it means to live off the land. To bend the wilderness to their will. Godly masters of creation. They're building a new society, and we're an important part of that," she said, her voice taking on a strange cadence, like she was repeating information she'd memorized.

"A new society. Do you mean ... with children?"

She nodded but still didn't look at me.

"Do you have any?" I asked, even though obviously she didn't. Surely I would have seen them by now.

Mary folded her arms across her chest and didn't answer. I couldn't see her expression with her face turned away from mine, but when she sniffed and moved her hand to swipe at her face, I knew she was crying.

"Not yet," she whispered. "So far I haven't been able to ... keep them."

"Keep them?" I prodded gently.

"I've had thirteen miscarriages," she whispered.

"I'm so sorry, Mary." I couldn't even begin to wrap my brain around what she'd been through out here, but this added a new and horrifying nuance to my understanding.

She whipped around to face me abruptly. "Don't tell Fred I said that. He gets angry when I talk about the ones we lost. I need to focus on the ones I'm going to bring into the world."

"What were their names?" I whispered, following my gut.

"I wasn't supposed to name them," she murmured.

"But you did. You can tell me," I said quietly. "You can trust me."

She clutched herself tighter, bony fingers digging into the dingy white nightdress she wore.

Then, finally, she whispered, "Annabelle. Benjamin. Caroline. Declan. Elijah. Frances. Gregory. Hannah. Isaiah. Jabez. Kedrick. Leona. Matthew."

As she said the names, I realized they were in alphabetical order. And gendered. They must have been late-term miscarriages. My throat constricted as I imagined her spending her life here, working her way through each letter as she lost child after child.

"I won't tell him," I promised. Then I squeezed my eyes shut and asked the question burning at the back of my throat. The one I hadn't asked since our tentative ceasefire. "Please, do you know where the key is for the padlock? I just want to stretch my legs a little more. If you let me out of these chains for just a little bit, I won't run away—"

She didn't react with anger, like I'd expected. "I can't," she said. "You'll run, rabbit, run, rabbit." She dissolved into song for a few measures, her voice so quiet I could barely catch the words. When I didn't press her again, she whispered, "You haven't been here long enough to fall in love with this life."

I wanted to shake her, but instead I asked, "And do *you* love this life?" with as much sincerity as I could muster.

She didn't hesitate. "Yes. The only thing that would make it better is a baby."

"You're only twenty-three," I blurted out. "We could leave this place. Together. Life outside is ..." I reached for the right word to describe what I missed the most.

All I could think of was Brent's face.

My throat closed so tight I could barely speak. "Life outside is worth everything," I finished.

Mary stood in silence, so I kept talking. "Rayna doesn't have to be dead—"

She spun around so fast I barely had time to react. A stinging slap against my cheek.

"She's *dead*. Do you know what they'd do to both of us if they heard you say that?"

"She's not—" I cried.

Slap.

Another hot sting on the same cheek.

"You want to get out of those chains, Ruthie Sue? Start by learning your place."

23

BRENT

It had been four days.

I tried to remember every story I'd ever heard of people going missing in the woods and surviving for days, weeks, months. I'd Google it if I had service out here. I was sure the news outlets were quoting the stats on repeat.

It was probably for the best. I'd probably come across other stories during those searches. Ones where they found remains in the end. My mind spun through all the possible worst-case scenarios on repeat, no matter how much I tried to stay positive.

Don't lose your shit and fall apart. Miley's voice echoed in my mind. But the stakes were higher than any race. I couldn't let the fears rising like a tide inside me take over. I needed to stay calm. Focus on finding her. Ignore the chaos.

A winding river ran parallel to base camp, and we searched up and down for any sign that Miles had been there. We combed the shores of a dozen alpine lakes.

The search effort was taking its toll on everyone. With each day that passed, smiles turned tighter and reassurances that we'd find her lost some of their insistence. The reporters, camped out in the parking lot of the Lodge, were the only ones who seemed eager as ever.

Some of the Hidden Springs staff members had already gone home. I couldn't blame them. They needed to work, to earn money, and the lodge was still closed. Each time someone said an awkward goodbye, it felt like a little more hope slipping through my fingers.

To his credit, Wes stayed. So did Jennifer, who didn't bring up the lodge's closure again—not to me, at least.

Today, we were on ATVs, taking a new route unreachable by car. The theory was that maybe her Jeep had gone off the road, into the trees. If she'd been disoriented, she might have wandered further into the forest instead of back to the road.

It was a horrifying thought, but options were running slim. I resigned myself to pairing up with Wes who was, of course, driving this four-wheeler just as badly as he drove his truck. At least I had a helmet. I gripped his skinny waist tighter as we hit a tree root and the vehicle jerked onto two wheels momentarily.

"Dude, relax. I can't breathe." Wes turned and barked at me over the sound of the motor.

"Sorry." I tried, without success, to find somewhere else to put my hands on his bony frame. There was just so little of him to hold on to.

As I let go, we hit another bump hard and my ass came off the seat. I scrambled to hold on, squeezing him tight again. He batted at my arms with one hand.

"Sorry! Quit driving so shitty and I'll let up!" I grumbled next to his ear.

He slowed down a little, but not much. I was okay with that. The faster we went, the more ground we covered. We just had to avoid flipping.

The narrow game trail we were flying down opened up, and red brake lights from another ATV flashed in the distance ahead, then parked. Wes slowed to a crawl.

The police officer in charge of the search—Connor—was just ahead. He didn't look back at us, even though he must have heard our ATV approaching. He was walking with purpose toward something through the tree line.

My heartbeat sped up, and I slapped Wes's shoulder. "Faster! Go faster!" I called over the sound of the engine. He didn't argue, just gunned it. Connor was pretty far ahead, but as we reached his ATV, I could already see what made him stop.

So did Wes. He braked and cut the engine so fast I slammed into his back. Neither of us mentioned it, though.

There, on a narrow dirt road that looked barely wide enough for an ATV let alone a vehicle, was Miley's teal Jeep Wrangler.

I didn't wait for Wes before charging through the brush to reach Connor. The police officer was standing next to the Jeep's driver's side door, looking inside the vehicle. I tried to read his face, unsure whether I should be hoping she was in there or not. The car didn't look damaged. Just abandoned.

"It's Miley's," I confirmed as I approached. I could already see from his face that she wasn't in there. Despair and hope clashed in my chest, both of them sharp enough to cut me up.

"Miley!" I screamed, in case she was somewhere nearby. "Miley!"

Nothing.

Connor waited for me to finish, a look on his face like he was already two steps ahead. His expression stayed neutral as he said, "Guessing she parked here and took that trail." He turned and pointed ahead to a thin squiggle of dirt snaking through the grass a few yards away that was so narrow the ATV wheels would mow down the foliage on both sides.

My heart leaped as my eyes landed on the barely noticeable trailhead. *Yes.* I looked behind me for Wes, desperate to keep moving. Connor held up a hand like he knew I was about to charge down the trail. "Hold on. Look at this." He pulled a folded-up map out of his back uniform pocket and flicked it open on the hood of Miley's Jeep.

"There's an alpine lake about three and a half miles from here. That trail should lead us to it," he said, his finger tracing a line that looked impossibly tiny on the huge map of the Frank Church. The speck of a lake was slightly larger than the dots near it on the map.

"This is it. Let's go," I said, unable to keep the excitement out of my voice. I whipped around, almost bowling Wes over in the process. His eyes widened as he took in the Jeep. "Come on," I told him. "We have a trail. And a good-sized lake."

He nodded and followed me back to the ATV.

Three more searchers pulled up, radios in hand as we headed out on the small trail. For the first time in a week, I didn't push down the hope rising in my chest.

This was it. I was sure of it. Miley usually aimed for six miles when she ran. The lake would have been a nearly perfect midpoint.

Connor waited for me and Wes to pull up before gunning his engine and speeding down the trail.

Wes cut in directly behind him, in front of the other searchers. I could feel his chest heave as he coughed in the dirt Connor's ATV was kicking up, but I didn't tell him to slow down.

We needed to haul ass.

24

MILEY

I expected Mary to go back to bed.

Instead, she puttered around the kitchen until daylight set in. I pretended to sleep, but I watched her instead, analyzed her.

There was a reason she'd wrapped her identity around *Mary* so tight.

The same reason I'd stopped arguing when she called me Ruthie Sue.

Pretending was tied to survival out here.

I had to convince her that I'd calmed down. That I was onboard with the idea of … *marrying* Hamish. The thought made me want to retch, but if that's what it took to trick her into letting me out of these chains, I'd do it.

I took a deep breath and stretched, pretending to wake up.

"Mary?" I asked.

She didn't turn around.

"I owe you an apology," I began, keeping my voice soft. "You were right to be angry with me last night."

She turned around and faced me, her hands covered in a gritty yellowish dough.

"I've been thinking about what you said. You really do seem happy out here. I was wrong to try to tell you otherwise. Maybe ..." I trailed off, like I was really wrestling with my words. "Maybe I *do* need taming. Maybe Hamish and Fred finding me was a blessing." I cringed at my own words but kept going, keeping my eyes on my hands. "If you're willing to teach me, maybe I could learn to be happy, too."

Mary put her hands on her hips, seeming to forget they were covered in goop. "Do you mean that?"

I nodded, made my eyes wide and earnest. "I've always loved being out in nature. I used to want to live in the woods. Maybe this is just the universe's way—"

"God's way," Mary interrupted sternly.

I blinked. "Yes, sorry. Maybe this is *God's* way of giving me my heart's desire. Saving me."

Her eyes lit up when I didn't argue. She walked toward me, nodding. "Exactly! That's right. Oh, I'm so happy you're starting to see it."

I smiled. "Can you take these off? I'd love to explore what you've built here." I raised a shackled hand and gestured toward the front door. "The cabin is so impressive, but I want to see it all."

"No." She shook her head like it was the dumbest thing she'd ever heard. "They told me to leave you like that until they got back. I obey."

Tears pinched at my nose, and a terrifying thought wormed its way to the front of my mind. *What if I do end up just like Rayna? What if I never leave this place at all?*

I shook my head hard, refusing to let the thought linger.

"It's all right." Mary kneeled beside me, close enough to stroke my hair. A few crumbs of dough from her hands skittered down my cheek. "Your hair is the color of cornsilk. Do you want me to wash it, make it shine for Hamish? We could give you a proper bath."

My stomach lurched. I desperately wanted that, but the idea of stripping off my last bits of clothing in front of her made me queasy. So far, the bucket of water and rags she'd used to wash my wounds had been little more than a sponge bath. I was cleaner now, but I still stank. And my scalp was itchy and greasy. "I'd love that," I said, swallowing my anxiety.

"Good!" Mary tittered, bouncing back up to her feet and disappearing into another part of the cabin.

When she returned, she lugged a long, shallow metal basin. She smiled at me and set it down just a few inches from my leg. Then she lit the propane stove and disappeared out the front door. I stood up to see her arm bobbing up and down through the front window. A water pump?

She made several trips with the bucket, warming the water until it boiled then filling the metal basin again and again. Finally, she topped it off with several buckets of cool water and handed me a washrag and a fresh, lumpy bar of soap. "You can use it on your hair, too," she said shyly. "It won't strip your natural oils."

I nodded along.

Without missing a beat, she reached around my waist and pulled down my underwear then helped me step into the metal basin. My cheeks burned as she wrinkled her nose and tossed the garment to the other side of the room like she was flinging away a particularly disgusting insect.

The water reached mid-calf and felt like heaven. I closed my eyes as Mary eased me down to sitting, trying to ignore the jarring clank of the chains pulling taut and hitting the side of the basin. As the warm water lapped at my stomach and thighs, it occurred to me that she would have to take me out of chains to remove my sports bra.

As she moved to soap up my arms and armpits. I nodded down at my bra. "Can we take this off? It's so dirty. I don't want Hamish to see me like this."

Mary frowned. Then she sloshed water onto my chest and scrubbed the soap into the material itself. "We'll make do. It'll dry."

I bit my lip to hold in my protest.

She paused and lifted my chin with sudsy hands. "Good girl. I promise that if you're ready to accept your life here, they'll let you out. Patience is a virtue. That's what my mom always said," she quipped as she gathered my long hair to one side and laid it across my shoulder. She dipped what she could in the water, then used her hands to get the rest soapy and wet.

"Tell me more about your mom," I said, grabbing hold of what she'd offered.

She stiffened.

To my surprise, though, she responded. "She was a good woman. Tried her best," she said. Her voice was wistful but firm, like she'd closed the door on those memories a long time ago.

I wasn't sure if she was using past tense because her mom had passed away or because she'd left her behind. When she didn't elaborate further, I didn't push. We sat in silence, except for the sound of dripping water as she rinsed my long hair, cupping water again and again to reach my scalp.

She hummed a little tune while she worked. Not the godawful "Run, Rabbit, Run" this time, but something I couldn't place. Something soft and sweet. A lullaby, maybe.

When she was finished rinsing my hair, she helped me step out of the basin onto a ragged towel. Then she used the bucket to empty the basin of dirty water until it scraped the bottom. When she returned with a comb, I cringed. My hair felt rough without conditioner, and her touch wasn't exactly careful. I imagined more hair being yanked from my tender scalp.

"I'll be gentle," she promised. Then she tilted her head to the side. "Long as you promise to stay away from Freddy."

I tried not to show my disgust. I'd rather eat spiders than go anywhere near Freddy. "Absolutely. I belong ... to Hamish."

"Good," she said, apparently satisfied.

She worked the comb through the very ends of my hair, slowly moving up toward my scalp. Unlike the bath, this actually felt good. Memories of Mom combing my hair then braiding it before bed floated to the front of my memory. For once, I didn't push them away. Instead, I let myself get lost in them so fully that they tilted into dreams as my head lolled against the cabin wall while Mary gently sorted through the tangles.

When she was done, she gathered my hair to the side and wove it into a French braid, tying the end with a scrap of cloth. Then she disappeared into her room for a few minutes, returning with a dress made of the same floral pattern she wore. She helped me step into the dress, letting it flop when she reached my chained arms. I knew I had to look ridiculous in the baggy dress hanging around my waist, but Mary didn't seem to notice.

"You really are pretty," she murmured, studying my face intently.

I smiled in response, but her face stayed expressionless.

"Stay away from Freddy."

25

BRENT

Connor's brake lights finally flashed red through the cloud of dust.

I was off the ATV and unstrapping my helmet, Wes close behind me, within seconds. As the dust cleared, a pristine lake revealed itself, shimmering in the sunlight.

It was just the kind of place Miley loved—remote, untouched, beautiful.

Connor was already on the shoreline, delicately picking something up from the ground.

I called out as I approached, my voice tense. "What did you find?"

He lifted the object, using tweezers he'd removed from his jacket: A piece of clothing, soaked with dark rusty liquid.

Blood.

My heart constricted.

So much blood.

My eyes landed on her running shoes, scattered a short distance from the bloody clothing.

She'd never leave those shoes behind in the middle of a run. No matter what happened. Unless she couldn't run anymore.

"No ... it can't be." A desperate whisper escaped me.

I approached him, hands trembling as I reached for the fabric remnants: light gray with little white stripes. Connor put up a hand and shook his head firmly. "Don't touch them. We'll need to test the blood."

"It's her tank top," I murmured in a daze. "She always wears that brand. And those are her shoes."

Connor studied me carefully. "Are you sure?"

Tears welled up in my eyes. I couldn't answer. If I tried to talk, I'd choke on the words. I nodded again.

The sound of the other ATVs growled closer. More volunteers. Likely a reporter or two.

The world tipped sideways, and for a moment I felt sure I was going to collapse.

Over the drone, Wes's footfalls thudded behind me. He stopped short when he saw what Connor was holding. "Oh God, no," he moaned. "I knew it. A bear."

I didn't give him time to say anything else.

I whipped around and punched him in the face.

He went down on his ass, hand covering his nose, glasses tipping at an angle. "What the hell?"

I didn't answer. Just wound up my fist again and was about to go for another hit when Connor grabbed my arm. His voice was stern enough to knock the fight out of me. "That's not gonna do anything, kid." He jerked a hand toward the sound of the approaching ATVs. "Don't give them anything else to report."

I stumbled toward the water's edge, away from both of them. Away from the bloody clothing and abandoned shoes.

Then I let the tears fall.

I stood there like that for what felt like hours while the horror behind me spiraled deeper. More people arrived. More gasps. More talk of bears. More horror. More footsteps behind me that started, then stopped, then slowly backed away.

A short distance away, I could hear one reporter filming, speaking in a sympathy-soaked voice about the search ending in tragedy.

I wanted to rip the camera out of her assistant's hand and throw it in the lake.

When I finally turned around, I saw Connor, Wes, and the rest of the small group of searchers. The reporter was, miraculously, gone. Maybe Connor had insisted she leave.

Nobody had that steely look of determination in their eyes anymore, or the weary persistence we'd all rallied around as the days wore on. Some people stared at their feet, shuffling dirt around. Others sat hunched on their ATVs, as if waiting for something.

Connor approached me slowly, eyes on my balled fists like he was expecting me to lash out again. I couldn't blame him. I wanted to.

He opened his mouth to speak.

"Don't say it." I held my hand up.

He stopped where he was, about ten feet away from me. "I'm really sorry, kid."

"I said, *don't say it.*"

"We'll take the clothing with us for DNA testing to confirm what we suspect. But given the amount of blood and the way the clothes are torn up, it was some kind of animal attack," he said anyway. "Fish and Game will take it from here."

I squeezed my eyes shut. "Maybe she got away," I managed. "Maybe she's still out there." I scanned the lake as if I might see her silhouette on one of the boulders that lined the shore, just waiting for somebody to look.

I barely caught the rest of what he said. I blinked, forcing myself to listen.

"I'm sorry to say that I think our search ends here," he went on. "We'll consult with Fish and Game when the DNA testing comes back, but given what we've found and how long it's been ..." He trailed off.

My gaze drifted to Wes. He was still covering his nose with a cupped hand, blood on his upper lip. He watched me like I was a wild animal.

"We have to find her. Bring her home," I choked out. The idea of leaving Miley out here—even if it was just her body—was too much. I couldn't accept any of it.

Connor sighed heavily. "I wish we had the resources to do that, son. I really do. Miley deserves that. But given what we've just found, the bulk of our volunteers will go home. We're already spread thin. There's a mudslide in Challis that's got people trapped in their cabins. An abandoned vehicle and a missing group of high school kids outside of Grangeville. A ten-year-old boy who fell into the river outside of Grandjean and was swept downstream." He rubbed at his eyes wearily. "Lots of other folks who need our help."

Lots of other folks who might still be alive, I translated.

"I understand. But I'm not going home," I said quietly. I physically couldn't walk away, no matter what he said.

"I know. But you need sleep," Connor said gently. "We're all running on fumes. Go back to the resort. Jennifer will put you up for another night. If you want to set out on your own tomorrow, I can't stop you. I'll even loan you one of the department's ATVs."

I swallowed hard but nodded. The idea of walking past the media in the parking lot tonight was almost unbearable. But it would be the last time I'd leave these woods until I found her.

"I'm coming with you," Wes said, shuffling beside Connor. He eyed me warily.

"Why?" I demanded.

He didn't look away. "Because nobody deserves to be left out here." He set his mouth in a tight line. "Besides, I'm out of a job. I heard Jennifer say there was no way she could reopen this season. The optics are bad."

I nodded slowly. I'd take all the help I could get, even if that meant Wes.

Connor eyed the two of us. "Good." He thrust the battered trail map toward me. "Stick together. And take this with you. It's easy to get lost out here."

"I'll drive the ATV," I said to Wes, my voice tight.

He nodded, still holding his nose. His eyes were rimmed red. He'd been crying, too.

Wes flinched when I reached out an arm, like I might hit him again. Then he slowly shook my outstretched hand.

26

Early morning mist still hung heavily over the parking lot when I spotted Wes by the ATV, his full Nalgene bottle reflecting the first glimmers of sunlight. We'd left parked halfway down the logging road, then cut through the cabins to avoid any lingering news outlets. I didn't want them to know what I was doing. I didn't want to be cast as the dogged, brave teammate in their stories. I just wanted to find her.

Wes had come prepared with everything I'd instructed: backpack stuffed to the brim with supplies—and a glinting can of bear spray clipped to the side with a carabiner.

"Have you ever hunted before?" I asked when I got within earshot, breaking the silence and setting down my own gear. It'd be a tight fit on the ATV, but I wasn't about to waste time shuttling back and forth between the camp every night to sleep. Based on the size of Wes's pack, he wasn't planning on camping. But that was his business.

Wes shook his head. "My dad always wanted to take me. Said his 'flower child' needed to learn to man up." He gestured to his neon-yellow T-shirt that sported scientific drawings of dandelions. "I never could stomach the idea of killing something just for the thrill of it, though."

"Hunting isn't all about the kill," I countered, passing him a helmet. "In biathlon, the hunt is about the chase. Tracking your rival, aiming for the target. That's how we're going to find Miley."

His eyebrows knitted together, and he eyed the .22 rifle strapped to my back. "What's up with your gun, anyway?"

I couldn't blame him for asking. The ultra-lightweight, slim-profile gray and red gun looked almost toylike in comparison to the typical hunter's weapon of choice. "It's a biathlon rifle," I clarified. "There are real bullets inside."

"Fine." He held up his hands. "You do you."

"It's a lot more reliable than bear spray," I murmured, nodding to the gun.

"You know it's not hunting season, right?" he added.

"We won't use it unless we have to," I muttered, situating my gear in the ATV's deep wire basket and starting the machine with a growl. Wes clambered onto the back, his grip tight around my waist. I didn't bother asking if he was ready before kicking into high gear and tearing down the trail as fast as the machine would take us.

With a clear destination and the ATV at top speed, the ride to the lake was mercifully short.

Even one night of sleep had been impossible to stomach while Miley was still out there.

We had to find her.

I wouldn't stop until I did.

When we arrived, we parked the ATV in the same spot on the shore of the lake. The dirt and sand was criss-crossed with tire marks and flattened weeds from yesterday.

"She's more than just your friend, isn't she?" Wes asked.

"What the hell kind of question is that?"

When he didn't respond, I took a deep, steadying breath, trying to quell the rush of emotions, the mix of fear, hope, and desperation. "It's complicated," I finally admitted.

Wes shrugged, his gaze a mix of sadness and sympathy. "You loved her."

"I *love* her," I barked, surprising myself with how loud it came out.

Wes took a few steps back.

I turned my focus to the pristine lake. Its water was so clear I could see the rocky floor.

As I scanned the pebbles a few yards from shore, I caught a glimmer of something out of place. The wrong color, my brain insisted.

I yanked off my shoes and waded into the freezing water.

"What are you doing?" Wes called, but I was focused on the glimmer of orange that, with each step I took closer, morphed into a rectangular shape beneath the surface.

"It's her fitness tracker," I exclaimed, plunging a hand into the water and grabbing hold of it. I turned the watch over to look at its dead, black face.

There. The scratch. I remembered the night in Beijing when she had scraped its face against an elevator door. It was a trivial memory, but like every other moment I'd shared with Miley over the years, it was deeply etched in my mind.

My mind spun back to the bloody clothes on the shoreline, the placement of the running shoes. How in the world had the fitness tracker gotten into the lake? Why was it separated from Miley's clothing by so much distance?

My gut told me that Miley had taken off the tracker intentionally.

I didn't know what that meant, but it was the first glimmer of hope I'd felt since we discovered this place yesterday.

27

MILEY

I must have fallen asleep after Mary finished braiding my hair, because the next thing I knew, Fred and Hamish stood in front of me.

"Well, don't you look nice, honey," Fred cooed, those nasty brown teeth and leering gaze barely a foot away from my face. "Feeling more at home now?"

"You look real pretty," Hamish whispered, then licked his lips. His eyes lingered on the purple sports bra that was impossible to conceal without pulling the dress up past my chained arms.

My stomach turned but I forced a smile, reminding myself that I was just playing a part. A means to an end. The only thing that mattered was getting out of these chains.

"Thanks. I feel much better," I said, keeping my eyes down. "Mary fixed my hair."

Fred nodded approvingly and looked over at Mary. She blushed and shrugged like she'd been given some award.

Jesus Christ.

I was desperate to ask when the chains would come off. But I held the question in.

"How'd she do, Mary?" Fred asked.

Her one eye darted over at me, then at Fred. "It was rough, but she did okay, Freddy."

I forced another smile. She could have said worse.

"Good," Fred said. "Can already tell it's gonna be an early fall —and winter. There's a whole lot of work to do, and we could use another pair of hands. Not to mention a wedding we gotta get on with."

I nodded along like I cared, hoping that meant he was going to let me out of the shackles.

Instead, he clomped across the kitchen and took a bite of the Johnnycakes Mary had baked.

"I'd like to help," I prodded, jangling the chains a little.

Hamish smirked.

Fred laughed out loud. "Eager beaver now, aren't you?" A few crumbs of the yellow cake spilled into his beard. "You're not ready yet. My pussycat Mary was the same way at first. The winter will beat it out of you better than I could."

I swallowed hard and nodded like I understood, trying to hold back the tears at the thought of more time against this wall. It was impossible, though.

"She's cryin'," Hamish observed, squatting down to get closer to my face. I wanted to turn away from him. Everything in me screamed *danger*. Instead, I forced a wobbly smile.

He wiped a tear from my face using his almost-black-with-dirt thumb.

I kept myself still.

In one swift motion, Fred strode over and smacked him hard over the back of the head. Hamish lurched forward, nearly smashing his face into mine.

"Swear to Christ. She'll be near impossible to live with if you pussy-foot around her like that. Stop it!"

Hamish scrambled to his feet away from me but clenched his teeth, jaw set in anger. I moved my eyes to the floral pattern on the scratchy dress Mary had put me in. I didn't want to get in the middle of whatever this was.

"Come on, honey," Fred said, grabbing Mary's arm by the elbow roughly. "It's been way too long." He didn't let go when she stumbled against him.

He winked at Hamish then shot me one last leering look before he disappeared down the hall with Mary and slammed the bedroom door.

Hamish sat down on the worn, orange-and-brown plaid couch against the opposite wall of the living room. Light from the big window made his strawberry blonde hair look like greasy gold. He put his elbows on his knees and just watched me.

Something slammed against the bedroom door.

Mary gave a muffled yelp. I couldn't even count to three before I heard the bed springs moving. Mary whimpered.

"He's hurting her," I said to Hamish, making my voice as soft and gentle as I could. There was something softer about Hamish. Like whatever had calcified in Fred's brain still had room to shift in his.

At least, that's what I told myself.

Hamish shrugged.

"Is that what you're going to do? Hurt me like that?" I tried, prying for the cracks.

"You're our women," he said, like it was a basic fact I should have learned by now.

I swallowed. I didn't have time to change his mind. I needed to work with what he already believed. "He's hurting her, though. He doesn't need to do that."

He narrowed his eyes. "Not my business."

"Okay, fine. But I'm your business, right?" I kept my gaze fixed on his, hoping I was broadcasting a sultry look. "I think we could have a good time together … if you let me show you."

I nearly gagged on the words, but I kept my eyes soft and inviting. If he took the bait, he'd have to remove my chains. And then the only thing I really wanted to show him was how hard I could kick, how fast I could run even if it meant tearing my healing feet up all over again.

His Adam's apple bobbed. "Not until we're married."

I nodded like that was totally reasonable. Kidnapping was fair game. Sex before marriage, not so much. *Right.* Before I could respond, the bedroom door flew open with a hollow thud and Fred strode back into the room, pulling up his suspenders. I glared at him, not bothering to mask my hatred this time. That had taken all of five minutes.

"Mary, get your ass out here and make us supper," he called over his shoulder. Then to Hamish, "The hell you sitting there for, drooling over her?" He kicked his son's boot, and Hamish stood to attention. "Go out to the shed and get me some of that brew you been working on."

Fred watched as Hamish left the room, brushing past Mary on his way. Her red-rimmed eye met mine for a split second, and I knew she'd been crying.

She hurried to the kitchen and began pulling things out of cupboards, humming a soft, frantic tune.

Fred glanced at her back then kneeled down beside me and picked my thick braid off my shoulder without a word. He sniffed it and smiled. I darted my eyes to Mary, not daring to make a sound.

Dear God, don't let her see.

Fred finally let go of my braid and whispered, "You make an old man feel like he could go again."

Everything in me recoiled. For a moment, I was afraid he was going to reach out and touch me. I wouldn't be able to stay silent then.

Just then, Mary dropped a plastic dish. It made a dull clatter on the wood floor, and her humming rose in volume in response. Fred snapped his head toward her. "Clumsy whore."

He turned his eyes back to me and drawled, "She might be tame, but that don't make her smart."

"Sorry," Mary mumbled, but her sweet, contrite voice contrasted with the murderous look she was giving me. Like she thought I was the one pushing Fred's buttons.

Fred grabbed my chin hard when he caught me staring at Mary. "Don't look at her. Look at me."

"The hell you doing?" Hamish yelled, walking into the cabin.

Fred winked at me. Then, without a response, he stood up and grabbed the brown jug dangling from Hamish's hands. He took a long, noisy swig, wiping the dribble of amber liquid off his beard as he let out a loud belch. "You're one lucky cat, boy."

28

MILEY

"We don't have time to tame her your way." Hamish's hushed voice filtered in from outside the cracked kitchen window. "We could use the help getting ready for winter. You said so yourself."

My ears perked up, and I strained to listen to the men talking. I'd been alone in the living room for hours today. At first, I braced myself whenever I heard footsteps thud back and forth past the cabin. But Fred and Hamish stayed outside.

Fred grunted in response. "No. The three of us work hard, and we'll get it all done."

"We've got another mouth to feed, so we need another pair of hands," Hamish insisted. "I think we should move up the wedding."

Fred laughed. "I'm the one who kept us alive all these years, so I'm the one who decides when that woman gets out of chains. You want her, I hear that. But if you don't wait 'til she's soft and ready, she won't be worth it. She'll bite your little pecker. Then run the first chance she gets."

Damn right I will.

"Been living out here my whole life," Hamish spit out, his voice rising. "Longer than you, if you come at it that way."

Fred laughed. "Your whole life ain't even half of mine."

I rolled my eyes. Of course they'd get into a dick-measuring contest.

"I'll tame her. You'll see," Hamish said. "I'll tame her faster than you could. By the time the snow comes, you'll be singing a different tune."

Tame her.

The first time I'd heard those words, they sliced like knives. But now, from the chains in this cabin, I felt like I was the one wielding the blade.

I'd be tame, all right.

I pressed my body against the cabin wall to finagle a push-up. My legs weren't going to save me if I never got out of these chains. Not unless I could convince Hamish and Fred I was on board with this whole situation.

So I would go along with whatever crazy thing they wanted me to do.

I had to get out of here by the time the first snow fell. Escape was just the first hurdle. Even if I managed to get away, I still had miles and miles of remote wilderness between me and any kind of rescue. If the weather turned cold, I'd never survive without supplies. Without shoes. Without a coat.

But if I stayed here through the winter as Hamish's wife pretending to melt into this new life, I was terrified I'd actually become *Ruthie Sue.* Like Rayna had become Mary.

I closed my eyes and imagined myself splitting in two. Untangling myself from the girl who wanted to lash out at these men, wanted to convince Mary that her real name was Rayna, wanted to run the first chance she got even if it wasn't the right moment. If I wanted any real chance at escape, I had to be able to walk free first. That meant I needed to be compliant, unopinionated. *Grateful.*

In other words, I needed to take a page from Mary's playbook. Not just for a day, though. I needed to go all in.

The thought sent a chill down my spine.

At what point would it stop being a playbook and simply morph into my life, like it had for her? Surely, Rayna had tried to escape. How long could I play with fire before I got burned?

I drew in a deep breath. *In, one, two, three, four. Out, one, two, three, four.*

I would find a way to escape before the snow came, when the moment was right. When they thought I was Ruthie Sue. When they thought all trace of Miley was gone, even though she'd still be there, hidden inside me.

I steeled myself to take the charade deeper.

Hamish walked back into the cabin, his huge boots thumping.

When he glanced at me, I offered him my sweetest smile then turned my face downward, like I was suddenly shy. "I was wondering ..." I trailed off.

"Need to get back to the garden," he muttered, but from the way he lingered in front of me, I knew he wanted me to continue.

"I keep thinking about what you said earlier. And I was wondering if there's anything I could do to help get ready for winter. I know how to work hard," I said.

He sniffed and then plopped down on the couch across the room from me, stroking his bushy red beard.

"You ain't tame yet."

"You don't have to let me out of the chains," I clarified quickly. "I mean, if there's anything I can do right here."

He raised an eyebrow, like I was talking nonsense. I kept my face relaxed, soft.

"Not much you can do in them chains."

I dipped my chin, like this news disappointed me. "I understand. I just want you to know ... I've had a lot of time to think. Mary helped me see this place in a whole new way. And ... well ... I appreciate the way you stood up to your dad for me like that. I think you and I could have a good life here, together."

His eyes widened, and I wondered if I'd oversold it. Surely he wasn't stupid enough to think I'd come around that quickly. Fred was right about that much.

"But you ain't tame yet," he repeated doggedly.

I swallowed back the irritation and nodded, like I understood. "That's fair."

He cracked his knuckles and looked at the ceiling for a long few seconds. "You've gotta stop talkin' back. Stop askin' stupid questions. Be more like Mary."

"I understand," I said simply.

He narrowed his eyes. "I still can't let you out. Won't go against my dad."

I choked back the retort I wanted to make about Fred.

Hamish cocked his head. Then he smiled.

I smiled back, imagining the blade of the secret knife I held getting sharper.

29

BRENT

I held Miley's fitness tracker like a talisman while we searched, even though somewhere in the back of my mind I knew I shouldn't have touched it at all.

It might be evidence. The police would probably be pissed I'd picked it up with my bare hands. But another voice, louder and more insistent, drowned out the thought.

They'd already written her off as dead.

Everyone, including the police, seemed convinced that Miley was just another statistic, taken by the wilderness. One of the 500,000 hikers, campers, and hunters who went missing in the forest every year, most presumed dead. But I wasn't ready to accept that. Not without doing everything I could to find her.

The fitness tracker itself felt like the last link I had to Miley herself. My last thread of hope that she was still out there—and that I'd find her, somehow.

With each step through the underbrush and along the shoreline, my eyes scanned for any sign of her. I turned the tracker over and over in my hands while I searched. How often had I seen it on her wrist? She never took it off. Not even to swim.

Wes and I kept looking as the day dragged on. Heavy clouds loomed on the horizon, getting closer as the wind picked up. Each time the sun broke through, it was higher in the sky, a constant reminder of how much time a search like this could take. After a while, the warm metal of the tracker felt like it had become part of my skin. It kept me going. Because it wasn't just a piece of tech; it was a piece of her.

When I'd combed every inch of shoreline, navigating thick trees and endless rocky outcrops that dead-ended in water so deep I was forced to wade up to my chest to continue, I circled back to the beach where we'd found Miley's clothing. The lake's glass surface had turned choppy with the rising wind, and I shuddered to think what would have happened if we'd waited to start our search by a few hours. I never would have seen the tracker through that dark, choppy water.

"Where are you, Miles?" I murmured softly, trying to imagine her slicing through the water at a brisk freestyle, pretending that her shoulder didn't hurt.

Maybe twenty yards to my right, I caught sight of Wes. His head was down while he combed through the grass at the edge of the treeline by the meadow. A place he'd already searched.

My heart sank. We were no closer to finding her than we had been hours ago. The day had started with so much hope, but it was sinking as quickly as the sun making its way toward the horizon.

"Brent, get over here."

The hair on the back of my neck prickled. Wes's voice came from somewhere within the trees. This was the first time either of us had said a word to each other while we searched.

I squeezed the tracker to my palm so hard I expected it would leave a bruise, but I didn't give a damn.

"Look," Wes demanded before I'd even broken through the treeline. "Those huckleberry plants."

He pointed to a thicket of shrubs swaying in the wind.

I took a step closer and saw the half-broken branches, some of them smashed into the ground.

At the base of the plants, the dirt looked scuffed.

Signs of a struggle, maybe? My eyes combed over the scene.

"There," I barked, pointing to a stand of sagebrush with one of its limbs nearly torn off. The raw edge of the torn branch, pale against the dark bark, flapped gently in the wind.

"And there," Wes added, hurrying toward the bent stem of a sapling a few feet away, deeper into the forest.

"Good tracking," I breathed, daring to hope even though I knew that anything could have made these disturbances. My heart beat faster as we fell into step, moving deeper into the forest, away from the lake, scanning.

Every few feet, there was fresh evidence that something—or someone—had thrashed this direction through the forest. More bent stems, more cracked branches, and tiny patches of upturned soil marked a tenuous trail.

With each step, each new sign, I became more convinced that it wasn't an animal that had left this path. Most of my experience with shooting had come from biathlon, but I'd learned a few things from my uncle, who took me hunting with him every November. He was the one who'd shown me how to set a trapline, how to track a wounded animal, and how to field dress a kill.

For the most part, forest creatures moved through the woods like shadows, barely making a sound—never leaving a wild trail like this. The one exception was when they'd been injured so badly that the only option left was to crash through the trees so fast, so furiously, they left a path.

Except, in that case, there was almost always blood. Fur. Hoofprints as a half-ton doe or elk ran for its life.

The stillness of the enormous forest suddenly felt oppressive, and I had to force my thoughts away from so many ominous possibilities. My chest tightened with anxiety and fear, wondering what might have prompted Miley to leave a trail like this. Had someone—or something—dragged her this way?

Miley's voice was in my mind.

Don't let your emotions run away with you. Keep your head.

Yes. I had to keep my shit together or I risked precious time.

A few feet ahead of me, Wes had gone still.

My heart leaped to my throat, both desperate and terrified to know what he was staring at.

"What is it?" I asked, moving quickly in his direction.

Wes didn't answer immediately, but he didn't have to. I saw what he was staring at, in a patch of dirt at his feet, as soon as I approached.

He crouched down slowly. I did the same automatically, not bothering to swipe the hair whipping across my face, as we both squinted at the faint imprint.

It wasn't a clear outline. But with some imagination, it began to resemble a boot print.

"That's not Miley's," I breathed. The footprint was enormous—at least a size thirteen. Miley wore a size six.

I pushed back the war of emotions clanging in my chest. Hope, terror, confusion. The print was huge. When I tried to picture the person who'd made it, my heart seized. I pushed the image away. Who was to say this boot print didn't belong to some hiker? Or one of the searchers? Had one of them made the trail of broken branches and scuttled leaves?

I'd been in a daze the day before, but what had the sheriff said? *Still early for backpackers.*

We followed the tenuous trail of disturbed brush for another fifteen minutes, silently scanning for any sign of more footprints. The ground here, deeper into the forest, was spongy, ideal for leaving footprints, but most of it was covered by a layer of old pine needles.

Just when I'd started to despair, I stopped dead. "Look," I breathed.

Wes was at my side in seconds.

This time, my heart hammered like a freight train when I saw the impression on the patch of dirt beneath a leafy shrub that had kept the ground bare, free of pine needles.

"Shit," Wes breathed.

It was another boot print. This one was far clearer than the last.

And right beside it was a smaller, more delicate print.

A bare foot that I'd bet my life was a size six.

Her, her, her, my brain screamed.

"Did somebody take her?" Wes asked, voicing the horrifying thought niggling its way through my mind.

"Who would even know she was up here?" I muttered, my eyes darting in all directions.

And who would drag her this way? This wasn't a trail. Not by a longshot.

Another realization hit me. "Did you see her bra in that pile of bloody clothing?" I asked Wes.

His cheeks burned crimson, but he didn't try to say anything cute. "No ... I mean, I don't think so. Everything was all torn up so bad, it was hard to tell what was what."

I balled my hands into fists, furious at myself for not connecting the dots earlier, but the sight of that blood-soaked clothing had short-circuited my system. I could hardly bear to think of it, but now I racked my brain, trying to remember exactly what I'd seen among the ripped fabric and rusty blood. "Did you see any purple fabric?"

Wes shook his head. "I ... I don't think so. Just black and gray."

"Dammit." My hands were shaking from the adrenaline now. Miley loved high-end, understated workout gear. Under Armour, Patagonia, Lululemon. Her sports bras were the notable exception. Always colorful. Usually purple, her favorite color.

My voice rose in excitement. "She must've been wearing the bra when she went missing. She always wears a purple one. I don't think it was with her other clothes."

Wes's face twisted in a war between horror and hope. "So she might still be alive?" The words came out as a strangled whisper, like this was the first time he'd let himself believe that what we found out here in the forest, if we found anything, might lead us to a living, breathing Miley.

I nodded. "Gather up your pack. I'll get mine. This storm is going to hit soon, but we can search until that happens."

Wes's mouth dropped open. "Hold on. We should go back and tell Connor."

It took everything in me not to shake him by the shoulders—or throw another fist at his nose, which looked swollen and painful up close. Instead, I lifted an arm skyward, my hand indicating the heavy black clouds poised to burst directly overhead. "Those clouds are going to drop buckets any time now. There won't be any prints left to find by the time we get back here."

Wes grabbed his phone from his pocket and leaned in close to snap a photo of the boot print and footprint. His face crinkled in disappointment when he saw the screen. "It's not a great photo, but we could take it back with us. Show Connor and—"

"It'll be nearly dark by then. And storming. It'll be tomorrow morning at the earliest by the time the others get here. I'm not letting nearly an entire day go to waste when she might still be alive. Go back if you want, but I'm following this trail."

I ignored the incredulous expression on his face and turned to scan the forest floor for more scuff marks, more signs of a struggle.

"Whoa, what about the ATV? We can't take it through here," Wes called from behind.

"We leave it for now. Go on foot."

"This isn't exactly a perfect trail of breadcrumbs," he argued. "Did you forget the small detail about how the Frank Church is *millions* of acres? It'd take a lifetime to cover it on foot. "

I stopped walking and spun around with a growl. "So, what do you suggest?"

He held up his hands, as if in surrender. "I'm not saying we just give up. But we go back to camp. Get more supplies. Tell Connor about the boot print. Set out in the morning and keep looking for as long as it takes to find her."

"Hell no," I spat the words out. "I'm going now. We can't waste all that time."

"We're just going to charge out there? What the hell are we going to eat?"

I glowered at him and shifted the rifle on my shoulder. "This forest is full of small game. We can trap at night. And I've got all kinds of gear in my backpack. We'll be fine."

He eyed my pack, skeptically. "Fine, but I don't even have a sleeping bag. And it's freezing out here at night."

I thought quickly. I only had one ultra-light sleeping bag in my pack, and I sure as hell wasn't going to share it with him. "I've got blankets," I fibbed, not telling him that they were the emergency tin-foil variety that crinkled every time you moved a millimeter. They'd keep us warm enough. That was the important thing. And if he agreed to come with me, I might even swap him for the sleeping bag once in a while. I hated to admit it, but I wanted him to stay with me. For one thing, he knew the area better. For another, he was a damn good tracker. It would have taken me precious time to find that boot print—or the trampled brush—without him.

He rubbed his cheek where the stubble had grown in. "I don't want to leave you alone. But this seems like a bad idea."

A shiver of doubt wormed its way through the adrenaline urging me to charge ahead alone, no matter how dangerous that might be.

He was right, though. This wasn't a small decision. Previously, we'd only searched as far as we could get in a day from the resort with the rest of the search party.

I mentally calculated the number of dry meals I'd crammed into my survival pack along with the tiny two-man tent. With Jennifer putting the volunteers up at the lodge, I hadn't had to eat any of them —or use the tent. Seven Mountain House meals, if I remembered correctly, a water filter, plus a big handful of protein bars. I did the worst math of my life, hoping it would hold. If we split all that and ate every day, we'd last a week, even if we didn't stop to hunt or trap. Sure, our stomachs would protest. Sure, we'd lose some weight. But if it meant the difference between losing the trail and finding Miley, it was an easy choice.

"How much food did you bring with you?" I demanded.

Wes frowned. "A handful of beef sticks? Some granola bars? I could probably eat all of them right now—"

"Don't." I cut him off. "If we ration, that'll buy us another week. If you're coming with me."

I held his gaze. The first drops of rain were already hitting my bare arms. I tugged on the thick hoodie I'd tied around my waist when I waded through the lake.

He set his jaw and looked back in the direction of the ATV.

I blew out a sigh and turned around. I couldn't blame him for balking at the idea of charging into the forest with a half-baked plan and haphazard supplies.

It was the only thing I could do, though. He had to know that. I scanned the forest floor, trying to find more signs of broken branches or trampled grass through the wind as I walked away from him.

"There won't be any ripe berries this early in the season," he muttered loud enough for me to hear. "But we'll find some rosehips. And the thimbleberries will come on quick. Then the salmonberries." To my surprise, his footsteps thudded toward me.

I shot him a look, but I had to admit I was impressed. I could handle myself in the forest, but I knew next to nothing about plants. "Okay, flower child."

He pushed up his glasses and scowled. "You fly off the handle easy, you know that?"

A smile cracked my lips for the first time in days. "So I've been told."

30

MILEY

Moonlight and cold air streamed through the gaps of the cabin's wooden panels.

I shivered violently but managed to keep the chains from clinking. The dress Mary had given me was significantly warmer than just my bra and underwear, but the nights were still way too cold to be remotely comfortable. When I slept, it was in fits and starts, like a cat.

Hamish's hulking form lay sprawled across the couch just across the room. It had become his makeshift bed ever since he'd returned from the hunt. I suspected he was worried about what Fred might do in the night.

His presence had effectively made it so I couldn't keep up my exercises. I'd tried at first, but it was almost impossible without clanking the chains. The sound startled him every time, sending the couch cushions squeaking under his weight as he sat bolt upright and stared at me through the darkness.

I blinked my tired eyes and tried not to despair. While the men were away, the night had been my refuge, a sliver of time where I could discreetly move, stretch, and keep my muscles strong. Now that my feet were healing, I could do even more—if I just had the chance.

With Hamish so close, that avenue was now firmly closed. My chest tightened, breath coming in shallow gasps until I wrangled it back under control. My brain still couldn't accept the premise that I was supposed to marry the hulking stranger on the couch. The idea of it would be ludicrous, laughable, if I wasn't fully convinced that he and Fred were very, very serious.

Every part of me wanted to squirm away from him.

I couldn't stop the hot, frustrated tears from rolling down my cheeks tonight.

When I squeezed my eyes to stop them, grasping for any thread of hope, it was Brent's face that drifted to the front of my mind.

What I wouldn't give to see him push his unruly hair underneath that dumb trucker hat. What I wouldn't give to hear the sound of his voice, feel the safe warmth of his arms around me.

Was he still looking for me? Did he still think there was a chance he'd find me?

His voice echoed in my mind like the words of a lullaby. *I got you.* It was what he said before every race as he took the last leg. I tried to imagine him saying it now, somewhere across the wilderness.

Please don't give up on me. The words spun through my mind again and again, trying to breathe life into the tiny flame of hope still keeping me going.

I opened my eyes and another tear rolled down my cheek, this one a cocktail of hope and pain. If anyone was stubborn enough—and emotional enough—to think I was still alive despite the evidence to the contrary, it was Brent.

But that was a big, fat *if.*

* * *

When I woke up to daylight streaming through the window panes, Hamish wasn't on the couch anymore. He was clomping through the front door, covered in splinters that clung to the flannel of his shirt and stained jeans.

I scrambled to sit up and smooth down my hair, plastering what I hoped was a radiant smile onto my face. "Morning," I greeted, attempting to sound upbeat.

His lips tugged into a familiar, lopsided half-smile. If I had to guess, he'd been chopping wood. I was surprised I hadn't heard the sound. "You look exhausted. I'd get you a drink of water, but ..." I jangled my chained wrists for emphasis and winked at him.

Hamish smiled wider. Without saying a word, he moved toward the kitchen and scooped a ladle full of water from the bucket they used for drinking.

A few seconds later, Fred came tramping through the door behind him. He didn't head for water. Instead, he fixed his gaze on me.

"Playing the sweet girl, huh?" His voice boomed, every word dripping with skepticism.

I stole a glance at Hamish, but he avoided my gaze. Feeling small, I tucked my knees close to my chest, staring intently at my bare feet. Some of the smaller scratches were little more than faint red lines now, but the bruises and deeper cuts had bloomed green and yellow at the edges as they healed.

Fred continued. "My boy's a little slow, but even he can tell you're tryin' to charm him. You've got him all hot and bothered, but I know you're still a Jezebel down deep."

He knelt beside me and I squirmed toward the wall, terrified he was going to reach out and grope me again. He chuckled softly. "You'll get used to the idea of being part of this little family, or you'll suffer." He inched closer, and I could smell the rot of his mouth. "I suspect you'll choose to suffer a while longer."

I forced myself to draw in a breath, even though it smelled like a compost heap. "I'm not trying to fool anybody. Like you said, I figure I've got two choices: keep suffering, or learn to love this life." I swallowed and kept going, never letting my eyes leave his. "I've made up my mind. And when I put my mind to something, I do it."

"You're a liar," he whispered so softly I wasn't sure Hamish could hear.

"Let me prove it to you," I insisted. "I promise I won't run. If I do, you'll just shoot me." The words popped gooseflesh across my arms as I said them.

His hand moved rattlesnake-fast, striking my cheek in a hot slap.

I gasped and touched the stinging spot. "What was that for?"

"If you were tame, you wouldn't have to ask," Fred muttered.

I turned to look at Hamish in the kitchen, but Fred grabbed my face by the chin, whipping it back so it faced his dead eyes. "Don't look at him when I'm talkin' to ya," he said through clenched teeth.

Mary peeked her head around the hallway and took a few tentative steps toward Hamish, into the kitchen.

"What's going on?" she asked, her voice soft and childlike.

"Nobody talking to you," Fred mumbled, eyes still lasering me.

"Weevils in the flour are getting bad," Mary whispered.

When Fred turned to face Mary, she flinched toward Hamish.

"The hell you cowering for, woman? He ain't gonna help you."

"Sorry," she whispered, letting her hand fall to her side and staring at the ground.

I looked at the ground too, hoping it would save me from another slap. The room was silent, except for the sound of Fred's ragged, rotten breath. Finally, he rose to his feet and took a few steps back, shoving his hands into his dirty coveralls. "Gettin' leaner," he mused, looking me over, eyes lingering on my arms and legs. I didn't dare try to tuck them back under the dress. "That's good. Women don't need muscles like men do. Just birthin' hips." He laughed at his own joke. Hamish joined in half-heartedly.

"I'm a hard worker," I insisted quietly, keeping my eyes down. "I can do more than—"

Fred raised his hand and darted toward me again, stopping just inches before striking.

I flinched and turned my face away from him.

"Don't talk back to me, honey," he murmured. "You'll learn better."

Fred turned to Hamish, a sly grin peeking through that dirty, wiry gray beard. "You know what? Now that I think about it, maybe we can let your girl out of those chains after all."

I held my breath, barely believing what I was hearing.

Hamish nodded eagerly, all but licking his lips. "Oh, yeah?"

Fred laughed softly, and my initial delight turned to suspicion. He'd changed his mind too suddenly.

He wanted me to know he saw right through my facade.

"We'll chain them up together," he said matter-of-factly, nodding toward Mary. "One hand, one foot."

He tucked his thumbs into his overall belt loops and rocked on his boots. I stared at the dirt crumbling from the soles, trying to process what I was hearing. Chain us together? Like some twisted three-legged race?

I forced my face to stay passive. *Don't talk back.*

"My woman knows better than to run," he continued. "Even if your little wildcat tries to drag her, she won't get nowhere."

He moved toward Mary and grabbed her hand. She protested but didn't pull away. "I've been good, Freddy," she simpered. "That's what you said. Winter's coming and—"

"Exactly," he crowed, like Mary was seeing his vision. "You'll both be able to help now."

To my horror, Hamish was nodding along eagerly with this plan.

"But the weevils are getting bad," Mary whispered. "I need my hands to strain them out of the flour."

Fred set his jaw in a frown, and Mary winced. A slap was coming if she said another word. Everyone in the cabin knew that. "You'll each have a free hand," he said slowly, like Mary simply didn't understand. "You'll just have to work together."

Mary looked down and nodded. Fred smirked at me and pulled a keyring out of his pocket to unchain my right hand. It felt so damn good that I wanted to cry. Before I could even relish the moment, though, Hamish had tugged my dress fully up my arms then produced a shorter chain to lock my right hand to Mary's left, then my right foot to her left.

I wasn't free. But I was finally fully dressed. And I wasn't shackled to the wall anymore.

I tried not to let any reaction spread across my face as I stood beside Mary. This wasn't exactly a win. From the way Mary tensed up the second my skin brushed hers, I had a feeling I was going to be the target of her wrath at this new development. But maybe it was a small step in the right direction.

31

MILEY

I followed Mary as closely as I could, trying to stay in step as we made our first awkward pilgrimage through the cabin door and onto the property.

I blinked in the sunlight, savoring the feel of it on my skin, in my hair.

The shackles around my arm and leg were so tight they bit into my skin every time I failed to step in sync with her. But my opposite arm and leg felt gloriously free as they finally moved unrestrained.

"Keep up with me," Mary muttered, yanking me forward and nearly tripping herself over in the process.

I refocused my attention on each muscle group in my arms and legs. Even this little small bit of movement revealed how much weaker I'd gotten over the past week, both from sitting still and from malnutrition.

I drew in a breath of fresh air, still cool in the morning hours, and tried not to let it dampen my spirits—or, worse, make me cry. I'd already shared too many intimate moments against my will with Mary. I hated the fact that she'd been forced to care for me, bathe me, feed me, even dress me like the baby she wanted so badly.

Mary stopped when we reached a worn-looking shed that sported a smatter of faded blue paint flecks. "This is where we keep the flour and other food storage." She wrinkled her nose a little then quickly shook her head, like she was trying not to show her disgust. "We've already got a bad outbreak."

"An outbreak?" I swallowed. I didn't know what weevils were, and this chore sounded worse with every passing second.

She rolled her eyes like I was truly stupid. "*Weevils, Ruthie Sue.* We have to pick them out of the flour. And then we have to check the other stores, too."

I swallowed hard when she pulled the shed door open. There were a lot of barrels in there. I don't know what I'd expected, but that was a lot of supplies.

"We'll start here, then move along the perimeter. We've got supplies hidden all over the property," she added, sounding proud. "When shit hits the fan, who knows what sort of drifters or looters will find their way out here, coming after our stuff."

"Oh," was all I could muster. "I don't think anybody's coming for this," I murmured, staring into the dark shed. The idea that anybody would find this cabin—where she'd been missing for four years—was laughable.

Mary pursed her lips. "That's not true. Anyway, it doesn't matter what you think. We have a job to do." Then she pulled me into the shed.

There were no windows inside, so it was dark except for the slit of light the open door allowed. There was floor to ceiling shelving and more white plastic gallon buckets than I'd ever seen outside of a hardware store.

Mary yanked me hard to the right before I could follow her.

"Stop doing that!" I snapped, thankful that at least it wasn't my bad shoulder she was pulling. It would have been screaming in pain by now. "Just tell me where you want to go and I'll follow."

"You don't seem like the following type."

"Well, people can change." *Or learn how to manipulate a little better.*

Mary scoffed while she grappled with a battery-powered lantern that illuminated the space a little more fully.

"Now," Mary began, sounding like a schoolteacher. "Let's start here." She pulled me toward the nearest bucket and opened the lid.

I leaned down and stared in horror. The grainy, brown flour was moving. Not on its own, though. It was teeming. Alive.

Hundreds of dark-brown dots churned to hide beneath the surface, away from the light. When I looked closer, my stomach clenched in disgust. Their minuscule black and tan bodies wriggled away from me, creating squiggle patterns in the flour.

Mary kept talking, apparently oblivious to my reaction. "They're probably in all the buckets at this point. I don't think we need to worry about the wheat berries, just the flour."

"Why?" I managed, no longer able to tell if I was seeing weevils or if spots were dancing in front of my eyes from staring at the flour.

"Because when we grind up the wheat berries for flour, the weevils will get ground up, too. You'd never know the difference," she said. "I'll grab a bucket so we can gather them up for the chickens."

"The weevils?" I almost screeched. This was too much. How could she not see how messed up this was? They were still going to eat this flour? I pulled away from the open bucket. "Rayna, look what they've done to you."

Slap.

My hand went right to my face in shock, even though I'd been hit so many times now I should have expected it.

"Why the hell did you do that?" I cried.

"I told you not to call me that. Do you want to get us both in trouble?"

"I'm already in trouble," I muttered, lifting up our bound wrists and nudging her with my leg. "You are, too."

She shook her head furiously. "No, I'm helping tame you."

I swallowed my response, hating that I'd let my facade slip. This wasn't going to make Mary trust me any faster.

"Here, you start with this one." She crouched down beside the open gallon bucket, forcing me to bend right beside her. She plopped down on the dirt floor and pulled another bucket between her legs. I mimicked her movements, even though what I really wanted to do was drag her screaming out of the shed.

"We'll need to seal the buckets up again afterward," she prattled like she hadn't just slapped me across the face. "We can't let them be exposed to air for too long, so you'll have to go through a whole bucket in one sitting."

"Do I just … stick my hand into the bucket and fish around?" I asked through gritted teeth.

"No. Here." She handed me a plastic scoop with crude holes punctured in the bottom. A makeshift sieve. "Scoop out a little flour at a time. Then drop the weevils into this jar." She set a huge Mason jar in between us.

"You've really got this system down," I managed.

She nodded, but it was hard to read her expression. The black eye patch faced me, so I couldn't see her working eye from this angle. "There's always plenty of weevils. We rotate through the wheat berries, grinding them up in batches, so the freshest flour buckets are the ones we eat last."

She dipped the scooper into the flour and tapped it against the side. The dingy flour sifted through the holes, leaving a thin layer of squirming weevils.

"Oh my god," I murmured.

"Don't take the Lord's name in vain," she snapped. Then, more softly, "The chickens love them."

She turned her face so she could see me and flashed an impossibly bright grin.

I smiled back in spite of the nausea churning in my stomach. Because for a split second I could see the person she used to be. Not a husk of a person teetering on the edge of sanity, but a teenage girl just starting her life.

Just Rayna.

32

MILEY

"I love the chickens," Mary announced suddenly, tugging on my arm to dump a new batch of weevils into the jar.

We'd been working in silence camped out on the shed floor for at least two hours. I was almost numb to the fact that I was sitting next to a seething Mason jar full of wriggling black bodies I'd pulled out of the flour with my bare hands. We'd each gone through two gallon buckets so far, and there was no end in sight.

The weevils were so tiny, I could half-pretend they were little balls of lint if I squinted my eyes enough. At least it was a relief to be tucked away from Fred and Hamish, whose voices had long since disappeared into the forest. I didn't know what they were doing today, and since it didn't include me, I didn't care.

I tapped my sieve on the side of the bucket. "Tell me more about the chickens," I prompted. I'd heard the way Mary cooed at the chickens in the yard while Fred and Hamish were away. She'd stopped when they returned.

"I'll introduce you to all of them," Mary said, clearly pleased I was taking an interest in the flock. Her voice dropped. "But you can't tell Freddy I named them. They're not pets. They're food. But they can be pets for a little while, can't they? As long as I don't make a fuss?" She shrugged and returned to her task.

I smiled to myself. "That seems fair. I love chickens, too. My mom and I used to have a few when I was little."

Mary tilted her face toward me again, a real smile playing on her lips. "Us, too. Bantams. The little guys with feathers all around their feet like booties."

I nodded. "I'm not sure what kind we had. Black with white speckles. My favorite was a big hen named Mr. Chicken."

Mary wrinkled her nose. "For a hen?"

I laughed. "I was like six years old."

"Ours were named Georgia, Virginia, Scarlett, and Tony," she rattled off. "Tony was the rooster."

"Sounds like a bunch of Southern ladies and a mob boss."

Mary laughed, leaning her mouth against her sleeve like the sound was too loud. "I guess it does."

We worked in silence for a few more minutes. I needed to keep her talking, but we had to dig a little deeper than chickens.

"How did that happen?" I asked as casually as possible, keeping my eyes on the tattered black cloth covering the eye nearest me.

When she lifted her hand from the bucket of flour and met my gaze, I was sure she was going to slap me again. I braced but didn't look away.

Instead, she dumped a few bugs into the Mason jar then went back to sifting flour. "My eye?"

"You don't have to tell me. I just—"

"I don't mind," she said nonchalantly, like I'd asked another question about her chickens. "Might even help you come around a little faster."

I tried not to react, eager to keep her talking.

"Like I said before, I used to be just like you." She flicked her eye to my free hand, and I realized I'd stopped working.

"Sorry," I rushed, dipping the scoop back into my bowl of flour and trying to act like we were still just talking about chickens. I knew from past experience that the switch could flip in her brain at any moment, and I'd get slappy Mary back. *Please keep talking,* I begged silently.

To my relief, when I got back to work sifting weevils, she did. "One day, after I'd gotten Freddy and Hamish to trust me enough to let me out of my chains, I ran."

The words sent a chill creeping beneath the stiff cotton dress, even though it was warm enough in the shed that I'd broken a sweat.

She continued, still scooping flour. "I planned it all out, waited for the right time. Then I ran like the dickens. I got pretty far, too. Maybe a few miles. Far enough to think I'd covered a lot of ground. But then I got turned around."

She paused, but I didn't try to rush her. After a few seconds, she kept going, her voice so soft I could barely hear her over the sifting flour. "I spent the night in the woods. It was freezing, but I covered myself up with pine boughs and told myself I'd find my way out in the morning. Spent the second night that way, too. And the third. That's when I recognized a fallen log I knew I'd already passed. I was going in circles."

She sighed and made a strange little sound that might have been a bubble of laughter. "Freddy came for me on the fourth night. When I heard him moving through the trees, I thought for sure it was a wolf. Maybe even a bear. I just knew I was going to die on the forest floor. But it was my Freddy. He'd been tracking me the whole time with his scope, letting me work out my disobedience while I ran in circles."

I fought the frown that tugged at my lips. How far had Mary really gotten? I knew Fred had a scope, but even scopes couldn't see through trees. Had it taken so long to find her that he fed her a lie to deter her from running again? What if she was closer to help than she realized?

When Mary met my gaze, her face was brighter, her smile a little sheepish. "I never thought I'd be happy to see him, but I was. He didn't give up on me. Didn't kill me, like I expected. He took me home. He saved me."

I clamped my lips tight to keep my cynical thoughts from blurting out into the silence.

She sighed. "I knew in my bones I couldn't survive on my own. I needed him."

"And your eye?" I prodded gently.

Mary tilted her head, stock still like a wild rabbit. "Actions have consequences," she said, like she was reciting the words from a chalkboard. "Freddy took it. He didn't want to, but it had to be done. Not quite a pound of flesh, but enough."

A hard knot tightened in my gut. I thought for sure she'd stop the story there, but instead she set down her flour scoop and stared at the dusty shed wall in front of us, lost in the memory. "He did it in the kitchen. Sat me down on his lap and took out his pocket knife, the same one he used for dressing game. The knife was so shiny, I could see the reflection of my own eye in it as he brought it closer and closer," she said. "And then ..."

She let out a long, shuddering sigh, her shoulders sagging like the weight of that story had been impossibly heavy on her chest.

I swallowed. "But why—"

She continued like I hadn't spoken. "Every time I look in the mirror, I remember the price of disobedience. I was so busy searching for a way out, I couldn't see the glorious life Freddy had prepared for me." Her voice turned singsong as she quoted, "'And if thine eye offend thee, pluck it out, and cast it from thee: it is better for thee to enter into life with one eye, rather than having two eyes to be cast into hell fire.'"

Numb, I dipped my scoop into the flour with shaking hands. "Mary," I began—

"Look at that teamwork."

I jumped as the door to the shed flung fully open, nearly hitting me in the side.

Fred stood looking down at the two of us, blocking the light.

Mary flashed him a smile and worked faster with her bucket and sieve. I did the same with my free hand, keeping my eyes on the flour.

Fred stood there for a few seconds longer. For a moment, I was afraid he'd been listening outside the door. That he was about to lunge forward and hit one of us. But instead, he just shook his head, muttered something unintelligible, then shuffled away.

Mary started humming that damn tune she loved. The one about rabbits.

Storytime was over.

I sighed and plunged my scoop into the soft flour for what felt like the millionth time. "This can't be sanitary. I can't remember the last time I washed my hands. Not since you gave me that bath."

To my surprise, Mary plopped her sieve down and stood, tugging on my arm before I could get my bearings. "Follow me."

"Give me just a second!" I muttered, trying not to fall headfirst after her as I scrambled to my feet.

When we reached the threshold of the shed, she turned her head both ways. "He's gone. Stay quiet," she hissed.

I nodded, not about to argue.

She picked up the skirt of her long dress and motioned for me to do the same.

And then we ran.

Not toward the woods. Just toward the back of the cabin. Still, it felt so good, so right after weeks of near immobility, that a lump rose in my throat.

All I wanted was to keep going. To pull her toward the treeline and drag her back to a trail I recognized, but with the price of disobedience on my mind—and the shackles on my arm and leg—I knew in my bones it was the wrong time.

When we reached a water pump, Mary stopped abruptly and looked around before motioning to the hand pump. "Quick." She snatched a bar of homemade soap sitting on a stump and handed it to me. I lathered it and handed it back to her. She did the same.

The second we'd rinsed, we ran back to the shed, pumping our arms and legs in unison more easily with each stride.

If this were a three-legged race, we'd win.

If only the stakes were that low.

When we reached the shed, Mary sat down with a big, happy huff and a strange little giggle.

I sat down beside her so I wouldn't be dragged to the floor. "Why did we have to sneak off to wash our hands?" I whispered.

Mary shrugged. "Freddy will get upset if he finds us off task," she said simply.

By the time the first jar of weevils was completely full, we'd made it through two more buckets of flour. I tried again and again to start up another conversation, but it was like Mary had closed the lid on those particular memories.

I couldn't blame her.

33

BRENT

The first night in the woods was a shitshow, to put it lightly.

The clouds broke loose maybe two hours after we made the decision to follow the faint trail of trampled branches and scuffed dirt into the forest.

We tried to keep searching, but even I finally relented until the storm broke. All we'd do was muddy the trail and destroy the delicate signs that Miley might have left for us to follow.

We managed to get the two-man backpacking tent up beneath the partial shelter of a rock ledge, but by the time we squeezed inside, shivering and irritated, everything was soaked and muddy.

The rain pelted thin fabric like a drumbeat, faster and harder.

I lay there next to Wes, feeling like a drowned rat, glad the sound of the rain was so loud that at least we wouldn't have to try to pass the time talking. It was too early to fall asleep, even though the dark sky beneath the canopy made it feel like night.

The only silver lining, if you could call it that, was that we were warm enough. But only because we were crammed into the tiny space like sardines.

Every time Wes moved, his aluminum blanket crinkled loud enough that I could just hear it over the storm.

"I thought you said this was a two-man tent," he said, leaning next to my ear and raising his voice loud enough that I jerked away.

"It *is* a two-man," I snapped, nearly shouting over the rain. He had a point, though. Tent math only calculated room for sleeping bags.

I squeezed my eyes shut and focused on my breathing.

In, one, two, three, four. Out, one, two, three, four.

I imagined Miley doing the same, wherever she was, whatever was happening.

* * *

We packed up the wet gear in the morning without saying much. We wouldn't have had a scrap of breakfast if it weren't for the rosehips Wes gathered while I broke camp. My stomach growled in protest at the tart, mealy berries, but they were better than nothing.

As we moved out, my heart sank. The storm had tossed the trees around enough that fresh limbs and pine needles littered the forest floor. It hadn't been easy tracking before, but this was a whole new level of difficulty.

I moved toward a trampled sapling, bent in half at the roots, my heart rate rising with fresh determination. The storm hadn't done that. If we just kept looking, surely we'd see another bootprint. Another footprint. Something else the rain hadn't washed away.

When I didn't hear Wes's footsteps behind me, I turned around, trying to keep the irritation out of my voice. "Come on, we need to get moving. We already lost so much time yesterday. Let's go."

He held up a neon-yellow strip of fabric that I realized he must have torn from his own T-shirt—the one with the scientific drawings of dandelions. He tied it around a tree and fixed me with a look. "I don't know about you, but I want to find my way home at some point."

I rolled my eyes but didn't protest. It was the smart thing to do, and if he wanted to give himself a crop top tearing strips off that T-shirt, he could be my guest. "Thanks," I said gruffly, knowing I needed to slow down and get a handle on myself.

We were already taking a risk with this rogue search. There wasn't room for errors, for cutting corners. And if Wes and I didn't find Miley—or got ourselves lost out here—I'd have failed her just as badly as if I'd called off my search with the rest of them. No matter how much I wanted to find Miley, I needed to be logical. Making rash choices was how people ended up lost and dead in the woods. I needed to remember that.

When Wes still didn't follow me, I gritted my teeth. "What's wrong?"

"Did you hear that?" he asked, standing stock still.

I forced the blood boiling in my veins to quiet down so I could listen.

After a few seconds, right as I was about to insist we move out, I heard it.

A soft *pop,* then a fleeting, whispery echo.

I froze and locked eyes with Wes. "That was a gunshot."

He frowned and raised an eyebrow. He was skeptical. I couldn't blame him. The sound had none of the sharp, booming menace of a close-range shot. This noise was so quiet, it was amazing he'd heard it at all.

I definitely wouldn't have heard it if I'd kept pushing through the woods just now.

I held up a hand and we both listened, but the sound didn't come again.

"If that was a gun, we need to be careful," Wes said slowly. "It's not hunting season."

The words hung in the air.

Whoever made that bootprint might also be the owner of that gun.

The thought set my heart thudding hard, but I channeled the anger into looking for more disturbed brush, more shoots and saplings bent at the roots where a footstep had landed. More evidence of Miley.

Please, help us find her, I prayed again and again as my eyes darted back and forth through the thick forest. I wasn't religious. I hadn't said a real prayer since I was in kindergarten, when I had a nightmare.

I did believe in an afterlife, though. The idea of ghosts had spooked me until Miley's mom died. Then the idea of dead spirits sort of comforted me.

I hoped against all reason that she was right here with us, pointing the way as each sign in the brush suddenly stood out from the sea of brown and green like a map.

A dark hole, like an ulcer, had been growing in my chest since the moment I'd found out Miley was missing. Whenever I lost the trail, when Wes took a break to retie his shoe or gather a handful of rosehips, when I started to wonder if this search was for nothing and if Miley really was dead or swallowed up by the woods, I felt myself tipping into it, falling headlong.

The warm tracker in my palm kept me moving forward. I'd find her, or I'd keep searching until I couldn't. I wasn't sure Wes felt the same way, but I was afraid to ask at this point.

All I knew was that life without her was a dark void. She was my best friend. My teammate. My family, even more than my parents, who I'd left behind the day I turned eighteen and saw only once in a blue moon. I wasn't parentless. Not like Miley. But spending time with her was the thing that brought me to life, made me realize that the kind of love I got at home was halfhearted and finite. Drops of water in a bucket.

Miley—and her mom, Jane—loved like the turquoise ocean I'd only seen in postcards. Warm and limitless.

The sound of chewing noises tore me from my thoughts. When I looked over my shoulder, Wes stopped moving his jaw. His cheeks burned red. "We divvied it up," he mumbled, tucking a wrapper into his pocket. "I feel like I'm going to pass out. The berries aren't enough."

I turned my face back to the forest floor without responding. I wanted to tell him he wasn't getting any of my food when his was gone, but it sounded petty, and right now I needed to keep my energy focused on the search. We'd have to start trapping at night. Maybe even stop to hunt or fish eventually if we stayed out here much longer. And I'd have to keep my emotions in check, or I'd drive away my only ally in this search.

Don't fly off the handle. Play the long game.

A few minutes later, the trees opened up to a grassy meadow.

My heart sank as I scanned the grass, wet and bending from the rain. No matter how much I searched, I couldn't find a single sign that anyone had walked this way. It all looked the same. Had they cut through the grass? Veered left through the treeline? Gone right?

I took a step in the direction we'd heard the distant gunshots earlier, but doubt kept me from moving forward.

Wes took the opportunity to tie another strip of bright yellow fabric around a tree branch at eye level. "I don't see anything," he said quietly. Then he cleared his throat. "I want to help you, man. I really do. I care about Miles—Miley." He ducked his head when I shot him a sharp look at the use of the nickname. He was right, though. It was going to take hours to comb the edges of this meadow, looking for more subtle signs of the trail. I'd known this search was going to be grueling, but facing the stark reality of it was something else.

Wes moved toward me. "Last night was rough. Maybe we should just go back, tell the sheriff about those footprints we found, about her tracker—"

I scanned the shrubs at the edge of the meadow, desperate for something. Some sliver of hope.

Help me find her, Jane, I begged silently.

My eyes stopped on something shiny clinging to a tall nettle at the edge of the meadow, shining in the light like nothing I'd seen in the forest before.

I moved toward it, hardly daring to believe what I saw.

"Brent? What are you doing?" Wes called after me, but again, I didn't answer.

The silvery threads were tangled in the nettle's spiky stalks like a spiderweb, but as I got closer, I could see that it was a thin cluster of hair.

Long, blonde strands of hair.

Miley's hair.

34

MILEY

Being chained up with Mary worked well enough for sorting weevils, but beyond that, it was a complete nightmare.

I still wasn't allowed to use the outhouse, so she crouched next to me while I went in the bucket that they moved to the front porch —on account of the smell. When she used the outhouse, I crowded in with her, keeping my face to the trees while she struggled with her skirt.

At night, we both slept chained to the wall in the living room, although neither of us slept much. It was impossible to get comfortable, and the second one of us fell asleep, the other inevitably tugged on a wrist or a leg, starting the whole misery over again.

Cooking and cleaning rubbed our wrists raw as the shackles tugged, even when we managed to find a strange rhythm in the tasks.

Whenever Fred walked into the room—or waited for us to serve him and Hamish at the dinner table, he chuckled like he was watching a slapstick routine. "They look like Siamese twins, Hame," he guffawed as we moved in tandem.

During dinner, Mary and I brought bowls of stew to the table. We'd spent all day making the meal, Mary careful not to let me near the knife.

As Mary leaned over to set Fred's serving of stew in front of him, she tripped on the corner of the worn rug.

The chain went taut and I grabbed onto the table to keep us both from tumbling head over heels—as the entire bowl of stew went flying onto Fred's lap.

"Clumsy whore," he shrieked, leaping from the chair and brushing the hot stew, boiling only a few moments earlier, from his pants.

Mary yanked my arm and leg as she rushed to help him, wailing apologies.

Before I could pull her out of the way, he backhanded her hard.

She gasped and fell to the ground on her rear. I had no choice but to land hard beside her, catching myself with my bad shoulder.

The pain rippled through me like electricity, and I yelped so loud that Fred stopped hollering and stared like he'd forgotten I was there for a moment.

The pause didn't last long, though. The next thing I knew, he was on top of her, punching her in the face like a playground bully. "You stupid bitch. Why'd you make the stew so hot?"

I tried to reach for her, put out a hand to stop him, but my shoulder was locked in pain.

I turned my head to look up at Hamish. "He's going to kill her. He's going to kill me," I gasped as Fred landed another punch to Mary's face.

Something sprayed against my cheek and I screamed, but the sound ripped through the room unaccompanied. Mary wasn't screaming with me. And she wasn't fighting back.

Was she still conscious? I squeezed my eyes shut and waited for the blows to start landing on my face, too.

Each time he hit her, the shock rippled through the chain to yank my arm and leg. I tried to roll away, tried to drag her with me, but there was no escape.

Hamish's chair leg, inches from my head, scraped against the wood floor. I looked up at him looming above me, desperate for him to intervene.

Instead, he scooted farther away, out of the reach of my hands. I didn't realize that my free hand had curled into a fist around the hem of his pant leg until he shook it off, sending a fresh wave of pain through my aching shoulder. "Do something," I demanded, tears running hot and wild down my face.

At these words, Fred finally turned his rage on me, smacking my cheek so hard my top and bottom molars cracked together in a white-hot explosion of agony.

I felt, rather than saw, Hamish stand up.

The sound of Fred's breath was ragged in my ears, and I knew he was inches away from my face.

A drop of hot saliva landed on my cheek and mingled with my tears. All I could imagine was a rabid dog about to bite. "Please, no," I begged.

Hamish took a step closer and leaned down slowly, carefully.

I opened my eyes a crack to see him touch his father's arm.

To my shock, Fred snapped his head toward his son and blinked, like he was waking up from the rage-filled stupor.

My eyes opened wider, staring back at Fred as he looked down at me, then Mary, seemingly confused.

I forced my breath to slow, to come out in measured lungfuls instead of loud gasps that might draw his attention again.

Fred finally looked at Hamish. Then he ran a bloody hand across his balding head to slick down the few hairs there. "Damn women," he muttered. "Hame, get me another bowl of stew." He nodded at Mary. "Her portion. She don't eat tonight."

I turned my head to look at Mary, bracing for what I might see.

She wasn't moving. I couldn't see her chest rise and fall beneath the shapeless dress, so many of its white flowers now red with her blood.

Fresh bruises spread across her face like spilled ink, already deepening to a sickly shade of purple. Her good eye, the one Fred had spared, was now completely swollen shut. Her nose, split and bloodied, bent at an unnatural angle. A deep gash ran across her forehead. The blood had dripped down her cheeks in rivulets, mixing with tears that left streaks across her face.

It was her neck that hurt to look at the most, though. The otherwise pale skin showed the angry red imprint of Fred's grip.

Fred took a seat at the table and stared at me until I looked up at him. The smell of the stew splattered across the floor, mixing with Mary's blood, made bile rise in my throat. I swallowed it down.

Behind us, Hamish dipped the ladle back into the stew with a clank.

"Get up. And clean her up. Look at this mess," Fred snapped, not looking at me.

I rolled over onto my side, toward Mary, trying to decide if there was any way I could lift her without injuring her further, without dragging her.

I couldn't stop the tears that continued to roll down my cheeks. "I can't lift her. She might be hurt ... bad."

Fred's lip curled, but he nodded to Hamish, who had just set a fresh bowl of stew down in front of his father. Hamish carefully pushed the bowl into the center of the table so there was no chance of another spill. "She'll be fine," Fred barked. "Hame, get them out of my sight."

Without a word, Hamish bent down and slipped an arm beneath Mary's free arm and another beneath her free leg, taking care to avoid the chains. I felt every movement through the links, the cold metal rubbing against my skin, pulling on me in tandem.

As he began to lift her, I instinctively tried to rise too, but the pain from my shoulder shot through my body, making me wince. Mary groaned softly but didn't wake up.

"Easy," Hamish mumbled, his voice strained with effort. He seemed to be trying to lift both of us, even though he was only holding onto Mary's arm and leg. I could feel Fred's eyes on us the whole time as he sat slurping the hot stew.

When I finally made it to my feet, we began the agonizing shuffle into the living room. It was only a few yards to the wall where we'd been chained each night, but every inch felt like a fight.

"Please, can you lay her down on the couch?" I asked softly, hoping Fred wouldn't object. "If she's propped up against the cushions, I can clean her up better. The blood's on her front … I won't let it get onto the fabric," I begged, knowing full well that if this wasn't the case, I'd be punished. The tatty couch was more valuable to them than either of us.

Hamish didn't reply, but he changed course toward the ugly couch, where he lay her against the cushions next to me.

Fred muttered something unintelligible.

Hamish finally set Mary down on the couch, the chains pooling between us as I sat beside her, our limbs awkwardly tangled together. The scratchy material felt like heaven.

Breathing heavily, Hamish walked away and came back with the same bucket of water, bar of soap, and salve Mary had used on my feet when I first arrived.

* * *

Hamish slept in his own room that night. It would have been a relief, but all I could think about was whether Mary was going to be okay.

She slept fitfully, whimpering occasionally as I tended to her injuries with the remedial supplies.

"Run, rabbit, run," I sang in a whisper while I worked, trying to make the tune sweeter. Trying to make her eyes flutter open at the sound of the song she seemed to like the best. Trying to make the words sink deep into her psyche.

After a while, I left out the rabbit completely.

"Run, run, run," I whispered. "Come back and let's run, Rayna."

She moaned but didn't open her eyes.

I stared out the tiny kitchen window at the moon, a scrap of light among the clouds.

When I'd cleaned Mary up as best I could, applying salve to the bruises and cuts, I took her hand in mine. It was impossible not to despair about how it was the first night they hadn't chained us both to the wall.

They knew we couldn't run. Not tonight.

Just as my eyes were closing, lulled by the soft cushions at my back, Mary stirred in her sleep and jerked my right arm.

"Run," she whispered, the word coming out in a lisp through her split lip.

I opened my eyes and stared at her, heart beating fast.

Her eyes were still closed. She must have been dreaming.

"Yes. We should run," I whispered. "Nobody should ever hit someone like that. I …" Emotion closed my throat for a few seconds. "I thought he'd killed you. I'm so sorry I couldn't do anything to stop it."

I nearly closed my eyes again. But that was when I saw the tear, glinting in the dim moonlight, as it rolled past her swollen eyelids and down her bruised cheek.

My heartbeat thudded faster. "Mary? Are you awake?"

She nodded, the movement so slight I thought I'd imagined it.

Then she said it again. *"Run."*

I didn't need to be told twice. "Do you think you can walk?" I whispered, barely able to believe what I was hearing.

She nodded again. "Can't … see."

"I'll help you," I told her. "We just have to be quiet."

The cabin was impossibly still. The chains would jangle unless we kept them tight and moved in sync. As far as I could tell, Mary's injuries were mostly concentrated on her face and neck, but he'd hit her so hard. Did she have a concussion? Could she really run?

The only thing I knew for sure was that this chance wasn't likely to come our way again anytime soon.

"Freddy … will kill us," she rasped. It hurt to hear her voice. He must have nearly crushed her windpipe.

I swallowed hard and grabbed her free hand with mine. "He'll kill us anyway," I whispered. "Maybe not tomorrow, but you know he will."

"I can't ... leave them," she said.

"Fred and Hamish?"

"No, the ... chickens."

My god, how she fussed over those damn chickens. Like they were her babies.

Her babies. I winced, wondering if Mary was talking about more than just chickens.

"They'll be okay," I murmured. "This is our chance, Mary. If we can just move together, like we did when we ran to the water pump, we can get out. I spent hours looking at trail maps, plotting my runs. Even if we can't find a trail, I can get us home. My mom ..." I fought to keep the words coming past the lump in my throat. "My mom taught me how to find my way home in the woods. I can get us out of here. And if we make it home, you can have as many chickens as you want. Dozens. Hundreds. Bantams."

I was overselling it a little. I wasn't nearly that confident I could find my way home, but there was no room for waffling right now.

Fresh tears leaked from her puffy, swollen eye.

She let go of my hand and moved it to touch her eye patch. I watched, dying to run but knowing I couldn't do it without her.

"He's taken everything from me," she croaked quietly.

"Not your legs," I whispered. "Can you still walk?" I asked again.

She drew in a breath.

I held mine.

Then she sat up, pulling me with her. "I can run."

35

MILEY

I wasn't sure it would work until we did it.

The chains connecting our arms and legs made even basic movement a coordinated dance. Trying to move quietly at a run was a new feat.

We lifted our legs in tandem, keeping our arm chains taut as we shuffled toward the door. I took the lead this time, gripping her with my free arm to reassure her that she wouldn't trip.

To my amazement, when we reached the cabin door, the simple lock clicked to open without a fuss. Why would they have deadbolts, I realized. The worst thing in these woods was already inside the cabin.

The cool, crisp night air tasted like hope. I filled my lungs with as much of it as I could and guided Mary over the threshold and onto the dirt, then closed the door quietly behind us.

I aimed for the shed at the back of the property. From there, we could make a break for the treeline and move through the forest, using the trees and the darkness for cover until we got far enough away that we could move faster, less precisely.

When we reached the dark silhouette of the shed, both of us pressed our backs to the cold wall, breathing fast.

I stared into the dark trees past the shed, across a short clearing. We could make it in under a minute, as long as we didn't trip.

Ahead, forest. Behind, hell.

"Are you ready?" I whispered. "Are you doing okay?" She was moving remarkably well for what she'd endured just a few hours earlier.

She hesitated as I tried to move away from the shed. "My babies … the chickens," she whispered.

The chain clanked against one of the wood planks, and I gritted my teeth. "The chickens will be okay. They'd want you to go."

She drew in a painful-sounding breath but didn't resist me anymore.

With that, we took our first step away from the shed, me leading and Mary holding on for guidance.

"I can't see," she rasped in panic when I tried to move into a run. For the first time, I was dragging *her* behind *me*. The chains clattered again, and I forced myself to slow us to a walk, settling into the same rhythmic cadence we'd worked out over the past three days. Despite the pain, exhaustion, and fear drumming through my veins, I was bursting with exhilaration.

We were getting out tonight.

The tender skin of the newly healed wounds on my bare feet met rough pine needles, pebbles, spiky weeds. I knew Mary must be feeling the same. But I barely registered the pain over the adrenaline rushing through my veins. None of that mattered as much as escape.

When the treeline was only a few feet away, Mary froze.

Creak.

The soft noise was a repeat of the one we'd heard just a few minutes earlier.

The cabin door opening.

36

MILEY

Panic surged through my veins, poker hot.

"Hurry," I hissed, dragging Mary with me.

"Hide," she wheezed, resisting.

My breath came faster, spiraling out of control. Should we make a run for it? Should we hide and hope to god they wouldn't find us before we could slip away?

There wasn't time to debate. I dove toward the treeline, pulling Mary with me. The chains clanked loudly in my ears, tangling around branches as we tried to bury ourselves in the foliage.

We held our breath, waiting. A moment later, a flashlight beam swept the clearing by the shed, where we'd been moments earlier. The rustling of leaves and the sound of footsteps grew louder.

"They're gone." It was Hamish, his voice carrying through the night.

He cursed and another set of footsteps approached.

"Told you she was a damn Jezebel," Fred's voice spat. "They won't have gotten far. We'll find them."

The flashlight beams darted closer, and Mary whimpered.

I reached for her hand and she quieted.

Then the footsteps and flashlights charged past us, toward the far edge of the property and the wooden sign announcing *Protected by God and Guns*. They hadn't seen us where we crouched in the brush.

With each step, the footsteps got fainter until I couldn't hear them at all.

My heart soared, but a voice in my head warned me to move slow, be cautious.

But they were gone. We had to take the chance and go, now. If we set off in the opposite direction the men had run, we could always circle back once we'd put some distance between us.

I nudged Mary and whispered, "Come on. We need to keep moving. That way."

"They'll catch us." Mary's tone had gone brittle with terror, and she balked when I tried to pull her to her feet.

"They won't," I promised, trying to pull her deeper into the forest in the opposite direction the men had gone. There wasn't time for this. We had to *move*.

With each step, each clank of the chains, I imagined a bullet hitting my back, ending everything in a split second. Just like the car accident.

My shoulder cried out as Mary stumbled on a root and reached for my arm. I almost yelped, but instead I clenched my teeth. "Almost there," I whispered, more to myself than to her.

Push, push harder, I told my body. *Faster. Farther.* Once we'd covered some ground, we could slow down and make a plan.

The sole of my foot landed on a sharp rock and I stumbled but caught myself.

Mary cried out as I jerked hard on her arm.

"Shh!" I hissed. "Just a little farther."

After we'd made it a few more yards, I guided her behind a wide pine trunk and we stood still again, backs to the rough wood, panting from exertion. I'd lost so much muscle, gotten so weak in my short time here.

"Okay, let's go," I whispered after a few more seconds, leading her deeper into the forest.

We were in chains, but we were free.

We were doing it.

I was doing it.

I was escaping.

We weren't going to die in that cabin of horrors.

Not today. Not ever.

A branch snapped behind us.

"Ruthie Sue? Mary?"

Hamish's voice.

Shit.

I couldn't tell if he'd already seen us through the darkness or if he'd called out our names because he'd heard the sound of our footsteps. Either way, he was so close I was shocked I hadn't heard him approach.

Mary came to a full stop. She was shaking so hard the chains were rattling softly again.

When I tried to move forward, she resisted.

The adrenaline that told me to run felt like it was pooling in my stomach with every second we stood still, making me sick with dread.

We couldn't stop now. We couldn't let him catch us.

I turned my head toward her in a silent plea, knowing she had no way of seeing me.

"Run, rabbit," I begged so softly I wasn't sure she could even hear.

She shook her head, and I knew before she opened her mouth what she was going to do.

"Hamish! Over here!" she screamed, the sound ripping through her throat, hoarse and loud.

"No," I choked, even though it was no use.

I tried to yank her forward, one last attempt at a headlong run.

She resisted, digging her heels into the dirt.

"She's trying to get me to run away!" Mary screamed again, the words distorted and harsh through her bruised windpipe. "I tried to stop her, but she dragged me. I'm hurt. I'm weak. Help," she mewed, like a desperate kitten.

Hamish's dark shape emerged through the trees just a few yards away.

I stared in numb horror.

"I knew I shouldn't have listened to you," Mary hissed to me.

Then she rattled the chains and cried out again. "Right here, help me!"

37

BRENT

It had been days of walking. Days of cramming into the too-small tent with Wes at night and trying to sleep even a few hours. Days of trying to get by on too-little food because the trapping was scarce, the berries were scarce, and the idea of stopping to hunt or fish until we absolutely had to was unthinkable. Days of following a trail that felt as scant as the hope I'd actually find Miley alive.

Minute by minute, hour by hour, we fought our way through the forest and meadows, following the strands of hair Miley had left like a meandering yellow brick road. The clusters of long, blonde hair were pretty evenly spaced, and always about the same amount of hair. I couldn't imagine how much she'd pulled out. God, she was smart. What would we have done if she hadn't—

"Look at this," Wes called from behind me, his voice urgent.

I stopped walking and turned around. He'd tried to ask me more questions about Miley, but when I answered in one-word responses, he'd given up. I didn't want to talk. Didn't want any chance of distraction. We couldn't risk missing a marker.

"Just over there. By those syringa." He pointed, and my eyes followed in that direction, but all I could see was tiny white flowers and groundcover.

"What is it?" I asked, not wanting to backtrack even a few feet unless it was important.

"It's a dead deer."

I stared at him. "So?"

"There's something weird about it. Hold on."

I took a deep breath, trying to be patient as Wes took big strides through the weeds. I put my hand into the pocket of my puffer jacket and felt the strands of Miley's hair that were quickly turning into a nest filling most of the pocket. I felt creepy doing it, but who cared? The idea of leaving anything of her behind was unthinkable.

I got you, Miles. Hang on.

Wes muttered something under his breath then called out, "Looks like it's been shot. Leg nearly blown apart," he added, voice filled with disgust.

"How long ago?" I'd been picturing a decomposing carcass until now. Old bones. But what if this deer had been killed by the same person who fired the gun a few days earlier?

He frowned. "You tell me."

I backtracked to get a better look. "Looks like maybe a week." The stomach was torn up from predators, which wasn't strange. But Wes was right to notice the leg. The knee was completely shattered. Definitely a bullet wound, and it wouldn't have been hard to track with all that blood. If I had to guess, someone wounded it then left it to die.

I frowned. "Keep talking. But let's keep moving." I settled back into my pattern of scanning the shrubs in a slow sweep as I walked away.

Wes hurried to catch up. "Way I see it, there's somebody living out here."

The words sent a chill down my spine, even though I'd been thinking the same thing. It wasn't hunting season. And even if it were, somebody this far out would be packing horses, gear. Even a small deer weighed about two hundred pounds. It was a whole operation to hunt big game off-trail, this deep in the mountains.

"I've always wondered if there were bugout spots out here," Wes said somberly.

My skin crawled. "You mean preppers?" I'd seen enough episodes of the TV show that I knew what he was talking about. People who went completely off the grid to prepare for the end times, get away from the government, or skip bail.

Wes cleared his throat. "Yeah, preppers. Idaho is sort of a hotspot for them. And the Frank Church is so huge ... well, it'd be ideal."

I frowned and made a beeline for a glinting cluster of hair a few yards away. Each time I found one, I felt like I could go a few more hours, a few more days. "Right now, all we have is a dead deer and a gunshot," I argued. "That doesn't mean—"

Wes cut me off. "I know. And maybe I'm wrong. Probably, actually. But Miles didn't leave this trail of hair because she's playing Hansel and Gretel. She did it because this was the only way she *could* make a trail."

I didn't respond. He was right.

After a few seconds, I stopped hearing the sound of his footsteps behind me. Finally, he called out, "Brent ... I still think maybe we should talk about going back. We don't know what we might be up against."

For the first time, part of me wondered if maybe he was right. But when I thought about Miley ripping out her own hair, hoping against the odds that somebody would find it and follow her, I knew I wouldn't be going back. Not without her.

"I'm not ready to do that yet," I muttered loud enough for him to hear, then stared him down. "Are you coming with me or not?"

His jaw, which was covered in scraggly, patchy stubble, twitched. For a moment, I thought he was going to fight me.

When I met his gaze, though, I realized that more than anything, he was genuinely scared.

He didn't want to walk back alone any more than I wanted to walk deeper into this forest alone.

"Are you coming?" I demanded again, taking another step away and knowing I couldn't blame him if he told me no. This wasn't camping. This wasn't backpacking. This was hell, and it might get much worse at any point.

At some point, the strands of hair would run out.

At some point, we'd cross paths with the person who had fired that gun, shot that deer.

If I had to walk toward that nightmare on my own, I would. No question. But I couldn't deny that part of me wondered whether I'd walk back out alive.

By way of an answer, Wes tore another strip off the hem of his shirt and tied the yellow fabric to a tree branch. He'd done it every single time I pulled a piece of Miley's hair from the brush. "The thimbleberries will be ripe in a couple of weeks. Let's keep going."

I turned around before he could see my eyes well up.

He still bugged me a little, but at the same time, I'd never been more grateful.

38

MILEY

When I woke up, all I knew was pain.

Then the déjà vu hit like a sack of bricks.

I was right back where I'd started. Chained to the cabin's living room wall.

As I drew in a breath of air and the rusty smell of blood filled my nostrils, it all came back. Hamish's hands clamping around my bad shoulder like a vise. The weight of his body as he slammed into me and grabbed hold of the shackles. Mary's bleating screams. Sharp pine needles pressing into my face and arms and he pushed us both to the ground. Then Fred's face hovering over me, his breath hot and rank against my cheek. The rough texture of his beard as he screamed at me, his spit landing on my face.

Unlike what had happened in the kitchen just hours earlier, I was the one who took the brunt of his blows this time, while Mary tried to stay out of the way.

The last thing I remembered was the clink of the metal links as they snapped taut again and again with each blow.

I wanted to explore my body for injuries, to find out whether anything was broken or worse. But Fred and Hamish were sitting on the couch across the living room, staring at me intently like I was their new favorite reality TV show.

"Mornin', Jezebel," Fred called, ribbing Hamish in the side. "Here we thought you was shaping up and gettin' tame." He raised his eyebrows and stared at his son with a clear I-told-you-so look.

Hamish didn't react, just glared at me.

A chair scraped at the kitchen table, and I looked over to see Mary sitting there with a plate in front of her. Her good eye was still swollen shut, and her face looked like an overripe banana in the light of day. But she held herself with the posture of a spoiled birthday child at the head of the table.

A strange smile stretched across her face, trembling at the edges like she'd crumple if she let it slip for even a fraction of a second.

In front of her was a small plate with a yellow square on it. I blinked, trying to keep my eyes in focus. They kept drifting into a blurry haze, and I wondered how many times Fred had hit me.

I was too sore, too sick to care.

"Mary got a little treat for being such a good girl," Fred announced, confirming my suspicions. "Go ahead and eat, woman."

He stood and took slow steps toward me. "Not you. Today, you get discipline."

The yellow square was cornbread, I finally realized. Had Fred and Hamish been waiting for me to wake up so I could fully appreciate this moment?

Mary reached for the plate with one hand to find it, then cut into the cornbread with shaking hands just as Fred backhanded me hard.

I slumped back against the wall, fresh pain forcing out a whimper. Red splotches danced in front of my closed eyelids.

He hit me again before I could sit back up, this time with a closed fist.

Hot blood burst from my nose. How could the pain be so constant but so fresh, every time?

The scrape of Mary's fork was loud, but was it really? Or was the sound echoing because my head had slammed into the wall?

I wanted to be angry with her. She was the reason I was here right now. But even as I thought the words, I knew better.

Mary wasn't the real reason I was here right now. Fred and Hamish were. All my hate belonged to them, no matter how much Mary betrayed me.

Another blow.

"Hurts to defy me, don't it?" Fred spat.

I curled into a ball as best I could despite the chains and tried to catch Hamish's eyes, silently pleading with him to intervene like he'd done for Mary the day before.

He just sat there, elbows on his dirty jeans, glaring at me with dead eyes.

I closed my eyes and pulled my knees into my chest, making myself as small as possible. My shoulder throbbed, but it was nothing compared to the searing pain in my face, my head, my nose.

"Just don't make her ugly," Hamish drawled after a few seconds. "Work somewhere else."

Fred laughed. "See, honey? Your man cares about you. Best try harder to please him." He kicked me in the side.

As I fell over, my bladder let go in a rush.

Fred didn't even pause.

He kicked me again, and this time I was sure he'd dislocated a rib. I heard the crunch. I gasped for breath and accidentally caught his eye. He didn't have the crazed, rabid-dog expression from the night before. He was fully in control. And somehow, that realization scared me even more.

"More than one way to tame a woman," Fred wheezed. "This ain't my favorite way, but you're too hard-headed for anything else."

It went on and on.

More kicks. More jabs. More moments where I wondered if the dusty wood floor was the last thing I'd ever see.

With each passing minute, the sound of Fred's voice got farther away until finally, I couldn't see or hear anything.

I welcomed the darkness. Anymore, it was my only friend.

39

MILEY

A splash of water across my face brought me back to consciousness, back to pain.

I blinked past the frigid water, wondering how much time had passed.

To my horror, Fred still stood in front of me holding an empty tin cup, breathing hard.

Mary still sat at the table, the yellow square in front of her only half gone.

"Won't learn your lesson if you sleep through it," Fred said, dropping the cup. It made a soft clank as it hit the wood floor. He looked over at the table, at Mary, challenging her to argue. She looked down.

"Eat your treat, woman. You earned it," he barked.

I watched in a blur as Mary felt along the table for the discarded fork and slowly cut another piece of cornbread, pushing it past her broken lip and into her mouth.

A tear trickled past the swollen slit of her eye. Did she regret what she'd done? Did she wish we'd run headlong into the forest?

It didn't really matter.

We'd lost our chance.

I'd lost my chance.

This was how I was going to die.

Fred approached again, and I flinched, cowering against the wall. I couldn't take another blow. "Please, no," I begged. "I'll do whatever you want. Just don't hit me again."

He took my chin and pulled it toward his face.

I didn't resist. Just let the tears run down and stared into his eyes.

"Gettin' there," he said with satisfaction, letting go of me roughly and taking a step back. "Won't be too long, Hame."

Hamish didn't respond, just sat there with his elbows on knees, staring at me. I swore to God, he licked his lips. "Well all right now," he murmured.

I wanted to retch. Instead, I found a spot on the wood floor and stared.

Fred had moved to the dining table, where Mary was still sitting.

"Finish your cornbread," he muttered. "It's your turn to clean this one up. She's gone and made another mess."

"Gonna leave her on the wall?" Hamish asked.

"Course. Although I doubt she can walk, let alone run in that state."

Through slitted eyes, I watched Hamish's face fall ever so slightly.

Fred laughed. "Don't worry, boy. She'll be right as rain by the wedding. I think we'll start makin' some real progress, now. That's how it was with my Mary, too."

I watched as Mary hesitated, the last bite of cornbread on the fork at her lips.

She looked like she wanted to vomit.

Instead, she pushed the crumbling bread past her split lips and forced another smile, like she suspected Fred might be looking.

* * *

I stopped speaking and eating altogether after that.

There was nothing left to say. No reason to think making myself stronger would help. So instead, I did the opposite.

Fred hit me when I wouldn't respond to a direct question, threatening that I'd stay chained up to the living room wall as long as it took.

He hit me when Mary returned to the kitchen with a full bowl of soup or mush, reporting that I hadn't eaten a bite.

I had so many bruises on my face that I wondered if it was possible to die that way. Battered to a pulp, little by little. My field of vision had narrowed to tiny slits that gave me the barest view of the ugly room. Just enough to see, day by day, that Mary's eye was finally healing.

As the days dragged on, I felt my body curling into itself.

The idea of dying didn't seem so bad anymore.

On the worst days, I wondered if I already had.

I knew my heart was still beating, the rush of blood spiking whenever one of the men came into the cabin. Whenever Mary came near me and attempted to force a few bites of mush into my mouth.

I knew I was still breathing, but I'd stopped counting my breaths or trying to think of ways to keep myself strong.

Most of the time, when I was awake, I kept myself as still as possible, bracing for the next blow.

It was only the small moments of anger I felt, bubbling red hot beneath my bruised skin, that reminded me I was still here. I was still somebody.

Barely, but still.

Sometimes, Hamish stayed in the room while Fred hurt me, like he was observing to learn. Other times, he walked away like part of him wanted to interfere. Or maybe he was just bored.

Fred was definitely getting bored.

One morning, when I refused Mary's offer of yet another spoonful of mush, he clomped into the bedroom and returned a few seconds later, dragging something on the ground beside him.

Mary darted back toward the couch, careful not to spill the mush. "Freddy," she tried. "Freddy."

I didn't look at her, just kept my eyes on the floor until he shook the object hard on the floor in front of me. The noise made me flinch.

When my narrow field of vision focused on what he held, I realized it was a belt with a thick, rusty buckle at the end.

I braced, waiting to feel the metal clank against my skull, hoping it would send me back into blackness.

Instead, a shadow moved from the corner of the room. Hamish darted toward Fred's side and grabbed hold of the belt.

"Enough," he demanded, his voice trembling with a mix of fear and defiance.

Fred turned sharply. "What did you say, boy?"

"I said, *enough*." Hamish took another step forward, moving his body between me and Fred, nudging the old man back toward Mary. "She's no good to me dead."

Fred laughed, the sound turning into a hacking cough. "Just doin' what you won't, boy."

"I can handle my own woman," Hamish insisted, his voice rising. "She's mine. And I won't let you take her from me."

He sounded almost protective of me, but I knew better. This was two dogs fighting over a bone. Nothing more.

To my surprise, though, Fred took a step back. I dared open my eyes as wide as I could and watched as the old man studied Hamish. He clearly hadn't expected this defiance.

Finally, Fred tossed the belt to the floor.

I stared at it. It was only when my body sagged with relief that I realized how hard I'd been bracing for impact.

Then he grunted and nudged the coiled belt toward Hamish. "Show me, then."

The relief flipped back to bone-numbing horror.

Hamish hesitated for only a moment, his eyes darting from the belt to me, then back to Fred. Then, slowly, he bent down to pick it up, testing the feel of it in his hand like he was hefting a snake that might bite if he made the wrong move.

I pressed my back against the wall. The room seemed to darken in front of my eyes, the dim light in the cabin playing tricks.

I couldn't breathe.

I couldn't move.

Fred's mocking voice cut through the silence. "Well?"

Hamish took a deep breath, and his eyes locked onto mine. There was a flash of something in them. Maybe it was an apology. Maybe it was just the glint of light coming through the window.

Either way, he suddenly raised the belt high above his head and swung it down hard.

The leather met my neck with a stinging slap.

The buckle caught my ear.

I couldn't keep the scream inside. It tore through my throat with as much force as the whoosh of the belt.

Hamish reared back and struck again. Then again. Each lash landed with cruel precision, each strike more painful than the last. The coarse leather tore at my skin each time it landed, leaving welts that bled whenever the belt hit the same spot twice. The buckle was worse, bruising and chipping bone.

And through it all, I heard Fred's grunts of approval.

The world blurred and I tried to force the darkness, the sudden slip from consciousness.

It wouldn't come.

40

MILEY

There were no more beatings after that, but I refused to be grateful.

For another long week, I stayed chained to the living room wall, still rejecting food. Drinking water only when my chapped lips split.

I was fading. Disappearing.

That was what I wanted.

There was no way out.

Each time Mary tried to feed me, Fred watched. Then he ribbed his son, making jabs that maybe he hadn't beaten me hard enough. Each time, Hamish calmly instructed Mary to take the food back to the kitchen and leave me alone. "I'll do things my own way," he muttered.

By the end of the week, my once strong arms and legs hung limp, the skin stretched tight over bones that jutted out sharply. I could feel the edges of my hips when I dared touch my aching sides.

The creaking of the floorboard announced Mary's presence in the dark room before I saw her.

She padded into the kitchen, carefully retrieving something from the larder.

I smelled it before she'd even come to stand next to me.

Cornbread. The rich, sweet scent made my acidic stomach churn harder.

I refused to open my eyes.

"Miley," she whispered. "Look what I have for you."

When I didn't lift my head to look at her, she knelt beside me, holding the bread under my nose. "Just a few bites?"

I squeezed my eyes shut tighter and turned my head.

"I'm sorry," she whispered, so softly I barely caught the words.

This made my eyes snap up to her. "We were so close," I rasped, surprised by how badly I needed an answer.

She flinched. "I just …"

"You just what?" I pushed the cornbread toward her. "Take that away from me. You don't care if I die. You don't even care if *you* die." My voice was getting too loud, but I couldn't stop the words from burning through my parched mouth. "Look around you, Rayna."

For once, she didn't hit me when I said her real name.

"Please eat it," she insisted, thrusting the food toward me.

"Why? So I can turn into you?"

Desperate, she tried to airplane a chunk of cornbread into my mouth like a toddler, humming that same frantic tune she always did.

Like the toddler she wanted me to be, I turned my face away again roughly.

When I opened my eyes and glared at her, Mary's face hardened. "I only have one eye left, that's why," she finally mumbled.

"It won't matter how many eyes you have left when you're dead," I whispered, but she was already on her feet, returning the cornbread to the kitchen without a backward glance.

When she tiptoed down the hallway, she gasped.

I shifted my eyes to the dark corridor and realized that Hamish had woken up.

He made an irritated sound in the back of his throat. "Go on," he said to her. "Get outta here before your man wakes up."

Mary didn't need to be asked twice. She hurried down the hall and shut the bedroom door quietly behind her, leaving me alone with Hamish.

I looked down at the floor, dully wondering what he planned to do now.

"We'll find another Ruthie Sue, you know," he said, his voice gentle but cold.

I slowly raised my eyes to meet his. I really didn't think I could feel anything else, but the horror had no limit.

He was already making plans to find my replacement.

If I died, Hamish and Fred would just find some other girl to chain up and torture until she melted into her own misery or agreed to love him.

Hamish shrugged. "I'd rather not go back at square one, needin' to tame another woman. But ..."

He really didn't care if I lived or died. The only thing I had going for me was that I was here in front of him. If I was a bad dog, they'd just put me down and return to the pet shop. Kidnap another woman. It was an inconvenience, but that's all.

Then I'd be dead, and for what? My pride? My anger that I was a prisoner, lumped in with Mary?

Hamish went on, "That what you want? If so, maybe we better cut to the chase because my patience is wearing thin."

Hamish reached to his side and drew out a pocket knife. It opened like a switchblade, and he held it in front of my face.

I searched his expression, but I couldn't find any bluff. He was ready to take more than an eye.

"If you'd rather be free, I can do that for you," he drawled, his breath hot on my cheek. "Just one little nick right here." He brought the blade to my neck, pressing hard enough that the steel bit into the soft skin where my pulse was thumping.

"It'd be a mess, but Mary would clean it up, and we'd have supper tomorrow like nothing ever happened." He let the words sink in. "Might be the last thing she ever does. Seems like she ain't meant to be a mother, and Fred's patience is wearing thin. 'Specially with you causing trouble."

I drew in a sharp breath.

"You want him to hurt Mary?"

I shook my head slowly. If I moved any faster, I might accidentally slit my own throat.

He smiled and stood up. "That's my girl." Then he walked to the larder where Mary had left the cornbread. "I think this calls for a little treat."

He shoved it into my hands so roughly that some of the crumbs smashed through my fingers.

I lifted it to my lips and forced the barely sweet, grainy bread inside.

41

MILEY

Hamish demanded that Fred let me off the wall and chain me to Mary again. And since Hamish had been able to get me to eat something, Fred agreed without a fight.

I was making good progress. Not toward escape, but toward a wedding.

That's how I forced myself to see it now, too.

When the men weren't around, Mary talked more than she ever had. She spoke to me like we were best friends, her voice sweet and full of warmth, as if the last conversation we'd had didn't involve me tearing her a new one.

As if we weren't both covered head to toe in bruises and cuts.

As if we weren't walking the knife's edge every moment of every day.

I didn't say much in response. The idea of rambling on about chores and chickens and the washing and the endless cooking with her level of enthusiasm was still a bridge too far. I kept my responses short and my eyes down while I mirrored her every movement.

Mary didn't seem bothered by the change in me. Maybe she just didn't care, now that I was eating again. As long as I nodded once in a while and made little noises, she was content to hold up the conversation, slipping into humming once in a while.

She seemed calmer than she'd been since I arrived. Like she, too, knew that I was inching closer to accepting the inevitable.

"Did you see, Ruthie Sue? The sunflowers near the shed have started to bloom. Brown centers that look like ants and those bright yellow petals."

"This morning, one of the hens laid a blue egg! Can you believe that? She's always laid green."

I nodded along, taking comfort in the fact that she sounded a little like Mom.

"Did you see the sunrise this morning? The sky was on fire, reds and oranges and even purples."

"The water at the pump today was particularly cold. Makes the washing a bit more challenging. The drying is easy now, with the warm days, but when the weather turns ..."

"The bread tasted good today. So nice to have another helper with the weevils. It's going to be a long winter, Ruthie Sue. Last year, it got so cold some of the chickens froze."

Every once in a while, she talked about her life from before, as if we both shared those memories. I couldn't help but tune in then.

"Do you remember that winter? The one when I got so sick?" Her voice was almost a whisper. She had a strange, distant look in her eyes I hadn't seen before. Like she was dreaming.

I nodded slowly, despite the fact that, of course, I couldn't remember.

Mary sighed, "Fred thought he was helping. He made that mint tea. So hot, steam was rising from it like smoke out the chimney." She paused. "Said it would purge the cold right out of me if I drank it like that."

Her voice turned so quiet I had a hard time hearing her. "It didn't. I coughed up blood all night."

When I didn't react, she kept going, taking a sharp left into a new topic like some wheel inside her brain had spun and landed. "You remember my friend Kari?"

I made an "mm hmm" noise, and she chuckled softly, but there was no joy in it.

"She had such a beautiful laugh," Mary continued. "She gave me a necklace with a rabbit pendant, said it was for luck when I ran my big race." Mary's hand went to her neck, fingers searching for a lucky charm that was no longer there. The skin on her throat still bore the faint outline of Fred's hand.

We worked in silence after that, crushing wheat berries into flour outside the shed, not bothering to pick out the weevils.

"Why?" I finally whispered when we stopped to open a new bucket.

Mary gave up trying to pry open the lid and whirled around so fast she yanked my arm. "What?"

"Why? Why did you call out to Hamish that night? We could have gotten away." I didn't want to cry, but I couldn't help the tears that dripped down my cheeks.

She looked down at the bucket. "We wouldn't have gotten away."

"But we might have," I cried, doing my best to keep my voice down. I had no idea where Hamish and Fred were today. Setting traps, most likely. The amount of squirrels, rabbits, and deer they'd brought home for us to skin and smoke over the past few weeks had been both impressive and horrifying.

"I couldn't ..." Mary started, but didn't finish.

"I'm waiting," I said, anger expanding inside me so hot and fast that I was afraid I'd explode and hurt her myself.

"I already told you. I couldn't let Freddy take my other eye."

"Why not?" I asked listlessly, already feeling the anger cool back into dull indifference. What did I think I was going to accomplish by bringing up our failed escape again?

When she didn't answer, I went on. "How long have we got out here, anyway? A few years? What's a life like that worth? He'll take your other eye eventually anyway."

"But they need me. Freddy needs me for—"

"Sex and hard labor," I interrupted.

"No. A baby," she hissed. "We're starting over out here."

I turned toward her, jerking her wrist a bit in the process. "He's tired of trying," I said in a low voice. "He's going to get rid of you."

"Why are you saying that?" Mary asked, voice full of pain, her one eye darting between mine.

I clamped my mouth shut, asking myself the same question.

To my surprise, the answer blinked like a lighthouse through the fog.

Because you still have a shot.

Just one.

Don't waste it.

As those words sunk in, I heard Brent's voice in my ear, clear as if he'd been standing next to me.

An extra seven seconds to load your rifle and slow your breath is nothing compared to a twenty-second penalty lap for missing your shot.

I blinked like the world was slipping back into focus.

I'd been so focused on my penalty lap over the past weeks that I'd lost sight of the race itself.

As long as I was still breathing, I still had another shot.

And next time, I wouldn't rush it.

My heart thumped harder, faster banging against my ribcage like it was suddenly too small.

The plan came to me in a rush like a breaking dam.

I'd bide my time and earn their trust. Make them believe my mind and body had been beaten. For real this time.

I'd slow my breath and heartbeat until both were so serene, everyone would think I'd accepted this life. Not just Hamish and Fred, but Mary, too.

But not me.

Never.

And when I finally had a straight shot, a real shot, I'd take it.

PART TWO

FOUR WEEKS LATER

42

BRENT

"We're down to the last of the rabbit jerky," Wes mumbled, huddled by the morning fire. He stared at the flames while he spoke, saying what we both knew. Even with the mountain berries starting to ripen, we weren't getting nearly enough calories.

We needed protein.

I ignored him and poked at the small fire with a stick, trying to spread out the coals so we could leave it behind and set out for the day. The farther we continued into the woods, the tinier I'd been making our fires. I didn't want to give anyone a heads up that we were out here.

"We have to stop to hunt again," Wes added when I didn't reply.

My insides squeezed painfully, but he was right. I'd started laying more traplines at night, and we'd been lucky enough to nab rabbits pretty regularly, but it wasn't enough. We were both losing too much weight, too fast.

From the number of deer I'd seen, I felt confident that I could bring one down if I took a day to stalk it. But it wouldn't be that easy. We'd have to dress it, preserve the meat. That would all take too much time.

There was also the fact that I was convinced, somehow, that we were getting close. The idea of firing a rifle and announcing our presence felt even riskier than the campfires.

I hadn't told Wes my hunch. Maybe I was worried he'd think I'd gone crazy after so long wandering through the forest with so little to eat, so many nights in the tiny tent.

Or maybe I was just worried I was wrong about everything. There was no reason for me to think we were any closer to finding her. We'd lost Miley's trail a full week ago and hadn't found a trace of her since. No more hair. No more trampled brush.

The forest had swallowed up all indication she'd ever passed this way.

We'd set up camp at the spot we'd last seen a clump of blonde hair strands, striking out in different directions every day.

And every day we came up empty.

I knew logically that it was the right call. When you got lost, you set a marker until you got your bearings. At the same time, the endless searching and hiking without any sign of her was slowly hollowing me out. We were getting nowhere.

Wes crossed his arms over his chest and leaned closer to the fire. When the sun broke through the trees and crested the mountain, it would warm up. For now though, it was miserable out here.

I closed my eyes and tried to focus on the feel of the fire on my face.

Wes finally cleared his throat and spoke. "I know you don't want to hear it, but—"

"Then don't say it," I interrupted. Every day we stayed out here felt like borrowed time. It had already been too long. This was turning into a suicide mission.

"It's freezing out here at night," Wes continued, his voice rigid. "The only reason we're still here is that we cram into that damn tent and spoon."

He slumped onto his knees, trying to get closer to the flame. "Even if she is out here, she's dead by now."

I closed my eyes and let it shred me. Best-case scenario, Miley was fighting for her life somewhere in these woods. Worst case, which felt more likely every passing day, she'd been dead all along. Would I ever feel like I'd done enough to find her? When would I throw in the towel?

Not yet.

When the silence stretched too thin, I blew out a breath. "I'll stop to hunt. Give me another week out here. If we don't find her by then, we can talk about it. But please don't bring it up again. Please."

He stayed silent for too long.

When I opened my eyes and looked at him, actually looked at him, I was shocked to see how sunken his cheekbones had turned.

He looked like a skeleton.

I knew I looked about the same.

Guilt wormed through my stomach, growling and gurgling so loudly I knew Wes must be able to hear it.

"Okay," he finally said. "One more week. But we have to get some more food."

"Tomorrow," I promised, pointing at the trees directly past his head. It was the one way we hadn't tried from this spot yet. "If we don't find anything, I'll spend the day hunting."

We sat in silence for a few more minutes, the fire's warmth struggling to fend off the morning cold. Then Wes stood up and stretched, his joints cracking audibly. "Then let's pack up," he said resolutely, already moving to douse the flames. "There's some serviceberries just over there. I'll pick us some."

As I packed our meager belongings and rolled the tent into my backpack, I glanced skyward, sending up another silent prayer.

All this time, I'd been hoping against hope that somebody was listening every time I begged for help finding Miley in this endless maze.

The lack of real progress was getting discouraging, to say the least. Maybe I'd been thinking about it all wrong, though.

Maybe it was Miley's prayers I needed to focus on. Not mine. Because if she was still alive, she'd be praying that somebody would keep fighting for her. Keep searching. Keep taking one more step through the trees no matter what.

That somebody was me.

I've got you, Miles, I promised her, same as I did every waking hour.

43

MILEY

Light the stove.
  Cook breakfast.
  Eat breakfast.
  Wash the dishes.
  Feed the chickens.
  Sweep and mop the floor.
  Wash the laundry by hand.
  Wrap my cracked and bleeding hands.
  Don't think about my shoulder.
  Don't think about escape.
  Don't think about what I did to Mom.
  Don't think about Brent.
  Don't think.
  Be seen, not heard.
  Smile at Hamish.
  Eyes down to Fred.
  Ignore Mary, except to move around.
  Slow breaths.
  Slow heartbeat.
  Quick obey.

I survived that way for weeks.

After a while, I took a certain pleasure in marking each day a success in disappearing. It was easier than I'd thought it would be. I couldn't do anything else, but I could do this.

Sometimes, I wondered whether I was pretending at all.

When those thoughts rose up, I shoved them back down. There were no guarantees I'd make it out of this mess, but if I was going to earn my shot, the only way out was through.

On day thirty-three of my disappearing act, Fred and Hamish sat down at the kitchen table, sharing a cat-that-ate-the-canary look between them.

I focused on following Mary's lead as we placed two bowls of mush between them.

"It's a beautiful day, Ruthie Sue," Fred said.

Mary stiffened beside me, but I didn't react. "Yes, lovely," I replied, keeping my eyes down and following Mary back to the kitchen. That was how he liked me to address him. Quietly. Reverently. We'd eat when the men were finished.

"Tomorrow's the wedding!" Hamish burst out.

I forced my reaction to match what they wanted. A half-smile. A shy look behind half-lidded eyes. A quiet, "Oh my goodness." Not too much enthusiasm, not too little.

I felt myself stick the landing in the smile I saw on Hamish's face.

"Oh, how wonderful!" Mary exclaimed, as if we'd just announced a real engagement. Like usual, I couldn't tell if she was playing along with them or playing along with me. I didn't care either way at this point.

"You could sound a little more excited," Hamish said, his smile falling a little as he pushed back from the table to stand beside me.

I forced my smile a little wider and didn't look away. I wasn't sure anymore whether Fred was the more dangerous of the two. Fred was a whirlwind of explosions. Hamish, on the other hand, hid switchblades beneath his bumbling exterior. At least you knew what to expect with a fireworks show.

"Yes, of course!" I soothed, forcing a blush to rise in my cheeks that I knew he'd interpret as shyness. I hoped he'd think I was imagining our wedding night.

Instead, I was thinking of Brent.

I let my imagination run wild in one spectacular burst, using it to feel the heat rise all the way down my neck as I pictured what it would be like to kiss Brent. To spend the night with him. To press my naked body against his, somewhere safe and warm and beautiful.

It worked like a charm, sending heat rising to my face and tears pressing at the back of my eyelids. I kept the tears down, forcing my gaze to stay steady on Hamish.

Seemingly satisfied by my reaction, Hamish took my hand in his, pulling on Mary's chained arm as he did.

I locked the mental image of Brent away where it wouldn't hurt so much.

"We'll leave the plannin' to you two. But let's have chicken for the wedding supper. A real feast," Fred said, rising from the table to stand next to Mary and watching like he expected this idea to hurt her.

I didn't look at Mary. I didn't have to. I felt her response in the way her arm tucked hard against her middle section.

She didn't protest, though. "How many chickens should we ... butcher, Freddy?"

"I think two. Roosters. We don't need them."

Mary nodded. She loved the roosters as much as the hens. "We'll dig roots, too. The ones you love, Hamish. Make a mash."

Hamish beamed.

So did I.

* * *

"It's not their fault they're born roosters," Mary mumbled, a hitch in her voice as we stood in the clearing near the water pump and shed.

I held the first rooster under my free arm.

The chicken bobbed its head, clearly wondering what was going on but not trying to get away.

It trusted us.

Don't care about Mary, I instructed myself in response to the pang of pity that throbbed in my chest.

"Do you want to hold the rooster or do you want to twist its neck?" I asked evenly. "It'll be quick."

She swallowed hard, and when she looked at me her cheek was wet. "Can I hold him?"

I nodded matter-of-factly, not quite able to keep the lump from rising in my throat. "Yes."

We knelt side by side, and I stroked his glossy black head softly. "I'm sorry," I whispered.

He couldn't understand me. But he was my friend.

Mary is your friend, too. The words sprang to the front of my brain before I could stop them.

They didn't make sense. I didn't want it to be true. But there was no way around it.

As I shifted closer, trying to finagle the best position to make the rooster's death quick, Mary clutched the bird tighter.

"I'm sorry I turned us in," she blurted out suddenly in a whispery rush.

I refused to let the surprise and hurt well up any further in my throat. "It's fine," I said flatly, cupping my hand around the rooster's neck.

"I'm glad you're okay," she added.

I looked at her blankly. "You think this is okay?"

"Things can always be worse," she whispered.

"Things could be better, too," I said, then clamped my mouth shut. Mary wasn't part of my plans any more than this chicken.

If you leave her behind, you leave her to die, a little voice in my head piped up. *Fred will blame her if you get away.*

I shoved it down and focused on the rooster.

"Stop it. Just stop it. You've been doing so good, Miley," Mary began in a low voice then stopped herself.

I looked at her, but she looked away.

"I mean, Ruthie Sue," she whispered.

The rooster made a low, worried warble and started to struggle in her arms. "Do it now," Mary murmured, then closed her eyes.

44

BRENT

We'd barely made it half a mile, moving southeast and combing the forest before Wes tripped on a root and rolled his damn ankle.

It wasn't a bad sprain. Honestly, it was a miracle neither of us had gotten injured before now. I didn't push him to keep going, though, even when he offered. If he didn't spend some time resting that ankle, things could go from bad to worse quickly.

Reluctantly, I took his arm and helped him limp back to the orange tent, the sight of which I was beginning to hate almost as much as the forest itself.

Then I promised him I'd spend the rest of the day hunting. The trap lines I'd set the night before had come up empty.

When I'd gotten Wes situated by a new fire—and a thicket of huckleberries—I set out alone with my rifle, moving southeast again.

I was looking for deer, but while I walked, I looked for any sign of those golden threads I hadn't seen in way too long.

I went farther than I'd intended, pushing myself to cover more ground. Time was running out.

In one week, I'd have to turn around and go home empty-handed. I owed Wes that much. Miley, too.

Hope was one thing. Delusion was another. There was a time to acknowledge defeat and go home. Miley knew that better than anybody. But she was also the last person to admit it, and so was I these days.

Then I saw it, shining like a strange spider web.

Cornsilk where there shouldn't be any.

I blinked, terrified I was imagining it at first. But no, there it was. A long, thin cluster of Miley's hair.

Hardly daring to breathe, I marked the spot with a rock cairn and a strip of fabric from my T-shirt. Then I pushed forward, continuing southeast.

I'd made it maybe twenty feet before I found another beautiful, golden signpost.

"Holy shit," I breathed.

Then I charged back to camp as fast as I could move.

"Wes!" I gasped, completely out of breath. I whirled around, trying to spot the tent. Between my compass and the markers I'd followed today, I knew I was in the right spot, but finding the tent tucked into the forest was always an unnerving game of trial and error. The enormous pines hid even the smoke from the campfire until it was so far skyward, the plume had mostly dispersed.

"Wes," I hissed again, not wanting to shout in case the sound carried through the trees. In some places, the forest amplified your voice into a booming echo. In other spots, it muffled like a blanket. It was difficult to tell which one you'd get, but I didn't want to risk it.

No response.

I moved faster, dodging weeds and brush, searching for the scraps of light blue material—torn from my own dingy T-shirt—that I'd left for myself this morning.

When I finally saw the orange tent—and Wes beside it—I let out a sigh of relief and charged toward him. He whipped his head up at the sound of breaking branches, his eyebrows shooting up in alarm.

"I found the trail!" I sputtered.

His mouth dropped open in surprise. I ran the rest of the way to the tent and stopped, catching my breath. "How's your ankle?" I managed, trying to catch my breath and not really caring what he said. We needed to pack up and move out. Time was ticking, and we had a trail to follow.

He shook his head in disbelief. "I thought you were going to say you shot a deer or something. My ankle's ... okay." He stood up to prove it, only wincing a little.

"Sit down while I clean up camp," I demanded, knowing he'd only slow me down if he tried to help. We'd been in this spot a while now, and our meager supplies were scattered around like a disaster zone.

Despite my insistence that he stay by the fire and rest his foot until the last minute, Wes poked his head into the tent like a rummaging bear. He reached for the foil blanket, folding it quickly and stuffing it into its place in the pack.

I shot him a grateful look. "Thanks."

He nodded and cracked a smile for the first time in days. "Yeah, man. I didn't think ..." He shook his head as if thinking better of this line of conversation. "Let's go find some more freaking hair."

I laughed, despite myself. "I think we can get back to the marker I left before dark. Then we'll set up camp and I'll find something for us to eat, I promise. It might be a squirrel, but meat's meat, right?"

Wes's smile stayed put, and he grabbed the water filter.

"You set the pace," I told him when we were finally packed up and moving southeast. "If you need to stop and rest, it's okay. I'll keep my rifle out in case we see anything edible."

Wes just nodded and shuffled forward. We moved slowly, but that felt doable. At least we were on the right track. That alone felt like an impossible win for the day.

When we were nearly back to the rock cairn and fabric markers I'd left, a large rabbit darted across our path, moving directly toward me as it dove into a thicket of brush.

Moving quicker than I would have believed I still could, I pulled my rifle out of its sling and peered through my scope. I steadied my breath and followed its path.

There. Its brown fur mottled with white, the rabbit sat stock still beneath the lacy leaves of a huckleberry bush. I fired once, missed, as it took off again. I clenched my jaw and forced myself to slow down, following it with the scope, anticipating its movements, and firing another shot.

This time, I hit it.

Wes cheered, limping only a little as he hurried into the foliage to heft the dead rabbit by its hind legs. My stomach growled. It would be good for both of us to have a solid dinner tonight. "It's a big one. Should we dress it out here or keep going?" he asked.

I wanted to insist we keep moving. We were so close. But daylight was already fading to gray, and this spot was as good as any to regroup for the morning.

I exhaled, imagining all my impatience moving out of my body in that one big puff of air. "Let's set up right over there. If you want to get the tent up, I'll start making a fire ring."

He looked so relieved—not just to eat, but to rest—that I was glad I hadn't pressured him to go any farther.

Tomorrow would be a different story.

This was our last push, and nothing would slow me down this time.

45

MILEY

"Today's the day," a sweet voice crooned near my ear as gentle fingers moved a strand of hair away from my forehead.

I opened my eyes to look at Mary as she pushed a tin cup of water into my hands.

I took it and stared, uncomprehending.

I could move both of my hands, independent of hers.

We'd been chained together at all times since I'd started eating again—except when Fred wanted Mary in his bed. Then I got chained to the living room wall by myself.

This morning, though, I was lying on the couch. Mary was standing over me.

She was free.

I was free.

I looked down at my hands holding the cup in disbelief. My wrists were red and scabbed over from so many hours of cold metal pressing into and rubbing against skin.

But they were my hands again.

"Surprise!" Mary tittered. "Hamish unlocked us early this morning. He wanted to wake you up, but I told him that wouldn't be good luck for the wedding," she added, pushing a stubborn lock of hair off my forehead again, as if I were her child.

I shook my head and sat up, still staring at my hands as they steadied the cup of water. How the hell had I slept through that? Was I so far gone?

Mary watched me drink for a few seconds. I took my time, savoring the simple act of holding the cup in one hand and wiping the droplets of water from my lip with the other.

I gave her a sweet smile, the one everyone had seen more and more of over the last few weeks.

Mary smiled back. Then her cheeks flushed, and she cleared her throat as she said, "I thought I should ask ... since it's your wedding night. Have you ever ..." She trailed off then nodded like she expected me to pick up the rest.

"Ever what?" I asked distractedly, rubbing my wrists and ankle gently. I could run out the door right now if I wanted to.

I wouldn't, of course. I wasn't going to waste this shot. Not this time.

"You know ..." She rolled her eyes and put a finger through the hole she made with her other hand.

I held back a laugh. "Had sex?"

"Yes," she said, clearly relieved to stop miming.

"I'm good." I offered that sweet smile again to reassure her that I appreciated the consideration. Sometimes Mary seemed like a child. Too young to have lived through so much trauma. Other times, she seemed ageless, like she'd always lived in the cabin with Fred and Hamish. I constantly had to remind myself that she was only a few years younger than me.

"Did you think you were going to have to explain the birds and the bees to me?" I asked, my tone teasing but gentle.

She shrugged. "I didn't know."

I laughed softly. When was the last time I'd laughed? It died on my lips when I remembered that we were talking about me having sex with Hamish. Tonight.

"What's wrong?" Mary asked, seeing the look on my face.

"I don't want to marry Hamish tonight," I admitted, watching her reaction carefully. "I don't even like being in the same room with him, let alone the same bed."

She wrapped her whole hand over my mouth and moved so close to me, we might as well have been chained again. Our noses were almost touching. "Don't say that," she hissed.

My eyes searched her angry face for any sign of the woman who had apologized to me the day before.

She'd disappeared completely.

"You don't have to love him," she said flatly when I didn't react. "You just have to cleave unto him. Like the Bible says."

Footsteps clomped down the hall. Mary pulled away.

"Got the roosters plucked?" Hamish asked, appearing at the mouth of the hallway and pulling up his suspenders.

I couldn't tell who he was talking to, but I answered anyway. "Yes. We'll start them slow-roasting right after we finish breakfast," I told him, impressing even myself that not a drop of the anger I felt bled through to my voice.

Hamish stood there and gave us a what-are-you-waiting-for look. He'd been carrying himself differently ever since that night with the switchblade. Like he was a real man since he'd tamed his own woman. Like he was in charge now, even if Fred still pretended otherwise.

"Yes, of course. I'll start breakfast now," I said, getting off the couch and reveling in the feeling of walking across the room without being tethered to another person.

Hamish grabbed my wrist when I walked by. "I'm still deciding whether you'll keep those chains off," he said, making sure I looked him in the eye.

I used my free hand to touch his shoulder. "Yes, of course."

Hamish squeezed my wrist tighter.

I met his eyes. "And ... and thank you. I was so surprised this morning. That was very kind."

That did it. He released his grip and let me go.

* * *

When both roosters were in the oven, set to slow roast until supper, Mary presented me with the wedding dress she'd worn years ago.

It was more stark than plain, more gray than white. She'd clearly sewn it herself. I doubted I could do any better if someone thrust a needle and thread into my hands and instructed me to make a wedding dress. The fabric was heavy and coarse, and the hem of the dress was uneven, a little shorter at the front and dipping slightly at the back. There was no train, no veil, and the stitches showed at the seams. But I could see the effort Mary had put into making it.

My eyes moved to the dark-brown spots in a telltale splatter at the hem.

I looked away, not wanting to know where they'd come from.

Around the waist of the dress, Mary had attached a thin, faded ribbon that wasn't quite long enough for a bow.

"It's beautiful," I told her sincerely. The dress wouldn't win any fashion awards, but it was impossible not to think of the girl who had sewn this dress a few years ago. No matter how much Mary frustrated me, I clung to the glimpses I saw of Rayna.

"Let's braid your hair, too," Mary said softly, touching the tangled blonde mess that had grown duller and greasier with each passing day. I didn't have a mirror, but I could see the way it hung over my arms like old straw.

I nodded, refusing to show my terror as she helped me into the dress and tied the ribbon snug around my waist.

* * *

The ceremony took place in the front yard while the chickens wandered at our feet, pecking through the weeds for bugs. The feathers of the roosters I'd killed the day before floated among them like morbid confetti.

The chickens didn't seem to mind.

Both Fred and Hamish had bathed, which was more than either of them had done in at least a week.

I stretched my face into the brightest smile I could muster as Fred said a few gruff words and declared us married.

When Hamish leaned in to kiss me, I shut my eyes and pretended I was somewhere else. Anywhere else.

We signed nothing. There were no rings. No one clapped or embraced.

Just a dress with blood on the hem and feathers that belonged to something dead.

Afterward, we ate chicken and cornbread.

I tried to taste every bite, desperate not to let the nausea in my stomach win, knowing the meal would be the only good thing about this day.

And after that, Hamish took my hand and tugged me toward his bedroom.

It was still full daylight out, but nobody batted an eye.

He shut the door behind us.

My mind begged somewhere else, anywhere else to go.

As he climbed on top of me, I let it wander where it wanted. It went straight to the last memory I expected.

Mom.

46

MILEY

It was Mom's idea to take the trip to Redfish Lake the summer after I graduated from high school.

A poor woman's celebration, she'd called it. Just two-and-a-half hours away, Redfish was the perfect distance for an overnighter. A chance to relax on the lake, hike, eat a fancy dinner in the lodge. It was closer—and less bougie—than Sun Valley, but it still held the same appeal for us. The mountains were our siren, the way bright lights and casinos were for Brent's parents. They left him home alone for the weekend so often to make the drive to Jackpot, Nevada that he'd started calling them the "Slot Jockeys."

I felt bad for him—and for anybody who wasn't lucky enough to have a parent like mine. To the casual observer, she looked like a caricature of a poor, single mom. Messy hair with box-dyed roots, wrinkles that had never been touched by Botox, and feet that constantly ached after too many late shifts at the diner.

I knew better. All you had to do was catch her eye to see that fire blazing. The one that made sure I never missed an opportunity for travel that would help me train. The one that saved for better skis, warmer gear, better food, anything I needed, even if it meant overtime shift after overtime shift. She wasn't a martyr, though. There was a joyful resilience about her. When she was home, her laughter filled the apartment, drowning out the sound of our old, creaky heater in the winter.

When I protested this celebration trip, saying it would cost too much, she pinched my arm playfully. "It's not just for you. It's for me. We're celebrating together, so get excited."

I was. Thrilled, actually. I'd gotten my first real sponsor for the upcoming 2018 Winter Games at PyeongChang. The sponsorship wasn't enough to live off, but it was a start. I wanted so badly to take care of Mom and make it so she wouldn't have to work so hard anymore.

It had always been the two of us against the world. On paper, I was the champion. But Mom was *my* champion. And that mattered more than anything I did on the course. She was the one who had introduced me to cross-country skiing as a kid in the first place. She was the reason I'd stumbled onto biathlon.

One winter when I was nine, we'd decided to try cross-country skiing—who knew why. Maybe because it was too cold in Idaho to do much else outdoors during the long winters. Either way, she toted me along with her adult skiing group, thinking it would entertain me.

She was right. I was only nine, but being on skis felt right. Natural. Pretty soon, I was outpacing her team. To call it an obsession would be an understatement. We tried downhill skiing, but I didn't like it nearly as much. It was too much letting gravity decide how fast I went. Too much waiting to get to the top. I like covering ground, being in control. It was a hard, aerobic workout. But I loved it.

One of the men in Mom's ski group told her about biathlon, an obscure sport that was extremely popular in his home country of Norway. She'd never heard of the event before, and neither had I. It combined cross-country skiing with rifle shooting. Not exactly a nine-year-old's dream sport, and Mom balked at first. Yeah, we lived in Idaho, but we weren't gun people. The man just laughed and watched me skating ahead of the whole group. "That's a shame. Because your girl's fast, and her form is really impressive. If she has some aim, she could be a champion."

That was all it took for Mom to set aside her fears—and every spare dollar—into helping me train.

We set out for Redfish after she got off work at the diner that night. It was a late shift, and I knew she was exhausted. I told Mom I'd drive, so she could nap if she needed. My car was tiny but reliable. We'd have all day to hike and play in the lake the next day, then drive home after dinner. She gave me a look like I'd suggested popping by Walmart to get her a pair of granny bifocals. Then she turned up the volume to "Just Like Heaven" by The Cure, threw back her head, and did a weird little dance that she probably learned in the actual 1980s.

I laughed, already sure that this trip was going to be one of my best memories. Hoping that when I was Mom's age, I'd be that full of energy. That full of life. That full of fire.

A few songs later, Mom turned the music down. "I hope Brent's not too upset he got left behind," she said, trying to be casual, like I didn't know what she was up to. "Did you talk to him before we left?"

I rolled my eyes. "He's fine. And we're just friends, Mom."

Brent spent almost as much time at our place as he did his own after practices. He'd sort of informally adopted Mom as his own since he didn't have a great relationship with his own parents. I'd wanted to bring him along to Redfish, but Mom said no, even though she adored him. This trip was just for the two of us. A mother-daughter celebration. We'd hardly had a weekend alone since I'd jumped headlong into Olympic-level biathlon in middle school.

"Okay, okay," Mom relented. "But if you ask me, that boy is in love with you."

I kept my eyes on the road, knowing the unspoken subtext was, *And you're in love with him.* "He is not," I replied, more out of habit than any real conviction.

I didn't tell her that I was pretty sure he'd been about to lean in and kiss me when he dropped me off after practice, right before Mom and I left for Redfish.

When we got to the porch, he pulled me into a tight hug. That, in itself, wasn't unusual. We were close. But the way his hands pressed into the small of my back, drawing me closer, was new. And the look in his eyes when I drew back told me everything I needed to know about why he wasn't pulling away.

I'd pretended not to catch the signals he was sending loud and clear, rushing into the house and blabbering about packing for the trip.

The regret I felt as soon as I shut the front door took me by surprise. Did I want Brent McGowen to kiss me? The heat in my cheeks, spreading down to meet the longing in my chest told a different story than the questions spinning in my brain. Would it be awkward if things didn't work out? Would the team fall apart? Would I lose him as a friend?

Mom laughed softly in the passenger seat. "If you say so."

"We're just friends," I insisted with a shrug.

"You say that like it's nothing," she said gently. "Look at what happened with me and your dad. If it's all flame, you'll burn out fast." She chuckled. "I mean, a pile of wet firewood won't ignite. You need kindling, too. But if you've got some sturdy, high-quality wood underneath ..."

"Mom!" I exclaimed, glad it was dark so she couldn't see how furiously I was blushing. We were *not* talking about Brent's ... wood.

She laughed. "You know what I meant. I see the way he looks at you. Do you?"

I shook my head. "If it didn't work out, it would be a mess." That was as much as I was willing to concede right now. *If.*

"Opening your heart is messy," I told her, knowing she'd understand what I meant. I'd had a string of relationships with guys who started out as friends. When the relationship ended, so did the friendship. I missed every one of them, and I wasn't going to take the risk again. Especially not with Brent.

"Opening up your heart *is* messy—and risky. But keeping your heart spotless is risky too," Mom insisted, and I committed the words to heart, even if I wasn't sure I believed them. Mom had a poet's soul.

I sighed and squinted into the dark at an upcoming road sign. "The PyeongChang Olympics are the only thing on my mind right now." It was true—sort of. PyeongChang was still a few months away, but it felt like nothing compared to how much practice time I wanted to get in.

Mom turned her body to face me, shifting in the worn-out bucket seat. "I'm so proud of you for how hard you've been training. I want more for you, though. Someone who loves you. I mean, besides me." When I didn't respond, she pulled her legs up onto the seat and snuggled with her jacket against the passenger window until she fell asleep.

I put the conversation out of my mind and focused on the road. Time to catch up on episodes of *My Favorite Murder.* Mom didn't like the podcast. There was too much banter and too much blood. But it didn't scare me.

Most of the time, I got lost in an episode. Tonight, though, I could barely follow the thread of the story.

Instead, I replayed the moment on the porch over and over, layering it with Mom's words still stuck at the front of my mind.

For the first time, I let myself wonder what it would be like to let Brent in. To consider what if it worked—instead of spinning out on all the potential pitfalls.

What it would be like to kiss him. Ease into him like a hot bath on a cold night. What his hands would feel like on my skin, my—

I didn't realize that I'd veered into the narrow oncoming lane of traffic until I saw the pickup's headlights, blinding through the windshield.

Illuminating Mom's terrified expression as she jolted awake and flung her hands in front of her face.

I reacted too late—at the same moment the truck driver did, trying to swerve around me.

The other driver hit us head-on.

Right where Mom was sitting.

Our screams filled the car for a split second that seemed to hang in the spinning darkness. And then there was only silence.

* * *

When I woke up, a scream ripped through my throat like it'd never stopped. Just paused.

"Miley, it's me. You're safe. You're okay." My wails dissolved into a whimper, and my blurry eyes focused on Brent's face for a moment before darting wildly around the room.

I tried to sit up, but everything hurt so much. Especially my arm. It hung in a heavy cast that extended from my shoulder to my wrist. I couldn't move, but that didn't do much to stop the adrenaline pent up in my veins from trying.

My eyes went back to Brent as he pressed the call button on my hospital bed. He squeezed my knee. His face was puffy, eyes rimmed red. He was wearing his rattiest sweatpants and soft white undershirt. It looked like he'd rolled straight out of bed to drive here.

"Where's Mom?" I asked before my brain could even fully put the pieces together about why I was in this hospital room with a jacked-up arm. All I remembered at first was broken glass and the sound of my screams mingling with Mom's like a chorus from hell.

When a nurse hurried into the room, Brent tore his gaze away from mine. "She needs more pain meds," he told her, voice shaky.

Then the haze in my brain separated into memories.

The headlights. The truck. The crash.

"Where's Mom?" I repeated, locking eyes with Brent.

He looked away, at the nurse, like he was asking permission to tell me.

My head felt floaty, fuzzy, like it was already trying to cushion me from reality, my worst nightmare that would rip me apart the second Brent opened his mouth.

What had I done? I just knew it was bad.

The nurse nodded and adjusted something on the saline bag hanging from my hospital bed. "I'll give you two a minute," she said gently.

Brent's eyes were filled with tears when he looked back at me.

I didn't ask my question again, suddenly terrified to know how bad it was. I'd never seen him cry.

He opened his mouth, but all that came out was a soft moan. He shook his head.

I stared at him, mute and unblinking until he closed his eyes and whispered, "Miles, she's gone."

My brain refused to believe there wasn't more to be said.

She's gone.

Gone where? I wanted to ask, like maybe Brent would keep talking. Tell me she'd been taken to a different hospital.

But the smell of antiseptic, the hum of machinery, the dull throb in my shoulder, and Brent's eyes, red and swollen from hours of tears, painted a grim picture I couldn't shut out for long.

She's gone.

The longer those two words hung in the air, the faster cracks spread through my heart until it finally shattered.

I let out a raw sob and screamed so hard I could feel the force of it pressing at the back of my closed eyes. "No!"

Brent's grief-stricken face hovered over mine, tear trails staining his rough beard. "I'm so sorry," he whispered, his voice trembling as he leaned his forehead against mine and caressed my hair.

The crushing weight of grief took on a new kind of agony as details from the car crash flashed before my eyes. My hands on the wheel. My thoughts a million miles away, daydreaming about the idea of dating Brent. The sudden realization that I'd drifted over the centerline in the dark. The deafening crunch of metal. The blinding lights. The frantic beat of my heart. The void after.

The guilt pressed down so hard I could barely breathe. "It was my fault," I choked the horror of it seeping deep into my bones. My vision blurred, but I could see Brent's confusion in the furrow of his brow.

"Miles?" Brent's voice pulled me from the depths as I sank. His hands cradled my face, searching for a connection.

"I need to be alone," I whispered, the weight of my confession bearing down on me. My mom, my unwavering supporter, was gone. Because of me.

Because I was thinking about *him*.

"I'm not leaving you," he insisted, and the set of his jaw told me I'd lose if I tried to argue.

I stared at the wall as he settled into the chair next to the hospital bed.

"I'll be right here," he said softly, but I didn't look at him. All I wanted was for the blackness outside the windows to swallow me whole.

I must have fallen asleep at some point, and when I did, I saw that Brent had somehow managed to pretzel himself into a ball on the chair.

He'd stayed there all night long.

I studied every line of his exhausted face, knowing how much I needed him even if the self-loathing and devastation boiling over inside me made me want to explode. But even that trace of tenderness buckled under the lead weight in my chest. There wasn't room for gratitude or peace or love right now. Pain filled every crack inside me.

When I was discharged two days later, Brent was there with coffee and donuts. I took them with trembling hands and let him push me to the hospital exit in a wheelchair, even though it was my shoulder that had been injured, not my legs. I was shaking so hard I could barely stand.

The idea of returning to the home I'd shared with Mom, to rooms echoing with memories of her, felt impossible. Every corner, every piece of art, every fiber of carpet would scream her absence. Her smell would be everywhere.

"You could stay at my place for a while," Brent suggested before even putting the key in the ignition, his voice gentle.

I turned to him with glazed eyes.

There was no romance in the gesture. Just kindness.

I nodded numbly, and Brent's tiny studio apartment became my haven as days bled into weeks, then months of grief, guilt, and medical follow-ups.

Despite the first surgeon's optimistic prognosis, the ache in my shoulder never went away.

Neither did the guilty ache in my chest. And unlike my shoulder, I didn't expect it to mend.

47

MILEY

FRANK CHURCH WILDERNESS, IDAHO

September, 2022

When Hamish was finished with me, he chained one of my wrists to the iron headboard.

Then he rolled over and went to sleep for a few hours while I stared at the sunlit chinks in the windowless bedroom until they stopped glowing.

A few hours later, he woke up and climbed on top of me again, not bothering to unchain my wrist.

The bed was small. A double if that, and he took up most of it. The sheets smelled sour, like they'd never been washed. Still, if it hadn't been for the fact that his bare skin pressed against me all night long, it was the most comfortable place I'd slept in a long time.

I squeezed my eyes shut and tried to fall asleep, lose consciousness, anything to force the smell of him and the memories of the past few hours out of my head.

Sleep wouldn't come, though. Red-hot anger, humiliation, and pain kept it at bay.

Everything hurt. For once, the ache in my shoulder felt almost comforting in its familiarity. It burned, even though it was the other arm chained to the headboard.

The memory of how elated I'd been when my hands were unchained earlier felt like a fever dream now.

When morning finally arrived and the dim light streamed through the cracks in the logs, I couldn't help asking if tonight I might be able to sleep without the chains.

Hamish gave me a long look. "A tame girl wouldn't ask that," he said thoughtfully, then led me to the kitchen where Mary was humming that same old song about the rabbit while she kneaded dough.

Then he chained us back together.

Mary didn't even look surprised.

The next night, as I searched for any escape from my body while Hamish climbed on top of me, I let my mind drift to more places I'd never allowed it to go.

I let the memories of Mom wash over me. Not just the accident, but everything else. The way she smelled. The way her voice sounded when she told me she loved me. The taste of our favorite foods— coconut korma from Bombay House and mashed potatoes thick with butter. The day we'd stumbled across an entire herd of elk when we skied around a bend in the groomed trail, and they didn't run. Just stared back at us with those soft brown eyes and pawed for grass. *Look, Miley. Just look.*

The Christmas she'd surprised me with a new coat. The one that cost so much it hurt to look at, a little. She was so proud. I knew then what all the night shifts at the diner had been for. Our tiny living room, cluttered with mismatched photo frames we'd collected over the years. Most cheap, most filled with candid photos instead of the professional portraits I saw in my friends' homes, but I loved them even more for that.

The way she'd brush my long hair after the shower some nights when I got home from training. The way she told me she loved me with so much conviction that never, not once, had I doubted it the way my friends seemed to do when it came to their parents.

Five years' worth of memories I'd shoved away so hard that I assumed I wouldn't be able to find them all again. But as the hours dragged past in this black abyss, I realized they hadn't faded. Instead, they'd just been waiting for me to pull them out one by one, like a hope chest.

Sometimes, I imagined what Mom would think if she could see me now. Half-naked. Half-dead. Half wishing I was whenever Hamish's breathing changed and I knew he was awake.

At first, my mind wanted her to be horrified by my condition. To pity me. To blame me, even.

But with the memories fresh at the front of my mind, wrapping me in a protective bubble that hurt and healed at the same time, I knew better.

It's not your fault, her voice insisted.

I shouldn't have gone running so far off the main road, I argued back stubbornly. Part of me knew I was just talking to myself. The rest of me didn't care.

You were always my trailblazer, Miles.

I should have been paying more attention that night. I shouldn't have been daydreaming about Brent. I'm sorry I veered into the other lane. I'm so sorry I swerved.

It's not your fault, baby.

I'm sorry I couldn't get to the podium after everything you sacrificed for me. I'm sorry I let you down.

I'm so proud of you. For all of it. I love you, Miley.

I love you, Mom.

Tears ran down my bare arms and chest and eventually turned my skin into a cold wash of goose bumps while Hamish snored next to me. I curled into a ball and clung to the words. *I love you, Miley.*

After a while, I realized they sounded like Brent as much as Mom.

The tears came faster. Did he have any hope I might still be alive? Where was he right now? When would he move on with his life, fall in love with someone else? Get married. Have a family. Find a new best friend.

Every time I thought about that part, I cried harder.

I love you, I told the Brent in my head.

I could finally admit it now, at least, after everything.

I knew he'd burn the world down searching these woods, even if he thought I was dead. But Rayna had family and friends who loved her, too.

And they'd never found her.

Please don't give up on me.

* * *

"Are you feeling alright, Ruthie Sue?" Mary asked on the third day post-wedding, pulling me out of my thoughts.

She wiped a hot tear from my cheek. I'd slept maybe two hours over the past two days.

I forced a smile and mirrored her movements as we scrubbed the morning dishes side by side in the empty cabin. The monotonous days were starting to feel like a refuge from the nights, since Fred and Hamish often disappeared for hours. "My shoulder hurts. That's all."

"I'll try to move more slowly," Mary said sweetly, taking care not to yank the chain.

"I'm used to it," I said, brushing it off. What did it really matter if she moved in tandem with me more smoothly to wash dishes?

"Pain's funny like that, isn't it," Mary stated, not taking the hint to drop the topic. "Things that used to really upset me feel small now."

She was always doing this. Trying to teach me a lesson that would help me see our situation in a rosier light. Most of the time, I ignored her. Today, I tried a different approach.

"What hurts you the most now?" I asked.

She shrugged. "Not having a baby."

"What if you could have a baby if you went home? Back at Yale," I clarified.

Mary jerked my arm, the one attached to her. "This *is* home."

"Okay," I said evenly. "But one of my teammates ... her mom couldn't get pregnant until she started taking progesterone."

Mary looked at me with wide eyes but recovered quickly. "God will provide."

"God helped somebody discover progesterone," I clapped back.

To my surprise, her eye welled up with tears, dripping down into the pot she was scrubbing.

I pretended not to see.

* * *

That night, I finally fell asleep from pure exhaustion after Hamish rolled over and pulled the stinky, scratchy blankets to his side of the bed.

The blackness closed in like a blanket of my own, and this time, I welcomed it.

I dreamed as hard as I slept.

Brent and me, standing side by side on the podium at the Milano Cortina Winter Olympics. *I love you,* I mouthed, the words coming so easily it was hard to believe they'd been stuck to the roof of my mouth for so many years.

Mom was there too, in the crowd, looking older but every bit as radiant as the last time I'd seen her. She was holding a little girl with a pink parka that covered everything but her green eyes and downy blonde curls peeking from under her hat.

Mom was too far away for me to tell what she was saying as she pointed at Brent and me, telling the little girl to look and clap. But I knew what she was saying. *That's your mama. That's your papa. We're so proud of them, aren't we?*

I woke up and realized that my face and chest were, once again, wet with tears.

This time, though, I felt warm to my toes.

Cicadas chirped like mad outside the cabin, nearly drowning out Hamish's snores.

I let out a shuddery breath and blinked into the darkness of the airless bedroom.

Hamish grunted and flopped out a hand in his sleep, slapping it down hard across my chest—and bad shoulder. His hand hit just where my original injury had.

The epicenter of the pain.

I drew in a breath and braced for the inevitable shot of white-hot agony that would follow.

It never did.

48

MILEY

My shoulder still didn't hurt the following morning. Not even when, without explanation, Fred grabbed my arm while he unlocked the shackles binding me to Mary.

He didn't offer any kind of explanation.

I didn't ask for one. Neither did Mary. We just broke apart with a polite "thank you," murmured in unison and went about the day's chores.

I swung my arm tentatively while I carried a heavy pail of water from the hand pump into the cabin and set it on the kitchen floor to wash the breakfast dishes.

Mary stared at me as I windmilled my arm. Still no pain.

I couldn't help smiling. The phantom pain was gone. It took becoming a ghost of myself to finally get rid of it, but it was gone.

"What are you doing?" Mary asked.

I forced my face back to its serene, empty expression. "Just stretching."

She gave me a skeptical look but continued stacking firewood by the stove, stopping every few minutes to smash a spider. "When you're finished with those dishes, get some powdered milk from the shed. The men will want some with lunch."

I nodded obediently and walked outside to the shed like she'd asked, still distracted by the fact that the pain was gone. I shrugged my shoulder up and down while I walked, marveling at the way it moved, relishing the feeling of the sun on my face.

I kept my eyes on the shed, not allowing myself to stare into the trees. If I let my mind go there, it would be too difficult to keep myself from rushing toward them. But I couldn't help imagining what it would be like to sprint into the welcoming arms of the forest and run like hell down any trail I could find.

Reality was quick to tether me. I'd be missed in a few seconds. I could hear the low murmur of the men's voices from where they were gathered, digging out a new latrine. The old one—which I was finally allowed to use—was nearly full.

The men were never too far off unless they were out on a hunt. And I wasn't stupid to think they'd leave me unchained while they went on a hunt. Not yet.

Today was a test, and I planned to pass it.

At least I wasn't barefoot anymore. Hamish had gifted me a pair of old wool socks the day after the wedding, with the promise that Mary would teach me how to darn them. They were full of holes and smelled like Hamish, but they felt like the ultimate luxury.

I'd be able to run faster in socks than bare feet. Maybe even faster than the clunky leather boots Mary wore when she tended to chores outdoors.

The shed door creaked when I pushed it open to search the stacks of buckets and wooden crates for the powdered milk. There. I finally saw it on a high shelf. Not wanting to make Mary wonder whether I was coming back, I hurried to pull up a little stool on the shed floor, reaching high for the right bucket.

It almost certainly had weevils. Mary and I hadn't gotten to this shelf yet. The last time we'd opened a new container of powdered milk, I'd watched her add water to each serving then skim the little black bugs off the surface when they floated to the top.

I drank the bug-riddled milk, too. I'd lost so much weight—and muscle—that the brown and white floral dress was beginning to hang off my shoulders in the same way Mary's did.

It was time to stop wasting away.

Stepping down with the bucket, I turned and gasped, nearly toppling the rickety stool.

Fred was standing in the doorway to the shed, leaning against the hinges.

I held my breath, surprised I hadn't heard him—or smelled him—until I turned around. The faint aroma of rot filled the shed as we stared each other down. He must have spent some time in the old latrine, dismantling the wooden planks that made up the seat.

His expression was steely, eyes as dead as ever, but for once he didn't have a word to say.

Fred glanced over his shoulder and drew himself inside the shed, blanketing both of us in foul-smelling darkness.

My breathing threatened to turn fast and panicked, but I held it back.

Hamish and Mary taking my chains off this morning was one test.

This was another.

My stomach twisted, but I stayed silent.

He took a step toward me, and I gritted my teeth, grateful he couldn't see the fear in my eyes.

"You know what I'm here for, don't you, honey," he whispered in a low growl.

My mouth went dry. I was numb with horror, but I wouldn't let my act slip.

I was tamed, through and through.

"Yes," I managed.

He took two quick steps forward and gripped my shoulder, pulling me against him before I could say anything else.

My shoulder didn't protest. Neither did I, even though all I wanted was to knee him in the groin and run like hell.

Wait for your shot.

"I said I'd get a taste, didn't I?" he whispered into my hair and then took a big whiff of it.

I squeezed my eyes shut in the pitch-dark room, needing the darkness to be deeper. *No, no, no,* was all I could think.

Just keep breathing, the voice in my head told me gently, firmly. *No matter what he does, you're still Miley. He can't touch that part of you.*

Hot tears streaked my face.

Fred brought his lips to mine, taking another step so I was forced to brace against the uneven rows of stacked shelves.

There was nowhere to run, even if I wanted to.

The shed door creaked open a few inches, spilling light into the crawling darkness.

"Ruthie Sue?" Hamish called from just outside the shed. To my surprise, he actually sounded worried.

I stayed frozen against the shelves, but Fred recoiled and faced the light as the door opened a few inches wider.

Hamish's eyes moved between Fred and me. They darkened as he took in my posture, my tears.

"What the hell are you doin' with my woman?" Hamish growled.

Fred shoved me away then pushed past Hamish and stomped through the yard. "Settle down," he barked but didn't turn around.

I kept my eyes on the dirt floor, refusing to meet Hamish's stony gaze.

"Ruthie Sue?" he demanded.

"I need to get the milk to Mary, for lunch," I said softly, grabbing the right bucket and slipping past him.

He held out a hand to stop me then thought better of it and turned to follow Fred.

In, one, two, three, four. Out, one, two, three, four.

I refused to look at Mary as I set the bucket on the floor beside her. But when she made a startled noise and came to stand next to me, I knew that all the deep breaths in the world couldn't erase the stricken expression on my face.

"What happened? What took so long?" she asked, turning to face me while wiping her hands on her apron.

The tears leaked down my cheeks in a silent stream. "Nothing," I managed.

She darted her eyes to the closed front door. Outside in the yard, the sound of shouting grew louder.

She shook her head. "Ruthie Sue, you tell me what happened right this instant."

When I opened my mouth, it all just rushed out. Once I started, I couldn't stop. Detail after detail poured from my lips in a forceful stream, acrid as vomit.

I told her what Fred had done.

I told her about my nights with Hamish.

I told her about my mom and the accident.

I told her about Brent and how I finally knew, deep in my bones, that I loved him.

I told her that I'd dreamed about a baby girl with my blonde hair and his green eyes and that if I didn't get out of here, I'd lose her before she even had a chance at existing.

Mary kept her eye on me while I talked, not moving a muscle.

The shouting from outside the door got louder then softer, like thunder from a circling storm as the men had it out.

I expected her to slap me when I finally gasped for breath and quit talking.

Instead, she reached out her arms and pulled me into a tight embrace. "Push it to the back of your mind and lock it up. Tell yourself a new truth. It can still be good," she whispered fiercely.

Her words hollowed me out.

I pulled back to look at her. I'd never felt so alone in my life, but I knew she was only repeating the words she'd told herself so many times to keep herself alive here.

I wouldn't be like her, though. Instead of shoving what had just happened to the back of my mind, I fed each sliver of pain to the tiny flame of resistance in my belly.

Someday, I'd let it blaze like a torch.

Not yet. But soon.

When I nodded, Mary's face crumpled into relief. "Come on, let's go feed the chickens," she said, cocking her head and listening.

The men weren't outside shouting in the yard anymore.

Wherever they'd gone, I was glad for it.

I obediently followed Mary outside.

As we scattered the mix of scraps and weevils on the ground, Mary counted each of her babies.

I scanned the property, trying to see where Fred and Hamish had gone, but there was no sign of them.

"They'll be off hunting," Mary said as if reading my mind. "Blowing off steam. So they don't turn their guns on each other."

I sent her a side glance, trying to decide if she was making a joke, but her face stayed placid and serious.

I wondered, not for the first time, if I could bear to knock her out—even kill her—if it meant getting away.

Yes.

No.

Yes.

No.

"One of the hens is missing," she said abruptly, eyes turning wide and worried. "We need to find her. She's my favorite. Annabelle," she added so quietly I almost missed it.

The name rang a bell.

It was the same as the first baby she'd buried, I realized.

I followed behind her in a haze as she led the way through the trees, forming a trail among the scattered pine needles.

Some of the trees were already starting to turn where the cold mountain air sank low at night. The yellow leaves warned that fall was coming fast—and early.

With every step, I imagined what it would feel like to grab a heavy branch or rock and swing it at Mary's head. Could I do it if it meant I could run right now?

If I didn't hit her hard enough, she'd scream for Fred and Hamish.

If I hit her hard enough to knock her out cold, she might easily die on the spot—or be so badly injured she'd suffer and then die.

I knew how Fred tended to his so-called wife's ailments. With burning hot tea and a punch to the face if you complained about it.

"Annabelle," Mary whisper-called.

I swallowed the fire in my belly back down, keeping the flame small for now. Then I forced my eyes to comb the forest for any sign of the missing hen.

I had no idea which one was Annabelle.

But Mary did. And that alone made me doubt whether I could ever knowingly hurt—let alone kill—her.

Mary might as well be me, if I stayed here in the forest with these sociopaths for years.

No. The answer wasn't to hit Mary over the head.

Wait for your shot.

49

MILEY

We're so far from the cabin.

We're not chained together.

If we get far enough from the cabin, the men won't hear Mary scream when I run.

With every step we took past the weedy property and into the forest, the thoughts took up more space.

Was this the moment I'd been waiting for?

My mind raced. I had no idea where Hamish and Fred had gone. Mary said they'd probably gone hunting, but what if they were nearby?

I knew Fred had a scope, but even a scope couldn't see through tree trunks.

Had we been walking for five minutes? Ten? Twenty?

My mouth had gone dry. Could I find my way back to the lodge if I ran? Would I get lost, like Mary had? Would Fred find me with his scope then dig out my eye when he did?

What would Mary do if I took off through the trees and tried to outrun her? I felt sure I could. My feet had healed enough. And even though my legs were weak and wasted from all that time in chains, adrenaline would push me faster.

Would she try to tackle me? Run screaming back the way we'd come?

Would she betray me again?

I honestly had no idea. Mary was less predictable than the men.

"Annabelle," Mary called, her voice louder now that we'd traveled some distance from the cabin. She barely glanced in my direction as I followed behind her, scanning the trees. Which way would I run?

Downhill. Find a stream. Follow it.

It was the mantra Mom had taught me when we set out into the wilderness on our first adventure cross-country skiing. I was faster than everyone else, which meant I usually led the pack. But if a storm came up—or I took the wrong fork in the trail—it also meant I had the best chance of getting lost.

If you can't see the stream through the snow, look for the trees and brush flanking the shore, Mom had said. *Streams lead to rivers, rivers lead to roads. Roads lead to people.*

I would run until I found a trickle of a stream—like the ones we'd crossed on the way here. The ones that had turned my feet into caked mud that cracked and bled. Only this time, I'd follow it downhill for days until I found something. Anything.

I stopped abruptly.

There was shouting in the distance, coming from the direction of the cabin.

Hamish and Fred.

But the sounds still weren't directed at Mary and me. It was the same growling fight we'd heard through the cabin walls earlier.

They were too focused on tearing each other to shreds to even realize we were gone.

Take your shot.

"Annabelle," Mary called again. This time, her voice wavered with fear. "Help me call her!" she demanded, whirling around to face me. "If we don't find her, something else will!"

It's just a chicken, I wanted to say. *And I'd trade places with her in a heartbeat.*

I kept the retort to myself, though. We'd just passed the makeshift sign I'd seen on my first day here, announcing the property edge.

My eyes followed a game trail leading through the foliage, down a slight hill. My mind flashed back to the day I'd arrived. This was the way the men had brought me to the cabin. That was the way I should run.

Almost there. Just a little longer. If I could still hear the men fighting next to the cabin, they'd be able to hear Mary if—when—she screamed.

"Maybe she followed that game trail." I pointed to the nearly invisible path in the underbrush. "There's a stream in that direction. I remember we crossed it the day I got here." This part was true, although the stream had been so small at that point I doubted it was more than a dry wash now.

I could follow that, though. "If Annabelle wandered off, she might have been thirsty," I added.

Mary nodded vigorously. "Yes, that happened once before. One of the roosters tipped the water dish over and I didn't notice for a whole day. The girls were so thirsty."

"Come on, I bet she's just a little farther that way."

Mary shot me a grateful look, her cheeks wet with tears. "Do you really think she'll be there? I can't leave her alone out here. I can't lose another one."

She took a few steps. Then started crying so hard she had to stop walking.

I knew the tears weren't about the chicken.

I approached her carefully, warily. "What if Annabelle did run away?" I asked quietly.

"But this is her home," Mary whimpered.

"Maybe she saw what happened to the roosters," I said.

"Freddy will find her if she ran," Mary sobbed. "He can see her through the trees. He'll find her."

"He can't see her through all these trees," I said firmly, linking my arm through hers. "Look at me."

She did.

"Freddy won't find her, because he doesn't know her. He thinks she belongs to him, but she doesn't. She belongs to herself."

Mary stared at me. Maybe I was seeing what I wanted to see, but I was sure she was listening.

My heart beat faster, and I went on.

"Fred is so sure she's tame he lets her wander around free. But Annabelle surprised him, didn't she?"

Mary shook her head so hard I felt dizzy watching her. "Annabelle," she called, stumbling away from me.

I drew in a deep breath and tried to catch the sound of the men arguing back at the cabin.

Their faint voices still dipped and swelled.

I followed Mary farther down the trail, glad we were gaining speed.

Almost there.

Almost.

When the cracked mud of what had once been a snow-fed stream appeared on the ground through a stand of trees, I crouched and got ready to sprint.

And that's when I saw it.

A scrap of fabric tied to the lowest branch of a pine.

50

BRENT

Wes's ankle gave out barely a mile from the spot where I'd marked Miley's hair.

This time, there was no question he'd sprained it bad enough that walking was out of the question for at least a couple of days.

It took everything in me to loop his arm around my shoulder, sit him down on a log, let him rest, let him eat the last of the rabbit jerky we'd been saving. Everything not to scream while I set up the tent I hated more than I had words to say.

That had been three days ago.

The trail had dried up again as quickly as it had reappeared.

No more strands of hair. No more clues as to which direction I should charge.

Wes hunched his shoulders as he sat on the log and watched me fuss with the campfire, his sunken face so sad I couldn't bring myself to look back.

He ran a hand through his long beard, looking older than I would have thought possible. "Look, Brent …"

I clenched my jaw and said it for him. "I get it. You want to go back."

I heaved myself down on the log beside him and put my head in my hands.

The idea of letting Wes fight his way back through the forest alone—without a tent, completely alone—had seemed cruel before. But now that he could barely hobble at a walk, it was impossible.

If he refused to keep going, I wouldn't leave him behind.

He sighed loudly and put his hands up in surrender. "I know you can't do that. Not yet. But ankle aside, fall comes early here, dude." He gestured to the bright yellow leaves fluttering in the breeze. "And that stupid tent is no match for the winters out here. When the season ends, you go home. Everyone goes home, whether they're ready or not."

Not Miley.

When I looked at him, he held up the ragged, neon-yellow—incredibly short—hem of his T-shirt to reveal stark ribs. "I don't have a lot left to keep going," he added sadly. "And neither do you."

I drew in a long breath. He was right. My clothes were practically falling off. I didn't look any better than Wes did.

When I didn't reply, he sighed. "That's why I'm still giving you three more days. If—and this is a big *if*—you swear to me right now we'll turn around and walk out of here at that point. I'll actually be able to walk by then. You can still search, but maybe you could find us some food, too?"

I winced at the pleading look of desperation in his eyes.

I held out my hand. "Okay."

He took it, not bothering to hide the surprise on his face. "Really?"

I chewed my top lip before responding. My mustache was growing so long that it curled into my mouth. I brushed a patch of dirt off the knee of my pants. "I promise."

As the words left my mouth, a bird squawked from somewhere nearby.

Wes's mouth dropped open. "Did you hear that?"

"The bird?" I cocked my head and listened.

"That was a chicken." He hobbled to his feet and craned his neck to see into the forest.

"A chicken?" I repeated in disbelief. "What makes you think that?" I knew my wilderness noises, and I had to admit it didn't sound like any bird I recognized, but it didn't sound like a chicken to me either.

"I'm sure," he said firmly. "Our neighbors had chickens. The coop was on the other side of the fence right by my bedroom window. They make the weirdest noises when they're stressed out. And that was definitely a chicken."

Heart beating fast, I stood next to him and strained to hear.

But I didn't need to, because prancing into our camp like it'd just gotten its stage cue was a big speckled hen.

I took a step toward it, and the hen froze in its tracks.

"Go slow," Wes murmured. "Talk to it."

"Here, chicky, chicky," I cooed, crouching down.

The chicken cocked its head at me then set to scratching the dirt with its feet. But when I took another step closer, it made that same squawking noise and darted back the way it'd come.

"Slower," Wes hissed, and I turned to give him an exasperated look.

I forced myself to slow down even more, taking tiny steps as I got closer and closer to the hen.

I could practically hear Wes salivating behind me, but food was the furthest thing from my mind. Chickens didn't live in the woods. And if they did, they got eaten by something higher up the food chain pretty damn fast. The hen clearly wasn't the sharpest crayon in the box, because when I dove toward it this time, I caught it.

It made a new, frantic noise, beating its wings against my face while I held it tight.

"Come on, let's cook it," Wes exclaimed.

I walked back toward him and thrust it into his arms. "You cook it. I'm heading that way." Without waiting to hear his response, I took off running in the direction we'd heard that very first squawk.

I made it only a few yards before something made me stop so fast, my hiking boots skidded into the dirt and pine needles at my feet, creating a tiny mound.

Voices.

Branches snapping.

I froze, mind spinning, not sure whether to call out or hide.

People were headed this way.

51

MILEY

I didn't have time to wonder what the scrap of fabric meant, because I heard a loud squawking sound.

Mary was already running toward it, leaving me behind. "Annabelle!"

Was this my shot?

I watched her retreat, itching to run.

My heart pounded harder as I took a step backward. *Find a stream. Move downhill. Find a road. Find people.*

The chicken squawked again, then made a noise like I'd never heard before. Scream-crying, almost. Like it was being attacked.

"She's hurt!" Mary cried, her voice already getting lost in the forest. I couldn't see her anymore.

I tensed to run. "Goodbye, Rayna," I told her quietly, wishing this wasn't how our story ended.

Then Mary shrieked.

It wasn't a scream of despair, like she'd found the chicken bloody and flapping in the throes of death, caught by a fox or a bobcat.

That sound had been pure terror. Mary had never made that noise around Fred and Hamish. Not even when they beat her.

I hesitated again, adrenaline bellowing at me to leave her.

Not yet, a gut instinct warned, humming quietly beneath the adrenaline.

I wanted to argue with it. Ignore it. Take off through the trees and follow the dry stream bed on socked feet as fast as I could go.

The woods were silent now, but my ears echoed with the sound of that scream.

Setting my jaw, I veered away from the stream bed and cut toward the spot where I thought I'd heard her scream, bracing for what I'd find.

When I broke through a copse of aspens, yellow and flickering in the breeze, I stopped in my tracks.

There was Mary, standing in front of two men. But not Fred and Hamish.

The one closest to her turned to look at me, and I knew that shape anywhere.

Tall, with shoulders a little broader than most biathletes. Painfully skinny. Hair and beard much longer than the last time I'd seen him, and with that damn trucker hat traded for a dirty beanie.

Brent.

I gasped.

His eyes widened.

In my peripheral vision, I clocked a second skinny, bearded man sitting on a log and wrestling a chicken.

Wes, I knew suddenly. *And Annabelle.*

Everything moved in slow motion.

I couldn't get my mouth to form words.

I couldn't get my legs to move forward.

"Miles," Brent breathed, sounding as incredulous as I felt.

I watched him take in my disgusting, ill-fitting dress. My matted braid. My dirty, sock-clad feet. The yellowing, barely healed bruises on my skin.

We stared at each other in disbelief.

I wanted to run to him, but my feet still wouldn't move. All I could do was stand there, tears pooling in my eyes and streaming down my face.

"Oh god, it's you. I can't believe it's you." His voice cracked, and he closed the distance between us fast, until I felt his arms wrap around me.

Mary made a move toward the chicken.

Through the haze, I heard Wes gasp. I shifted my gaze to look at him, but his eyes weren't on me anymore.

"Rayna," he stated. Just that one word.

She didn't correct him. Just let out a stifled cry and darted forward to pluck the chicken from his arms.

I breathed in the smell of Brent. Dirt and campfire and a funk that might have made me wrinkle my nose any other day. But today, all it meant was that he'd been out here searching for me, starving his way through the wilderness until he stumbled onto Mary and that damn chicken.

I buried my face in his neck. "Brent," I repeated, like it was the only word I knew.

The moment lasted only a few seconds.

"Ruthie Sue!" Hamish's voice cut through the woods in the distance.

I recoiled like I'd been slapped.

My stomach yanked itself into a tight knot. "We have to go, we have to run, they have guns," I said to Brent in a rush, looking around wildly. Wes was standing up now, but he wasn't moving toward me and Brent. From the way he held his right leg, gingerly shifting his weight while leaning on a stick he'd picked up, I knew he was injured.

My euphoria evaporated into terror.

"I have my rifle." Brent reluctantly let go of me and made a move toward the small, orange tent.

He had no idea about the monsters headed right for us. And as far as I knew, Fred was right behind Hamish.

My brain flew through the calculations. Hamish's voice was too close. Brent was too far away from the tent. He couldn't make it to the tent in time to grab the rifle. Wes was closer, but he didn't look like he could even walk.

"Ruthie Sue! Mary!" Hamish cried out, even closer. It sounded like he was running now. If I had to guess, we had maybe fifteen seconds before he burst into the clearing.

Brent's eyes widened at the sound of the unfamiliar names and the snapping branches. We had to get out of here, *now.* "Hurry. We have to go," I stammered, darting forward and grabbing his hand. We'd have to leave the tent. Lose Hamish in the woods.

My eyes moved to Wes and Rayna.

"He's got a bad sprained ankle. He can't run." Brent's face darkened.

"Ruthie Sue!" Hamish bellowed louder.

No. No, no, no.

Mary was already walking toward his voice, holding the chicken tight. Any second now, she would scream for him. Alert him to where we were.

"Can you get back to the resort?" I asked Brent desperately. "Bring help?"

He looked at me, incredulous, but nodded.

"If they find this camp, they'll kill you—and Wes. They won't hurt me if I go back with Mary," I promised, making eye contact with her, praying to God she didn't open her mouth and scream.

She held out her hand toward me, eyes narrowing.

"Come back for me," I managed through the lump in my throat, eyes flicking to Wes who was staring at me open-mouthed, leaning against a tree for support.

Before Brent could argue, I pulled away from him and grabbed Mary's free arm that wasn't holding Annabelle.

"If you tell Hamish they're here, I will kill you the second I get the chance," I promised her through clenched teeth, dragging her toward the sound of Hamish's footfalls.

She made a small, surprised noise.

At first, I thought it was my threat.

Then I looked ahead and saw that she was staring right at Hamish.

52

MILEY

Hamish didn't ask questions.

He just cocked the rifle and pointed it past me.

The disbelieving look on his face gave away his surprise, though.

My heart thundered in my chest. I couldn't speak. Couldn't move.

He was aiming the gun directly at Brent.

"Don't you move a damn muscle," Hamish growled when Wes tried to put up his hands in surrender, then was forced to lay one back against the tree trunk for support.

My eyes cut to Mary.

Unlike the three of us, she hadn't frozen. She gave me a small frown then took another step toward Hamish.

Hamish flicked his eyes toward her, then back at me. "Who are they?"

I begged Mary not to repeat the word I was certain she'd heard me say. *Brent.*

She knew exactly who he was. The man I loved. The man I thought I'd never see again. And of course, she knew Wes.

If she told Hamish, he'd fire the gun without another thought.

Mary locked her eye with me and took another step toward Hamish but didn't speak.

"Just hikers. Campers," I blurted, finally finding my voice. "We were trying to find Annabelle—the chicken."

"Put your hands up and keep 'em up," Hamish barked.

Brent obeyed. Wes did too, teetering only a little this time.

"Sorry, man," Brent began, playing along. "We didn't know this was private property. We'll pack up our stuff and leave."

"Whole mountain's mine," Hamish spat. "So where you think you're gonna go, jackhole?"

"They'll leave us in peace if you let them go," I whispered to Hamish, trying to soothe him. "No way they can find their way back here," I added, even though I prayed to God that wasn't true.

"You keep your mouth shut, woman," Hamish snarled, keeping his gun trained on Brent and Wes.

Brent's eyes narrowed and his lips pursed. I could see him taking in the details that had rushed past when we first laid eyes on each other.

The healing bruises on my face and body.

The awful, identical dresses Mary and I wore.

The man with the gun calling me *woman.*

Brent slowly dropped his hands and clenched his fists at his sides.

Hamish grunted. "You deaf? Keep your hands up."

Keep your cool, I pleaded with Brent silently, shaking my head again. There was still a chance Hamish would let them go, if he would just calm down.

Not if Fred showed up, though.

"We'll just get packed up," Brent repeated, taking a small step back toward the camp.

As he did it, he glanced at Wes, who looked terrified and shaky. Like at any moment his ankle would give way and he'd topple over.

I wasn't sure if Brent was trying to reassure him that everything would be okay or send him a silent message. Wes was closer to the tent. Closer to Brent's rifle. If he could just make it a few yards—

Hamish didn't wait to find out what Wes might do.

It all happened so fast.

First the rifle blast, deafening as the bullet rang past.

Then the scream that ripped through my throat that I could barely hear through the ringing in my ears.

Then the expression on Wes's face as he looked down at the red liquid pouring from his belly, staining his ragged yellow T-shirt patterned with flowers.

He took a single step toward the tent—then crumpled to the ground like a rag doll, falling onto his face.

Mary gasped and dropped the chicken.

Tears dripped into my open mouth.

Wes wasn't moving.

"Hamish," I choked. "What did you do?"

Brent's hands were back in the air as he stared between me and Hamish. His face had gone white.

Hamish lowered the gun ever so slightly, like he couldn't quite believe he'd done it either.

"He's not moving," I said, covering my mouth after the words came out, trying to stifle another scream.

Seconds passed. Nobody flinched. Nobody spoke.

Hamish's face twitched. He took off his cowboy hat and rubbed his cheek, scratching his red beard.

"Well, damn, maybe I did kill him," he murmured, almost proud.

"We're with a big search party, looking for her," Brent said, nodding at me and rubbing his right eyebrow.

The eyebrow was a tell. Brent was lying. There was no search party.

I was so close to Hamish that I felt him stiffen.

I shook my head at Brent. *Stop talking.*

"They'll be here any minute," he pushed. "Especially after hearing that gunshot," he added, only stumbling a little as he felt his way around the lie.

Hamish's face twitched. This wasn't working. Brent had never been a convincing liar.

"Brent, no," I began.

It was the wrong thing to say.

Hamish sent me a stunned look. "You know this little prick's name?"

When I didn't answer, Hamish's face turned a shade of deep red that was just shy of purple. He narrowed his eyes and studied Brent.

The gaunt face. Dirty clothes. Bedraggled beard that looked just like his.

There was no organized search party. I could tell Hamish knew it.

He raised the rifle back into position.

Brent's mouth hardened into a stiff line.

The world shifted down into slow gear again as I watched Brent charge Hamish head on, the look of determination in his eyes like he was launching into a race.

Hamish didn't flinch.

He just fired.

53

BRENT

A roar of pain in my chest.

A blow to my back as I hit the ground hard.

He shot me.

My eyes blinked open long enough to see Miley shoving the man in the chest, crying, screaming.

No, Miley.

Fighting was the wrong choice.

Next thing I knew, Miley's long braid hung over me from above. Warm tears dripped onto my nose, down my own cheeks, like they belonged to both of us.

She felt around my neck, probing for a pulse, leaning down to hear the sound of my breath.

"Close your eyes," she breathed in a stern, threadbare whisper. "Be still."

Then she pushed up on her hands and turned to face the man. "You killed him," she cried, her voice so full of horror I wondered if maybe she really hadn't found a pulse. Was this what it felt like to be dead? If I stood up right now, would I leave my body behind?

The pain radiating through my body told me otherwise.

"There's no pulse," she sobbed.

I stayed perfectly still.

"Good riddance," the man with the rifle muttered.

I can't breathe, Miles.

I'm going to die.

I love you.

I found you.

I'm sorry I couldn't bring you home.

My mind raced, but I said nothing.

I listened through the thunder of blood in my ears as Miley stood up and walked past me, toward the tent. Toward Wes.

"What you doin', woman?" the man barked.

"Giving them some dignity," Miley said through her tears.

A few seconds later, she laid the aluminum blanket over my body.

Then everything went black.

54

MILEY

It took everything I had to force my lips into a tremulous smile and throw myself into Hamish's arms. "I'm sorry," I said over and over while Mary watched, silent and staring. "I was so scared. I didn't want him to take me, but I've never seen anybody die before."

His body relaxed against me ever so slightly, and I tried to hang on to that victory. He didn't seem to question Brent being dead.

A lie that might shift to truth at any time.

The tears pouring down my cheeks were real.

I refused to think about what I'd seen when I draped the sleeping bag over Wes's body. I'd leaned close to him, just like Brent. But unlike Brent, there was no pulse beneath my fingers.

Wes was unmistakably dead, shot in the stomach. A dark pool of blood seeped into the dirt where he lay face down.

I wanted to vomit.

I wanted to scream.

Instead, I let Hamish put an arm around me. I ducked my head to his chest and whimpered, trying to prove I was the tamest woman he'd ever known. After a moment, his gun dropped limp by his side.

"It's all right," I whispered into the funk of his clothing. "You did what you had to, defending us."

The words had the exact effect I'd hoped they would.

He relaxed a little more and started shaking, sweat beading from his forehead as he craned his neck and looked at the orange tent.

I made eye contact with Mary. She held my gaze. I read nothing in her big, brown eye, but I told myself she could have ratted me out long before now. Especially about the fact that I was in love with the man Hamish had just shot.

Maybe she told herself I really *didn't* want the men to take me away.

But if I had to guess, she knew the truth.

"I think we need to get Fred," I said quietly, forcing the tears back. "Even if there isn't a search party, these guys might still have friends out there in the forest. Fred will know what to do."

It was just the push Hamish needed to crumple.

"Oh god," he muttered, tearing the cowboy hat off his head and crumpling the brim into his fist.

I stayed silent, unsure if he regretted what he'd done or if he was imagining Fred's reaction to learning what he'd done. I suspected the second option.

When he turned to look at me, his face was hard again. "You did this, too," he said. "You're in just as much trouble as me. "

"You're right," I told him, knowing that, in part, he was. I'd gotten all of us into this situation.

He read the shame on my face and softened.

"Mary and I will take down the tent and clear the campsite," I offered.

Mary frowned, but Hamish nodded before she could say a word. "Yeah, good. Then go back to the cabin and get a shovel. Mary knows where they are. Then start digging. We gotta be quick. Might need to bug out."

I glanced at the fluttering yellow aspen leaves, grateful for the constant white noise that would cover the sound of Brent's breathing.

God, I hoped he was still breathing.

The aluminum blanket was shifting a little in the breeze, but as far as I could tell, Brent himself hadn't moved.

Hamish looked back in the direction of the cabin with fearful eyes, like he was expecting to see Fred burst through the trees at any second. To be honest, I was surprised he hadn't after the two gunshots.

Then again, he probably thought Hamish had shot an animal.

Good. That was good.

"He'll understand," I told Hamish gently. "Fred will help us figure things out. Is he close by?"

"Yeah," Hamish muttered, replacing his hat. "I know where he hunts. Won't be too far."

With that, he turned and ran back toward the cabin, leaving me and Mary alone.

The second he was out of sight, I sprinted over to Brent and moved the blanket to the side, terrified of what I'd see.

He blinked and released a slow, measured exhale. His face was pale, and a dark splotch of blood was getting bigger just beneath his rib cage on the right side.

I tried not to let the horror I felt show on my face. This wasn't a flesh wound. This was bad.

"Brent," I choked, pushing his hair off his sweaty forehead.

Mary hovered behind us, a few feet back.

In the back of my mind, I registered the fact that she wasn't calling for Hamish to come back, to tell him that Brent was still alive.

I turned my attention back to Brent. He was opening his mouth, trying to say something, but I put my fingers on his dry lips. "Don't try to talk."

Now that I was close to him, I could hear that his breathing was ragged, wet, gurgly.

He tapped his chest lightly, trying to tell me something.

"It's hard to breathe," I said, interpreting.

He nodded, and I winced.

"Mary, look for a first-aid kit. There's a backpack in the tent," I told her. I'd seen it when I retrieved the sleeping bag and foil blanket.

Brent nodded again. Yes. There would be something we could use to stop the flow of blood.

Was it possible the shot had somehow missed major arteries?

I held his hand as Mary flew toward the tent, doing as I asked. A few minutes later, she returned with a small box and set it at my feet.

I carefully pulled his shirt up and tried not to gasp at the sight of the bullet hole.

It was bad, but not as bad as I'd been bracing to see.

Less blood than I'd expected. No gushing, like an artery would. But the bullet had entered beneath his last rib.

I leaned in and heard a soft whistle. It'd hit his lung.

No. All signs pointed to a collapsed lung. "Keep your breathing steady," I told him sternly. "Count every single one," I added, knowing I was preaching to the choir.

The fact that he'd managed to stay so still, while conscious, under the crinkly aluminum blanket was a minor miracle in itself.

"Hand me the gauze," I barked at Mary, who obeyed without a word. Then I packed the wound as tight as I could, taped it shut to create a seal, and motioned for Mary to kneel beside me. I didn't know why she was helping me without a fight. I wasn't about to question it.

"We need to roll him onto his side. I think it'll be easier for him to breathe without the pressure on that wound," I said, hoping I was right. I wasn't a doctor. Nobody within millions of acres was a doctor.

All I could do was listen to the voice that whispered deep in my gut.

Brent made a desperate moan as we rolled him slowly onto his side, but when we repositioned him, his breathing seemed to come a little easier.

I tucked the foil blanket beneath him as best I could, trying my best not to change its position too much. Thankfully, the stiff way it tented hid the shape of Brent's body.

As I tucked the back of the blanket, I saw the exit wound in his back. No bullet left inside to fester. Also good. I patched his back up as quickly as I could with shaking fingers.

Then I looked at Mary and hesitated, unsure what to do now.

"Hamish and Freddy will come back here. See him alive," Mary said, her one eye wide with terror.

I nodded, unable to speak past the lump in my throat.

If I ran now, I felt pretty sure I could make it back to civilization one way or another.

But what would Mary do while I was gone? Would she tell the men Brent was alive? Would she try to follow me? Would she scream? I couldn't leave her with Brent. I could barely bear the idea of leaving Brent at all, even though it was the only way to help him.

All I knew was that I had to act, now.

"Hamish killed Wes," Mary whispered, still holding my gaze. "Like it was nothing."

I rushed past her without responding. I couldn't spare the time to help her process this. "Where are you going?" she asked fearfully, like she thought I was going to dart into the trees right then.

I continued ignoring her and made a beeline for the tent.

"Miley," she said.

That word finally made me look. "Getting Brent's rifle," I told her. There it was on the tent's floor, cradled in his sling, extra magazine attached. It was too big for me, but that didn't matter. I put the straps on and came out again.

"What about the search party?" she asked, looking into the woods. To my surprise, she sounded almost hopeful.

"There's no search party, Mary," I said bluntly, pulling the rifle out of the sling and adjusting the scope, checking the two magazines. Both were full.

Her face fell, but there wasn't time to deal with her back-and-forth bullshit. Not when Brent's life was on the line. Not when I held a rifle in my hands.

"My name's not Mary. It's Rayna," she said sharply, even though her voice wobbled.

That made me stop.

"Rayna," I repeated, searching her face.

She nodded firmly. "Rayna."

"Rayna right now, then Mary in five minutes?" I demanded.

She lifted her chin defiantly, and the next words out of her mouth made me want to sink to my knees in shock. "Mary is dead."

"Okay. Rayna," I confirmed, not letting the tremble in my gut work its way into my voice.

She nodded again. "I want to go home to Boise. I want to have babies and my own chickens." Fresh tears ran down her cheeks. "Wes was a good person."

My throat closed so tight I could barely speak past it. "Yes, he was," I managed.

"And that's your Brent," she said, kneeling next to him and resting one hand lightly on the foil blanket. It moved ever so slightly beneath her hand. "The one from your dream. The one you love."

"Yes," I told her without missing a beat. There was no controlling the wobble in my voice anymore. "He's the one."

I had no idea if Brent could hear us right now.

But I hoped so.

55

MILEY

"Why are we going back to the cabin?" Rayna asked fearfully, clutching the back of my dress in a vise grip, like she might lose me otherwise.

"Do you trust me?" I asked her, when we got to the end of the game trail by the sign that announced, *Protected by God and Guns.*

"Yes," she said simply.

I fixed her with a hard look. "I trust you, too," I said with slightly more conviction than I felt.

All I knew right now was that our chances of survival, of finding help for Brent as quickly as possible, would go up if we ran together.

I didn't tell her that I had no actual plan. But there was no question I had to deal with Hamish and Fred as my top priority. I couldn't run yet, knowing I'd be leaving Brent alone out there, where they'd try to bury his body—and inevitably realize that Hamish hadn't quite finished the job.

I squinted into the blue sky, trying to gauge the time. The sun was already beginning its descent toward the horizon. In a few hours, it would be fully dark. There wasn't time for any of us to mess around.

Part of me dared to hope that maybe Fred would be spooked enough by the intruders near his property that he'd bug out with Hamish—without me and Rayna. Maybe we'd show up at the cabin and find it already empty, with the bugout bags gone. Rayna hadn't returned for the shovel like Hamish asked her to, and they definitely would have noticed that by now.

I knew better, though. Fred would want to take his belongings with him. Especially when those belongings made his breakfast and scrubbed his underwear.

We kept moving toward the cabin, pushing ourselves faster even when a sharp pain in my lung paired with a side ache and a metallic taste in my mouth. I couldn't remember the last time I'd felt this way during a run, but my body wasn't used to this kind of activity. Not anymore.

I ignored the uncomfortable sensations and kept moving. Rayna gasped behind me but didn't slow down or let go of my dress.

When we reached the edge of the trees and caught the first glimpse of the cabin, I finally came to a stop.

Rayna pointed at the rifle without touching it. "Do you know how to use that?"

I nodded but didn't elaborate just how familiar I was with the weapon on my back. How many times I'd shot at targets with deadly accuracy.

Part of me still worried that Rayna might still flip if we got cornered. And I needed her to underestimate me just as badly as I needed Hamish and Fred to. Like they'd done all along.

We took a few steps closer to the clearing where the cabin perched at the top of a slight rise.

Shit.

There were supplies and gear strewn across the weeds outside the cabin. Beyond that, there was a more organized pile of stuff on a tarp.

They weren't gone yet. But they were definitely bugging out.

A flash of movement near the cabin made both of us go completely still.

It was Hamish, with an enormous duffel on his back. He turned his head and glared into the trees, clearly getting impatient that Rayna hadn't yet come back for the shovel.

I lifted the rifle to put him in my sights, finger on the trigger, just in time to watch him disappear inside the cabin.

He shouted something unintelligible.

A deeper voice shouted back.

Shit. Fred was in there with him.

"They're getting the bugout bags ready," Rayna whispered between labored breaths. I tried to calm my own heart, my own breathing, but it was far more difficult than it had ever been.

"Do you know where their bugout spot is?" I asked Rayna.

She nodded. "I've been there once. A day's hike." Her face puckered. "They'll walk right past Brent on the way there …"

She didn't have to finish the thought.

Running wasn't an option yet.

I had to do something, now, but what? Hide in the trees until they finished packing, then hope I got a clean shot on both men? Unless I managed to take down both Fred *and* Hamish, the survivor would almost certainly hunker down, take cover, and shoot back. A standoff like that could last for hours.

Brent didn't have hours.

How much longer could I bide my time, trying to avoid a penalty lap? When was the right time to take my shot and hope for the best?

The window to save Brent was closing, if it hadn't already.

The possibility of losing him—again—made my insides seize up.

An idea brewed in the back of my mind, though.

It was a longshot. It was crazy. But it was the only way out that didn't pin us in a desperate standoff against Fred and Hamish, or worse.

The chances it would work felt slim at best—and it hinged on Rayna cooperating.

The hope that Brent would survive long enough to see it through was just as slim.

But it was the best of so many bad options.

I fixed Rayna with a hard look. "Can you pretend to be Mary again?" I asked.

The way her face went pale and her lips curled into a disgusted grimace gave me the reassurance I needed.

"Mary is dead," she hissed.

I shook my head. "Mary's not dead. She's part of you. She helped you survive out here. And we need her one more time, okay?"

I watched her expression as her wide, brown eye scanned mine. "I can do it," she whispered.

God help me, I trusted her. "Good. Here's what we're going to do."

56

BRENT

I couldn't hear Miley's voice anymore.

Each breath was a struggle. Each inhale and exhale made a tell-tale liquid rattle. Was that blood in my lungs?

I lay still, pretending I was dead, wondering how long it would be a ruse.

It was easy enough. Even the tiniest movement made me want to pass out from the pain—or scream with air I didn't have.

I was so cold, even though Miley had tucked the blanket around me as best she could.

I knew it wasn't the temperature. Not yet, anyway. I was in shock. But when night came, the pain would take on a new, dark flavor.

I never thought I'd miss Wes's sharp elbows in my back and his whistling snore in the too-small orange tent.

Now, I'd give anything to have him back.

He was dead. I hadn't heard everything Miley said, but I'd heard that much.

Wes was dead.

The thought made my lungs contract, whooshing more air and a louder whistling noise.

No.

In, one, two, three, four. Out, one, two, three, four.

I opened my eyes and tried to gauge what time it was beneath the blanket that covered my face. Late afternoon. Almost dusk, if I had to guess.

I forced the image of Wes's last moments from my brain. How I told him to go for the rifle at the tent. I needed to focus on two things if I was going to make it through the night: staying warm and controlling my breath like my life depended on it.

Because it did.

I was no medical student, but I'd studied the lungs more than most people. My ability to breathe—and breathe well—was as important as my ability to ski and aim at a target.

I knew enough about lung collapse to realize that's what had happened. It wasn't a small injury. It was a death sentence if you panicked, let your pain and fear trick you into taking big, fast gasping breaths that would exacerbate the wound.

Slow in, slow out. Make the most of every inhale and exhale, I reminded myself with each passing minute. I imagined the oxygen coming into my body little by little, keeping me alive.

But I was so cold.

I drifted toward unconsciousness, felt my body start to sag in a way that would roll me onto my back again.

No.

Then I heard him.

Don't fall asleep yet. Don't talk, either, man.

Wes.

His face was in front of me, and he smiled.

You're not dead. I wasn't sure if I said the words or thought them.

His smile softened, and I realized he'd shaved that awful beard and gotten a haircut. His eyes weren't sunken and bleary anymore. He was wearing a new hoodie—and a new neon-yellow T-shirt with dandelions on the front.

Hang on, he told me gently. *She's got you.*

I opened my eyes abruptly and realized that my face was wet with tears.

I drew in another breath, shallow and steady.

Then another.

Then another.

57

MILEY

When I finished explaining my plan in a rush, Rayna stared at me, her eye wide with shock.

"You can do it," I told her. "You know you can."

The plan was gutsy bordering on stupid, but I knew in my bones it could work.

She'd already done it once before, and Fred had no reason to doubt her.

He wouldn't second-guess what Mary told him. He'd praise her for ratting me out.

"Remember, tell them you saw me running *that* way," I repeated, pointing in the direction opposite of where Brent lay dying at the wrecked campsite.

She nodded but didn't move.

"Go. Now. All you have to do is walk into the clearing and call for them," I said. "I'm going to be right here, hiding. You just need to get *both* men out here together. In front of the cabin. Tell them I ran away. I'll take the first clean shots I can get off."

Her face paled. "What if you miss and hit me instead? Do you really know how to use that thing?"

I tilted my head to the side. "I'm an Olympic biathlete. I've been shooting guns since I was thirteen. Just hold still and you'll be fine."

Her mouth made a shocked O shape. "You've won gold medals?"

I tried not to let my irritation show. "No, but if you're good enough to get to the Olympics, you're damn good. Okay? I'm damn good."

The truth of it made the fire in my chest blaze brighter. I'd never won a medal, and I'd definitely never carried the Olympic torch, but today I *was* the torch.

"What if you can't get a clean shot?" she asked in a small voice. "What if it doesn't work?"

"It'll work," I insisted, with more confidence than I felt. It had to work.

"What if Fred kills me because you ran away, like he said he would?" Rayna asked, her voice thick with fear.

"You're going to have to make them believe that you really tried to stop me."

We'd been over this. And we'd already been over the fact that it had to be Rayna, not me, as bait. They'd never believe that their Mary ran—and I didn't go with her. Plus, I was the sharpshooter.

We didn't have time to argue.

"Don't scream no matter what," I directed firmly, knowing she could hold it in. I'd seen her do it countless times. "I'm really sorry in advance."

Her eye went wide, but before she had a chance to react, I hit her hard in the face.

Like I'd hoped, she let out only a muffled grunt as blood spurted from her nose.

I winced and touched my knuckles as she staggered backward, tears already running down her cheeks.

"I'm sorry," I whispered again. My heart constricted when I thought about her walking right back to Fred and Hamish. Alone. Vulnerable. Could I really do what I promised?

Yes. This was finally, *finally* my shot.

With one last backward glance, Rayna stumbled through the trees and into the clearing by the cabin, shouting for Fred and Hamish.

I put my back against a big Douglas fir and took slow breaths to calm my heart down.

I couldn't panic now. Not if I wanted the element of surprise on my side. Both Fred and Hamish were terrifyingly good marksmen—and used to hitting moving targets.

I was a terrific shot—when it came to static targets in a controlled range. But I knew I could hit the men if Rayna could get them in the open. If I kept my breath steady, if I waited for a clear shot, if I spent my seconds wisely, I could do this.

I had to. Because I refused to let myself think about what the penalty for missing my mark would be this time.

58

MILEY

I pressed my body tighter against the trunk of the big Douglas fir and listened.

The lodgepole pines surrounding the cabin creaked in the chilly breeze, whispering a warning. The underbrush rustled, hinting at creatures seen and unseen. Some hunters. Some prey. Some both.

No footsteps. No voices.

What was taking so long?

The sky had settled into early dusk the color of a bruised plum. Still milky indigo at the edges, but shriveling fast. I had maybe an hour until it was fully dark. Already, the round moon peeping into view above the treeline felt like a spotlight, daring me to step into the open. Take my chances and run before they realized what was happening.

Not yet. This was my last shot. I knew that in my bones.

If I wasted it, we all died tonight.

I shivered hard in the thin, long-sleeved dress that rustled whenever I moved an inch. The stiff, ugly fabric should have at least kept me warm. Instead, it seemed to absorb the chill, drawing it close to my skin. The mountain air turned crisp the minute the sun slipped behind the nearest ridge. In a few hours, it would dip near freezing.

By then, I'd be gone.

Either tearing through the forest at a dead run—or just plain dead.

It took everything in me not to sink down beside the enormous tree. Close my eyes, just for a minute. But if I did that, my leg muscles would cool too much, making it so I couldn't run when it was time.

I couldn't let that happen.

This was the closest I'd been to escape since they'd brought me here. I'd imagined this moment so many times. The adrenaline, the dizzy desperation, the terror. Never the raw hesitation rooting my stocking feet to the forest floor.

I stared at the tree trunk, eyes blurring in and out of focus as I traced the pattern of the bark. *Just breathe,* I reminded myself. *Just listen. Just wait. Then run.*

In, two, three, four ... I tucked my face into the neck of my dress to hide the warm exhale, a white cloud that might easily announce my location to scanning eyes. *Out, two, three, four.*

Where were the men? What the hell was taking so long?

I squeezed my eyes shut and focused on counting my breaths to calm my pounding heart. Just a little longer.

Bam.

My eyes flew open at the sound of the cabin door, followed by footsteps.

"Ruthie Sue!" Hamish bellowed. His angry voice was distant, and I imagined him standing on the front porch. I shouldn't look. If he was staring in my direction across the clearing, he'd see the movement.

If Fred had the scope out, he'd definitely see me.

I forced down the adrenaline begging me to tear through the treeline. I breathed into my shoulder again, trying to hide that white cloud.

Fred's voice cut through the silence, a little lower, a little meaner. "Ruthie Sue!" he yelled alongside Hamish like I was a dog that would come running. "Told you she weren't tamed," he spat.

"We'll find her," Hamish said calmly.

I knew that tone. And it scared me more than if he'd raged.

Pine needles crunched beneath heavy footfalls. They were crossing the clearing, heading my way now.

I fought to keep my breaths steady and even, even as terror wrapped its hands tighter around my throat, turning the blood in my veins to ice water.

"Ruthie Sue," Fred crooned, switching tactics. "You'll die out here if you run," he added, just as sweetly.

I gritted my teeth. I'd been their pet for months, but they didn't know a thing about me.

I carefully leaned forward a few inches so I could get eyes on them. I had to know exactly where they were.

The quick glance showed familiar, unkempt beards. Heavy coats. Thick boots. Shotguns at their sides. They were maybe fifty yards away, moving fast in my direction.

If either of them looked directly at the Douglas fir, they'd see me, too.

The thinner shadow, Hamish, stopped near the water pump and whispered something I couldn't hear.

I took a step out from behind the tree.

It was now or never.

But I had to get eyes on Rayna before I took the first shot. Before I ended this once and for all.

Her voice suddenly rang out, loud and shrill. Sounding just like Mary. "She took off that way right after she hit me."

A shadow moved near the cabin.

There she was. Maybe twenty feet away from Fred.

Now.

Without wasting another second, I shifted into shooting stance and registered a clean shot at Fred.

I released my breath in a smooth exhale as I squeezed the trigger.

Bam.

He fell to the ground without so much as a moan.

I shifted the crosshairs to Hamish, expecting to trail him while he rushed to his father's side.

To my horror, he was making a mad dash back toward the cabin instead.

Back toward Rayna.

"Miley, run!" she screamed. The words had barely left her mouth when gunshots winged past me into the woods, one after another.

He was firing wildly, a hail of bullets, in my direction.

I ducked behind the tree trunk and braced until the bullets stopped, desperate to hear Rayna's voice.

There was only silence. Just a few brave cicadas starting up again in the deepening dusk.

"Where is she? How did she get a damn gun?" Hamish's voice cut through the stillness, loud and sharp.

I peered around the tree, weaseling my rifle barrel through the low branches and trying to make sense of the figures struggling near the cabin. Soon, it would be dark enough that the rifle scope would be useless.

As it was, I could just make out the pistol Hamish pointed at Rayna's head.

His other arm held her firmly in front of him. She was crying.

"Ruthie Sue," Hamish boomed. "Best come out now. Unless you want me to do to her what I did to those backpackers."

I squeezed my eyes shut. I didn't have a clean shot on him. He was hidden too well behind Rayna.

Shit.

Then an idea came to me. It was a longshot, but it was all I could think to do. I only hoped Rayna would understand what I was asking her to do half a second before Hamish.

I started singing. "Bang, bang, bang goes the farmer's gun … run, rabbit! Run, rabbit! Run, run, run."

I heard Rayna let out a little gasp. Then she grunted and spun around. *Yes.*

Hamish cried out as she kneed him in the groin then fell flat to the ground.

It was all the room I needed to squeeze the trigger again.

Pop.

But Hamish was already diving for Rayna.

He howled in pain as he miscalculated and hit the ground hard as Rayna scrambled to her feet and bolted toward the trees.

Hamish followed, hot on her trail.

Both of them ran toward me.

Yes. Hamish clutched his shooting arm. Blood seeped through the fabric of his shirt. I'd hit him. Not fatally, but it was something.

I trained my rifle on him and took another shot. Missed. He let out an ugly howl and fired at Rayna. Missed.

I squeezed off another shot at him. Missed again. He was moving too much, and it was getting darker, harder to see.

When I fired a final shot, he ducked into the brush at the edge of the trees and disappeared.

Dammit. I'd already used one magazine. I had five bullets left.

I heard Rayna's ragged breathing as she got closer to where I stood.

"Here," I whispered as quietly as I could, hoping she, but not Hamish, could hear me.

My mind spun, trying to find the words to tell her to take cover while I stalked Hamish through the dark underbrush.

To my surprise, her whispered voice was firm and clear. "I'll meet you at the camp. With our boys."

My heart constricted, and I nodded. *Our boys.* "Make sure he stays warm. Change the dressing on the wound," I choked quietly, keeping my eyes on the place I'd last seen Hamish, greedy for any sign of movement.

Rayna nodded. Then, without another word, she ducked and ran toward the edge of the property, toward the spot we'd left Brent.

I expected relief, but instead my heart seized with fear as her footsteps crunched through the trees, loud enough for Hamish to hear. Was Brent still alive? What if Hamish managed to sneak past me and follow her?

"Where'd you learn to shoot like that, Ruthie Sue?"

I kept my mouth clamped shut and squinted through the foliage. Something bobbed up and down near the treeline.

Hamish's head. Had to be. He was trying to get eyes on me.

Do that one more time.

59

MILEY

The seconds turned into minutes, each one an eternity.

I could hear Hamish rustling around in the weeds a hundred feet or so away like a damn gopher. What was he doing? All I needed was for him to pop up one more time.

Darkness was closing in. I could barely see anything through the scope now.

All I needed was one more shot.

Rayna must have reached Brent by now. Was she building a fire, changing his bandages?

Or had she found him cold and unbreathing, like Fred. Like Wes.

I blinked away the tears. They'd only blur my vision. Brent was strong. And he was counting on me.

The weeds rustled louder, grass rubbing against fabric, pine cones crunching.

Ragged breath and grunts betrayed Hamish's rough condition. He must be losing a good amount of blood from that wound.

All I could see through the scope was the clearing, darker by the second.

I listened hard. The noises he made were getting louder—but further away.

I took a few cautious steps past the tree to get a new position.

Then I saw him.

He was army crawling along the grass toward the shed and making pretty damn good time for having an injury, too.

I took aim and missed—again. *Four bullets left.* I bit my cheek, beyond frustrated with myself.

Slow down.

Before I could take another shot, Hamish popped up and slipped behind the shed in one smooth motion.

Dammit.

Now he could move along the back of the shed and make a break for the treeline in any number of directions.

He'd have a clear path to Rayna—and Brent.

I felt sick at the thought.

Moving as quietly as I could, I slipped through the trees, angling up so I'd have a better view past the shed.

There.

A shadow shuffled between the dark shape of two trees, headed uphill.

He was trying to get past me, moving in the same direction Rayna had gone.

I darted behind the nearest tree trunk. Had he seen me yet? He'd managed to grab an enormous backpack by the shed, and he looked barely human in silhouette. More like a tall, lumpy monster. He was moving so fast I wouldn't have believed it if I weren't seeing it with my own eyes.

I couldn't get a clean shot, and the scope had gone dark.

But the moon hung full and heavy overhead.

I'd just have to be quieter, faster—better than this douchebag.

Good thing I was.

But this was taking too much time. Brent's time. I had to be smart, not cocky.

Hamish and I moved further into the woods, closer to Brent's camp.

I didn't dare fire again until I knew I could hit him. Until I got a little closer. But time was running short.

That's when I saw an orange light flicker in the distance.

A small campfire.

Rayna. I pushed back a rush of tears. Did that mean Brent was still alive? Or was she just waiting for me beside his body, standing vigil, thinking I'd already killed Hamish? The thought sent cold fingers of dread snaking around my heart. I'd told her I could take care of the men as long as she did her part.

She'd done it so well.

I was the one letting her down, and she had no idea.

Hamish darted into the open for the briefest moment, moving one tree closer to the campfire.

He must have seen it, too.

My mouth went dry. Rayna would be a perfect target around that bright blaze. Hamish could sit in the darkness and take them down in two shots, like the sniper he was. Fury flared inside me.

I had to warn Rayna.

"Rayna, hide! Hamish is coming," I screamed as loud as I could.

I couldn't see her. Had no way to tell if she heard me, but I had to believe she did. *Keep Brent safe,* I wanted to add. But that would only make things worse.

"Bitch," Hamish muttered in the distance and fired in my direction.

The bullet grazed so close that I felt the splinters from the tree bark sting my cheek when the bullet exploded into the pine.

That's when the tiny speck of light in the woods disappeared as the campfire went out.

My heart soared.

Yes, Rayna.

I didn't dare peer around the tree again. He knew where I was now, and I had no doubt he'd hit me if I ran into the open. Unlike me, he had plenty of experience gunning down living things while they ran for their lives.

I kept my ears trained on the place I thought he was, listening for any evidence that he'd moved.

There was none.

The minutes ticked by.

I had to look. Had to try for another shot.

Leading with my rifle, I whipped my face around the tree trunk and back again in one smooth motion.

No Hamish.

Where was he? Had he moved closer to camp without me hearing?

My heartbeat tried to thunder past my control, but I kept it down. My breath tried to hitch, but I held it even.

Then I heard it.

Another crunch, closer toward camp. Hamish was on the move again.

No.

I swung my face around again but couldn't see a thing. Just the Frank Church, as wild as it ever would be.

60

MILEY

Finally, I heard a branch snap.

The sound made my stomach twist.

It was much further toward camp.

Was Rayna hidden? What about Brent?

Holding the rifle up in a ready position, I moved through the forest like a Navy SEAL. I stepped so carefully, slowly, tiptoeing on socked feet that kept my footsteps almost inaudible.

Where was he?

I pulled myself behind another large pine tree. When I quieted my breath, I heard a rustling in the weeds ahead.

A shadow darted out.

I nearly reacted by firing, but something in my brain screamed *no* so loudly that I didn't squeeze the trigger.

That wasn't Hamish's silhouette.

I'd barely processed the information when something that sounded like an aerosol can but louder, more violent, rocketed through the night.

Then deep, bellowing screams. Distinctly male. I might have mistaken them for an animal if I hadn't known better. Brent couldn't make those sounds in his state. They had to be coming from Hamish.

"Miley!" Rayna screamed over the sound of Hamish's anguished cries. What had she done?

I barreled toward the sound of her voice, toward the shadow dipping between the trees in the direction of camp.

A tiny white light flicked on. A headlamp across Rayna's forehead.

When she tilted her face toward the ground, I saw Hamish writhing at her feet, clawing at his face.

His pistol lay glinting a few feet away where he'd dropped it, out of reach.

The skin on his face was so red and angry that I stopped in my tracks and stared back at Rayna in disbelief. Hamish's eyes were swollen shut.

In Rayna's hand was an enormous can of bear spray.

Wes. He never would have come into this wilderness without it. The image of his wide blue eyes set above that scraggly beard flashed to the front of my mind, and my heart broke a little more for what he'd sacrificed. He'd barely known me, yet he'd been out here searching all this time. And now he was gone.

Hamish made a strangled, choking noise and Rayna sprayed him again, coughing as the acrid aerosol spray wafted back in the wind. "Shut up," she screamed, wide-eyed and panting hard in the tiny flickering headlamp.

Hamish curled into a ball and screamed louder.

"Brent," I gasped, keeping my eyes—and rifle—trained on Hamish. Beneath the pungent, stinging smell of the bear spray there was a new foul odor that told me he'd lost control of his bowels. But I wasn't about to take the chance that he might suddenly roll toward the gun a few feet away on the forest floor.

"Brent's alive," Rayna choked.

I looked at Hamish and raised the rifle to my shoulder but still didn't shoot. Firing while he was stalking through the trees to kill the people I loved was one thing. This felt like an entirely different choice.

"We have to do it," Rayna said, her voice hard, like the old Mary.

I nodded. She was right. I couldn't leave him out here with Brent while Rayna or I ran for help. That wasn't possible. Which meant I had to shoot him.

When Hamish rolled again, still wailing, Rayna bent down and snatched away his gun, then took hold of his backpack and dragged it off his body while he screamed louder, flailing like a fish out of water.

I gritted my teeth and lifted the rifle to aim it at Hamish as she stepped away from him.

"No, Ruthie Sue," Hamish clamored, bloody drool spilling from the corners of his mouth. "I love you. I'll be good to you."

I squeezed the trigger and fired one last time.

61

MILEY

I dropped to my knees and felt Brent's face carefully, hungrily, still not quite able to believe he was still breathing. "I'm here," I said, not bothering to wipe the tears dripping down my chin while I stroked the unruly beard covering his face. "I've got you."

I kissed him gently on the forehead.

His eyes flashed, and he tried to reach for me, pushing the blanket away that glared in the light of the fire Rayna had rekindled nearby.

He looked bad. His lung sounded worse, a gurgling sound creeping in with the whistle, and he'd flopped onto his back again. Rayna and I helped him roll onto his side as gently as we could and propped Hamish's giant pack behind him.

"There's a sleeping bag in the tent," she said. "I'll get it for him. There's food back at the cabin, I can get that too. I'll see if he'll take some broth. Care for him. Keep him warm. You need to go, now."

"Don't you dare die, Brent McGowen. I love you," I said fiercely. "Just breathe, okay? That's your only job. And you'd better do it like a gold medalist."

He closed his eyes and didn't respond. My throat tightened.

The fire blazed up as sparks caught kindling when Rayna added another branch.

"No. I can't do it. I can't leave him." I sent her a pleading look.

She furrowed her brow. "You're faster. *You* have to go. Now." Then she tilted her head and looked at my socked feet. "Hold on."

I watched her disappear into the forest, confused—until I realized that she was headed right back toward Hamish's body.

My stomach rolled. A few seconds later, Rayna returned with a grim, blank expression on her face—and two pairs of thick wool socks.

Then she removed the shoes from her own feet and handed them to me. They were at least two sizes too big, but with the socks, they'd fit. I'd be able to run in them.

I looked down at Brent's face, desperate to believe this wasn't the last time I'd see him.

"You'll need this, too." Rayna removed the headlamp and handed it to me.

I slipped it on numbly as she bent to unzip Hamish's bugout bag, careful not to disrupt Brent. "Good," she said, pulling out handfuls of prepackaged food. "It's expired, but you've had worse." She handed me a bottle of water from Hamish's pack. "When I went to look at Brent's wounds, he pointed me to this key."

I took it from her. It was squatty, with a little black cap on top. An ATV key. I pocketed it, not sure where they expected me to find it. "You keep this," I said, handing her Brent's rifle. "It has one more magazine."

Then I bent over Brent one more time. He blinked through half-lidded eyes. Conscious, but barely. "I love you," I told him again firmly, hoping that at least once, he'd hear me say it.

I wanted to say so much more. That I couldn't couldn't imagine living without him. That I was sorry for the time I'd wasted holding him at arm's length. That I was sorry my guilt over the car accident got tied up with my feelings for him. But there was no time for that.

His lips looked gray in the firelight.

He was already fading.

"Go," Rayna whispered, sitting beside him protectively like the mother hen she wanted so badly to be.

I ran.

62

MILEY

The dry streambed wasn't nearly as easy to follow as I'd imagined.

In the darkness, the snaking path the water had carved was difficult to see, covered in pine needles.

I managed to follow it maybe for an hour at a run, but when the moon set behind the mountains and the night turned darker, I lost it, darting down one wash then another before forcing myself to admit that I was turned around.

I was still heading downhill, but even that was difficult to gauge without another set of landmarks. The land rose and fell in dips and valleys.

I was terrified that at any moment I'd trip over a tree root and sprain my ankle—or worse.

Wes.

Brent.

Rayna.

Their names spun on repeat. I forced myself to run slower than I wanted, place my feet more carefully, keep moving in the direction I hoped would take me back to civilization.

It had taken three days to reach the cabin. But that was at a slow walk, in chains, in bare feet. Surely I'd be able to find my way out much faster than going in. And then there would be cell phones and helicopters and help. Brent just had to hold on long enough for me to make it happen.

My body churned, trying to keep up with what I demanded from it, but after a while, even the adrenaline started to cool in my veins.

I was exhausted. Hungry. Thirsty. But there was no time to stop and deal with any of those physical needs.

Every minute felt impossibly precious, each second ticking away a sliver of hope for Brent's survival. My breaths came in ragged gasps as I strained my ears for the sound of a stream I could follow.

That's when I saw it—a scrap of neon-yellow fabric tied to a tree.

It matched the ragged T-shirt Wes had been wearing when I saw him in that brief moment at camp.

The puzzle pieces clicked into place. The blue fabric I'd seen right before Rayna and I ran into Brent had matched his T-shirt.

These were markers. They'd left them to mark their way through the woods from the resort, just like I'd done with my hair.

If I was lucky, I could follow them back.

Relief exploded in my chest, so powerful it almost made me dizzy. I stumbled toward the scrap of yellow fabric, running my fingers over the rough texture of the cloth, then searching the darkness for another.

It took a few minutes, but there it was, not far from the first—a fluorescent beacon against the darkness. The sob that broke free from my lips was half relief, half desperation. The bright material practically glowed.

"Thank you, Brent. Thank you, Wes," I whispered, as if they could hear me.

The scraps were like stars guiding me home.

I moved as fast as I dared, keeping my eyes fixed for the next gleaming piece of yellow caught in my headlamp.

The markers led me steadily downhill. With every step, the forest felt like less of a labyrinth and more of a final gauntlet that would lead me back to civilization, to safety, to help, if I could just last.

My vision tunneled with exhaustion in the dark, but the scraps were just enough, reflecting what little ambient light there was left.

My hands were numb, my legs aching, and my heart pounding against my ribs like a drum, but the fabric markers didn't let me down.

My mind churned while I ran and scanned for the flashes of yellow.

How long had it been since I'd left Brent and Rayna? Two hours? Three? It felt like days. How long had it been since I'd set foot outside this forest? It felt like years. In one moment, my life had been stolen, and in the next, it had been given back to me.

I'd do anything if it meant Brent wouldn't be snatched away from me again.

As the night wore on, I stopped only when I couldn't see another fabric scrap quickly enough.

My lungs were on fire, scratching inside my body for relief, but it wasn't a good enough reason to stop. If Brent could control his breath with a collapsed lung, I could do the same with fussy, uncollapsed lungs.

More scraps of fabric. More running, until my mouth was completely dry and I started to cough. I needed to stop and take a sip of water. *Next piece of fabric,* I promised myself. *Then you can stop.*

I pushed on for ten more strips before I stopped to sip water. Instinctively, I started counting them. As if I were in a race and had just arrived at the shooting range.

I worked to slow my breath down fast in the seconds I spent drinking from the cheap plastic bottle.

I put the water back in the side pocket of the pack Rayna had given me and started running again, not feeling the least bit of pain as the straps dug into my shoulder.

It was all blackness of night, weeds, and neon-yellow stars. How much farther?

I wanted to lie down and cry. The despair of not knowing how much longer I'd have to scramble through the night until I could send help to Brent was too much.

But crying would make running more difficult, so I refused to allow the tears. I cleared my throat and picked up the pace. At some point, I knew I'd hit the wall and would feel like I could run all night. Good thing too, because if I could, I would.

I ran until the night turned gray with the approaching dawn. How much farther? How many miles? I felt like I was flying, moving much faster than I should have been able to in the too-big shoes that were rubbing my feet raw at the ankles.

The first glimmers of golden light flickered over the mountains in the east just as my headlamp reflected off something shiny in the distance.

I stopped and stared.

Water.

And not just any water, but an alpine lake. I darted closer and looked around the lake's rim incredulously.

Could this really be the same lake? Had I made it this far?

My brain refused to believe it even as my gut confirmed that yes, this was it.

Adrenaline surged, pushing me forward. I ran harder, knowing now that I had just a little more than three miles.

I could do this.

And then I came to an abrupt stop when the light illuminated something else.

An ATV.

63

MILEY

The look on Jennifer's face when I burst into her unlocked cabin at the crack of dawn was unforgettable.

She actually screamed.

"Life Flight," I gasped. "I found Rayna. Brent's been shot," I barked, not caring whether she understood me. All that mattered was getting help.

Jennifer snapped on her nightstand lamp and got out of bed in almost the same motion, pale-faced like she'd seen a ghost.

She shook her head back and forth, disbelieving. "You're alive. You're here," she managed, reaching for the landline phone on her bedside table and dialing.

I sagged with relief that she wasn't going to waste any time prodding me for details.

"We've been looking for Wes and Brent," she stuttered while she held the receiver to her ear, eyes huge. "We didn't think ..."

Wes.

I didn't have the words to tell her what had happened to him yet. I didn't have words for any of it, yet.

She snapped to attention. "Yes, hello, I need emergency services," Jennifer barked into the phone.

"Tell them we need a helicopter. Life Flight. Brent is dying," I insisted before finally sinking to the floor.

* * *

The aerial view of the Frank Church at sunrise was probably beautiful. But even up here, all I could see was pain. All I could feel was that tug of dread that we might be too late. That Brent might be gone.

There was nothing I could have done differently, but it didn't stop the terror from clinging sticky to my heart.

Jennifer had wrapped a robe around my shoulder, made me sip water, and asked me question after question while we waited for the police and Life Flight. But I was numb, both mentally and physically. So exhausted that I couldn't form words.

"The Frank Church is millions of acres wide." The pilot's voice came into my headphones. There were two of them and one of me, and I swore to god, if I had to hear someone else share that fact about the Frank Church ever again, I would slap them.

"She's got a campfire going. Look for smoke," I demanded.

"Not sure we'd see a small campfire from this far away."

I ignored him and strained my grainy eyes. I'd told the police about the trail of neon-yellow fabric, but I hoped to God we'd reach Brent and Rayna much quicker than they would on foot.

We just had to—

Then I saw it, a tiny curl of smoke through the trees. "There!" I shouted, pointing. The helicopter banked right and started making a descent.

My stomach recoiled as we flew past it, toward the clearing just visible beyond the treetops.

The cabin—and the shed—came into view.

As the chopper touched down, I stared at the body lying in the weeds.

Fred.

"Is that him?" the pilot asked, his voice grave through the static.

I shook my head. "No. That's one of the men who took me. And he's already dead."

I tried to lead the way to the property line, to the place I knew I'd see the orange tent, running even though I felt like I could barely stand. The EMTs outpaced me easily, rushing ahead as I called directions with the last of my voice.

When I stumbled through the trees, I saw Rayna.

My heart skipped faster.

"Brent," I croaked.

"He's still breathing," she cried out, tears streaming down her face.

They were the most beautiful words I'd ever heard.

EPILOGUE

MILEY

MILANO CORTINA OLYMPICS, 2026

Four Years Later

I squeezed Brent's hand, and he turned to look at me, his smile radiant. Brighter than the light of the flashing cameras and glittering snow. Brighter than the silver medals we each held for another photo op on the podium.

We'd placed second in the Mixed Medley race.

I'd made every single one of my shots. Brent had skied his ass off.

It wasn't enough for gold, but I didn't care. Not even a little.

Just the fact that I was standing here, next to him, meant everything.

It was a miracle he'd made it here at all. The headlines all shouted it in the months and years after the helicopter lifted us out of the Frank Church. *Olympic Miracle Couple,* and *From Hell to the Hillside.* And those were the tame ones. I didn't bother reading the rest. Especially not the ones that showed brushed-up photos of Fred and Hamish, praising the ingenuity of the cabin they'd hidden in the Frank Church Wilderness and the "Olympic belle" they'd captured.

It wasn't all miracles, though. Both of us still woke up with nightmares. Still woke up thrashing in the sheets, covered in sweat on the bad nights.

But never alone.

Brent's thumb grazed my gloved hand, feeling for my wedding band as we looked into the crowd.

I followed his gaze, knowing exactly who he was searching for: A woman with a neon pink parka, enormous sunglasses, a Day-Glo yellow hood, and lavender hair that peeked out from beneath it. She stood out in any crowd. Especially since I knew she'd have muscled her way to the front, iPhone at the ready, telling anybody who refused to move that she was eight months pregnant and Miley Petrowski's real-life friend—so make way.

She always looked like a flower in full bloom these days.

And she was.

"There she is," I said to Brent, leaning close to his ear and squeezing his hand.

Rayna held her iPhone above her head, already filming, just waiting for us to find her in the crowd. Waiting for us to do what we'd promised our two-year-old daughter, Jane.

My throat squeezed tight when I thought of my blonde-haired, green-eyed baby in the lodge, wearing her footie Cocomelon pajamas, sitting with Wes's mom. Waiting for Auntie Rayna to send the video of Mama and Daddy on the podium.

Brent and I lifted our fingers to our lips in unison and blew a kiss. Mouthed, *Love you.*

Rayna grinned and turned her attention to the phone screen to send the video. Then she looked back up and pulled something shiny from the front of her parka. It flashed in the sun as she held it up, too far away for me to see the details. I knew what it was, though.

A rabbit pendant, identical to the ones she'd given Brent and me right before the race.

For luck. For speed.

For the reminder that no matter what happened, we'd already won.

Author's Note

Miley Petrowski's story was inspired by real events that took place in the summer of 1984, the year I was born.

Kari Swenson grew up in rural Montana. An avid outdoorswoman and athlete, she became a trailblazer in the Olympic event of biathlon. Her tenacity and exceptional talents carved a path for other women to compete in the sport at a time when biathlon was just emerging on the world stage (and dominated by male athletes).

In 1984, at the age of twenty-three, Kari was abducted, assaulted, and ultimately left for dead by two men—a father and son—living off-grid in the Montana wilderness near Big Sky. Her friend and coworker, thirty-six-year-old Alan Goldstein, was one of the first searchers who found Kari. Her abductors shot and killed him in the rescue attempt. Kari, who was shot in the lung in the aftermath, kept her heart rate and breathing steady and controlled until more rescuers were able to find her.

Kari's athleticism, ability to remain calm in an unthinkably traumatic situation, and her grit meant that she not only survived but, as part of a long road of healing, went on to compete as a biathlete. Kari took fourth in the Oslo Norway Olympics in 1986, two years after her abduction and assault.

Her story inspired a media frenzy that romanticized and sensationalized the events as a "Seven Brides for Seven Brothers" frontier adventure instead of treating it with the compassion and solemnity it deserved. Onlookers showed up at the courtroom hoping for a photo of the father and son. Local bars held look-alike contests for "The Nichols boys." Newspapers ran articles that sympathized with the "last real mountain men."

Nothing could have been further from the truth.

While this novel was inspired by Kari's resilience and tenacity, it is a complete work of fiction. This is not Kari's story. While some details do parallel the events that took place in Montana in 1984, they are not her experiences. Kari's real-life story, with all its complexity and distinctness, is hers alone.

Kari Swenson's legacy as an athlete and survivor, her courage in the face of an unthinkable nightmare, her return to competitive biathlon, her ongoing advocacy for young athletes, and the life she has built speak to a remarkable woman. It's my hope that this novel honors the spirit of survivors everywhere.

P.S. If you scan the QR code below, it'll take you to a free bonus story called "After the Dark" (It's about Rayna!)

Acknowledgments

I couldn't have written this book without a remarkable group of people.

First of all, thank YOU for reading this book. Even my fastest readers (and some of you are *fast*) have been generous enough to share a few hours of your time with this story. *Gray After Dark* is my fifth thriller, and I still read every single review you write—whether it's on Amazon, Instagram, Meta, or TikTok. I'm always blown away by your kindness and your insights into these stories.

To Steph Nelson, Anna Gamel, Faith Gardner, Caleb Stephens, and Brett Mitchell Kent: Your support means the world to me, and your feedback is an invaluable part of my writing process. Thank you for keeping me on track and encouraging me. I'm lucky to know you.

To my husband Nate, thank you for always having my back. I like you and I love you. To Luke and Max, thank you for being proud of your mom in your teenager-nonchalant ways.

A shout-out to the crew at *My Favorite Murder* and Phoebe Judge of the *Criminal* podcast. Your portrayal of Kari's story was a masterclass in storytelling. It was refreshing to see the narrative focus where it belonged: on the protagonist's resilience and strength.

ABOUT THE AUTHOR

Noelle lives in Idaho with her husband, two sons, and two cats. When she's not plotting her next thriller, she's scaring herself with true-crime documentaries or going for a trail ride in the foothills (with her trusty pepper spray).

Gray After Dark is Noelle's fifth thriller-suspense novel. You can find her on Instagram @noelleihliauthor

*Read on for a thrilling excerpt
from Noelle W. Ihli's novel* Run on Red

"Still recovering from this heart-pounding read.
Keep your smartwatch on, because your pulse will be racing."
- Sara Ennis, author of *The Dollhouse*

RUN ON RED

A THRILLER

NOELLE W. IHLI

BESTSELLING AUTHOR OF *ASK FOR ANDREA*

1

"They're still tailgating us," I murmured, squinting into the lone pair of headlights shining through the back windshield. The sequins on my halter top caught on the lap belt, snicking like ticker tape as I shifted in the passenger seat.

"Maybe it's the Green River Killer," Laura said evenly, keeping her eyes on the road.

I snorted but kept watching as the headlights crept closer. "They caught the Green River Killer. I thought you read that blog I sent."

"It was twenty pages long. Anyway, why do I need a crime blog when I have Olivia Heath in my car?" she asked. As she slowed down to take the next hairpin turn, the watery yellow headlights behind us turned a pale orange where they mingled with our brake lights.

I ignored her and kept staring at the headlights that had been tailgating us relentlessly for miles on the dark rural highway.

Everything is fine, I chided myself. There were "No Passing" signs posted every other switchback on the narrow road, and our ancient Volvo was going ten miles under the speed limit as we chugged uphill. Of course they were tailgating us.

When I blinked, two mirror-image red spots flashed behind my eyelids. It was impossible to see the drivers—and I was getting carsick. I glared into the headlights a little longer and committed the license plate to memory: 2C GR275.

"Liv? Earth to Liv. They're probably late to the bonfire. Same as us." Laura was the Scully to my Mulder: ever the optimist, ever reasonable. Ever the one who talked me down from my imaginary ledges. But the question always tapped at the back of my mind: What if there really *was* a ledge?

"The license plate *does* say GR," I grumbled, but turned around, smoothing down my wonky sequins and drawing in a slow breath to calm my sloshing stomach.

"GR?" Laura prodded, glancing at me as we came out of the curve.

"Green River," I clarified with an exaggerated sigh. "Or Gary Ridgway, same guy. Go easy on the turns." I rested one hand out the uneven window ledge, so the cool night air hit my face in a slap that smelled like sage.

The Volvo's passenger-side window had collapsed inside the doorframe a few weeks earlier. Laura's sister Tish had talked about taping up a sheet of plastic in the hole, but since the car didn't have air conditioning, the window just stayed open. I rubbed at a smattering of goosebumps on my bare arms. I should have brought a jacket. The hills were at least twenty degrees cooler than the city, but I'd been too rushed—and too sweaty—after work to care.

The bonfire at the reservoir had started more than an hour ago, and as far as I could tell we were the only car on the road—aside from the tailgaters. Laura had waited until my shift ended at the Pie Hole to make the tedious, winding drive through the hills.

The interior of the Volvo grew brighter as the headlights edged closer. Laura glanced in the rearview mirror. When I craned my neck to do the same, she sent me a warning glare. "Stay facing forward. The only thing you need to worry about is not getting barf on Tish's car." She flicked the fuzzy dice hanging from the mirror. "I can't believe she bailed on us again tonight."

"I'm fine," I insisted, even as my stomach lurched danger-ously. I inhaled slowly through my nose to stave off the nausea. "But—"

"Breathe, Liv," she soothed. "They just want to pass us. I'll find somewhere to pull over."

"There's nowhere to pull over," I mumbled, wishing I'd gone to the library with Tish instead of "putting myself out there" tonight. "And this is definitely a no-passing zone." The isolated two-lane rural highway made me nervous, even in the daytime.

"Look, right there." Laura signaled and angled the Volvo to-ward a shallow gravel pullout carved into the hillside to our right.

The headlights stayed behind us, moving toward the same shoulder at a crawl.

"Why aren't they passing?" I demanded, even while I scold-ed myself for overreacting. I didn't trust my anxious brain to cor-rectly identify a real threat. It had steered me wrong way too many times.

As soon as the words left my lips, a vehicle with one head-light out—only the second car we'd seen since leaving city lim-its—whipped into view. It passed us from behind, going way too fast and nearly clipping the driver's side mirror of the Volvo. Once its brake lights disappeared around the next bend, the tail-gaters eased back onto the road and zipped past us as well.

Within a few seconds, the hills were dark and quiet again, except for the Volvo's idling mutter.

"See? They were just letting that idiot pass," Laura insisted triumphantly, flashing me a grin before hitting the gas and easing back onto the road. "No serial killers."

When I didn't respond, her eyes flicked toward me. "Have you heard anything from Tish?"

Shaking off the useless adrenaline rush, I sighed and reached down the front of my high-waisted denim cut-offs to open the slim traveler's pouch where I'd tucked my cell phone. Laura snickered at the sound of the zipper.

I ignored her and flipped open the phone. "You know she hasn't texted. You just wanted to see me open the magic fanny pack." I snapped the elastic of the traveler's pouch, tucked just beneath the top button of my shorts, for emphasis. "My pockets can hold half a Saltine, at most. Where the hell am I supposed to put my cell phone when I go out?"

"And your rape whistle, and your pepper spray," Laura chirped.

I rolled my eyes and laughed. "You really should read the blog."

My phone screen showed one service bar. I didn't have any new messages, but I took the opportunity to text Tish the car's license plate: 2C GR275. *Just in case.*

She wouldn't see it until she got home from the library later tonight. And even then, she wouldn't think anything of the text unless the apartment was still empty in the morning. Tish—like Laura—had come to expect the occasional license plate number— or blurry photo of some rando at the gas station who looked like a police sketch I'd seen on Twitter.

Laura shifted in the driver's seat to face me. "You know, we can turn around if you want," she offered gently, the bright white of her teeth slowly disappearing with her smile. "If you're not feeling up for the bonfire—"

"I'm good," I insisted more gruffly than I intended, avoiding her eyes. I could deal with jokes about my red-alert texts and travel pouch and rape whistle. But any hint of sympathy for the underbelly of my social anxiety … not so much.

I zipped my cell phone back into the slim travel pouch, refusing to imagine the last bar of cell service flickering out as we drove deeper into the hills. Then I reached over and turned the volume knob on the ancient boombox propped between us, where the glove box in the old Volvo used to live. It was an indestructible monstrosity, like the Volvo itself. I absolutely loved it.

"I did not wear scratchy sequins to turn around and go home," I sang off-key over Britney Spears. Laura had spent hours making this party mix, first downloading the songs, then burning them to a CD, then recording the CD onto a tape that would play in the ridiculous boombox.

Laura's smile brightened. "Atta girl."

2

The music pumping through the old boombox lasted until we approached the final turnoff onto the long dirt road that led to the reservoir.

The tape turned over with a loud click right as the Volvo clunked over a shallow pothole. When Britney's voice reemerged, it was slow and distorted, like the song had been dunked in syrup.

"Brit? Stay with us," Laura coaxed as the song subsided to a tinny whine. The boombox made a sudden, harsh buzzing noise, coughed out a burst of static, then went completely silent.

"I guess not." She laughed and wiggled the volume knob one more time.

I smiled and rested my arm on the edge of the open window, dipping my hand down, then up, then down in the breeze. *The bonfire will be fun,* I reassured myself. *You always have fun once you get there. Just stay with Laura.*

The nervous fizz deep in my stomach remained wary. I leaned out the open window a little and followed the smoky trail of the Milky Way until it disappeared behind the hillside looming to our right. The sounds of night creatures worrying among themselves took center stage in the quiet night as the Volvo slowly chugged up the incline.

A muted scratching coming from the dash suddenly broke through the geriatric drone of the engine. The seatbelt caught as I shifted in my seat, leaving a drooping curl of fabric across my chest. There it was again: a soft skittering. "Do you hear that? I swear there's something inside the dash."

Laura let go of the wheel with one hand to rap on the plastic of the dash. The sound stopped. "I think there might be something living in that hole, gnawing on the wires," she said, then shrugged as if she'd just made a comment about the weather. "Sometimes I hear that same scurrying sound while I drive. Tish said she does too. It's probably a mouse."

I looked at her in disbelief. "If I see a damn *mouse* come out of your dashboard, I am hurling myself out of the Volvo." I shuddered. "I still can't believe Tish spent money on this thing. It's amazing that it runs."

Laura shrugged again, unfazed. "She got it cheap from Tony's friend. It was like, five hundred bucks." Then she added, "The guy actually said he'd give it to her for two hundred if she threw in a blow job."

"Okay, pull the car over." I mimed gagging and grabbed the door handle.

"Olivia!" Laura shrieked and hit the brakes.

I laughed. "I'm kidding. Mostly. He actually *said* that to Tish?"

She rolled her eyes dramatically. "Yep."

"While Tish and Tony were together?"

"Uh huh."

"Gross." I sat forward in my seat, studying the sloping hills looming in the distance. If I remembered right, we were about twenty minutes away from the reservoir once we turned onto this dirt road.

"How is Tish doing, anyway?" I asked after a minute. "If I didn't see her cereal bowl in the sink, I wouldn't even know she'd been sleeping at the apartment lately."

Laura sighed. "She's okay—I think? I've hardly seen her lately either. Ever since the breakup, she's been weird."

I nodded, still half-listening for the mouse scurrying around in the dash, but Tish's drama was a welcome distraction. Tish and I were friends—but we'd never been especially close. Not like me and Laura, who had been inseparable since the seventh grade. "I thought she was definitely coming tonight," I pressed. "She even RSVPed on Facebook. Why did she stay home?"

Laura slowed the car down to skirt another pothole in the dirt road. "No idea. She texted a few minutes before you got home from work, saying she was staying at the library late." She shrugged again. "I think she just doesn't want to risk running into Tony at the bonfire."

I nodded slowly. "Do you think he'll be there? It's not really a Delta vibe."

"A Delta vibe?" Laura giggled. "You mean like, an AXE Body Spray commercial?"

I burst out laughing. "Pretty much."

Laura raised her eyebrow and smiled. "Are *you* hoping Tony will be there?"

Heat rose in my cheeks. "No way. Tish was *engaged* to him, dummy."

I'd seen plenty of photos of Tish's boyfriend—briefly fiancé—on Facebook, but I'd only really met him a couple of times. Once across the room at a party, and once on the apartment couch in passing. We didn't actually know each other. Not really.

I pictured the smiling, sun-kissed boy I'd seen on Tish's Facebook profile, wearing a Band of Horses T-shirt. He was incredibly good-looking.

Laura sighed and brushed her bangs away from her face. "It's true. He's ruined for all of us now."

"I'm surprised Tish ..." I trailed off, not totally sure how to finish that sentence. Both Laura and I had been surprised when Tish started dating Tony last year. He was what my dad would call a "big man on campus." Handsome, charming, and one of the chosen ones who had been accepted into the Delta fraternity freshman year. As much as I loved Tish, it was impossible to deny that she was Tony's polar opposite: quiet, shy, and maybe a little boring if I was being mean. Basically, she was like me. Laura had always been the designated social butterfly of our little cadre.

Laura giggled. "Hey, at least you've got *Ziggy*."

I snickered, but my stomach tightened at the mention of his name. "Stop it. We aren't discussing him tonight."

"Ziggy," which I now knew was short for "Zachariah," was the supremely awkward humanities TA who stared at me during class. Laura and I had found his Facebook profile one night and learned, to our horror and delight, that he was a member of the Pen and Quill Society: a LARPing group on campus. Ziggy was a "mage": which Laura and I had to Google. It meant he was some kind of magician.

Last week, in an effort to "put myself out there," I'd made the horrifying mistake of accepting a date with a cute guy I'd met on MySpace. His profile photo bore almost zero resemblance to the tall, painfully quiet, acne-covered senior who wrote things like "me likey" and "bomb diggity" on the margins of my papers. I didn't realize it was Ziggy until we met up for happy hour at SpaceBar that night. Things went from bad to worse when I learned he had recognized *me* from my profile photo. I'd made an excuse about a family emergency and booked it out of the bar, vowing to delete my profile the second I got back to the apartment to lick my wounds.

"Did you hear back from your professor?" Laura prodded.

I nodded slowly. Laura had convinced me to email my humanities professor about what had happened, but I still felt weird about the whole thing. "Yeah, forgot to tell you. He wrote back yesterday with a long apology about how this happened earlier in the semester to someone else. Long story short, Ziggy's not the humanities TA anymore."

Laura shot me an impressed look and took a turn in the road a little too fast. "Nice job, killer. What a creep."

I held my breath as our wheels edged toward the thin shoulder that petered off into the darkness beyond our headlights. I tugged on my seatbelt again, hoping it had been engineered to outlast the rest of the car despite its obvious fatigue. "I haven't been up to Coffee Creek in forever. How much farther is it to the reservoir?"

"Coffin Creek," Laura corrected me sternly.

I rolled my eyes. "I hate that name. Do we have to call it that? There's no coffin. Just muddy water and beer cans."

"Because it's fun. And because the freshman who went missing is buried there." She shrugged, then flashed me a wicked grin.

I sighed. "Her name is Ava Robles. And if they knew where she was buried, she wouldn't be missing, would she? If you had read *that* blog post, you'd know they never found her body."

Incoming freshman Ava Robles had gone missing near Coffin Creek three years earlier. The same year Laura and I had started at University of Idaho. I hadn't known her. Neither had Laura. We weren't on the guest list for that particular party.

Ava had been one of the few freshmen who attended the exclusive sorority party that night, at the end of Rush week. Her story had been firmly embedded in campus lore almost as soon as the news broke that she had gone missing. For weeks at the start of the semester, cops stalked sorority and frat houses to interview anyone who had attended the huge toga party.

When rumors—and a few bloggers—started to spread that her body had been dumped in Coffin Creek, the detectives even sent divers to troll the murky waters. They'd found absolutely nothing. From the blog I'd read, the police believed that the rumors might have been intentionally started as a way to throw off the investigation. It worked. And the rumors—as well as the unfortunate nickname—stuck like glue around campus ever since.

The only things they'd ever found of Ava's were her purse and phone, tossed into the sagebrush at the edge of the reservoir. They'd trolled it too, with zero success. All anyone really knew was that Ava had been at that party one minute—and the next she hadn't.

There were no traces of blood. No signs of a struggle. No witnesses who had noticed anything strange.

Everyone assumed she was dead. There was even some speculation that maybe she'd been pulled into the hills by a cougar. It wasn't likely, but it wasn't impossible. Despite the university nearby, this part of Idaho was mostly wild. The hills went on for miles and miles in all directions with sportsman's access.

I shivered. Thinking about Ava Robles was not helping my state of mind. "How much longer until we get there?" I asked.

Laura shrugged. "We'll be there in fifteen minutes, give or take. Is your stomach feeling better?"

"All good," I insisted, not counting the anxious bubbles. "But I'm freezing." I rubbed my arms, wishing again that I had brought my jacket. The last bonfire we'd attended—stoked by overeager freshmen— had burned so hot that somebody's bumper had melted by the end of the night.

"Me too, but this top looks like an old paper bag if I cover up my arms." She gestured to the high-neck cotton blouse that looked nothing like a paper bag. "I never learn. See if you can get the heater to work. Tish swore it did."

I turned my attention to the large knob next to the radio dial, cranking it all the way to the red side. It made a clicking noise, followed by a soft *pop*. "That's a no. It might be time to take the Volvo to a farm." I patted the window frame. "We love you, but you're falling apart."

Giving up on the heater, I settled against the bucket seat, reaching up to touch my hair. I'd cut it from waist-length to a trendy lob with bangs a few days earlier, and my head still felt weirdly untethered without the extra weight.

I shifted slightly to study Laura's long hair in my peripheral vision. It hung down her back and was such a pale white-blond that it seemed to glow against the gray seat. The summer before sixth grade, we'd both tried highlighting our hair with a combination of Sun-In and peroxide. Laura's hair had turned an ethereal white. My dark brown hair had turned Sunny-Delight orange in splotches I hadn't fully eradicated until eighth grade. I made a face and asked, "Was it a mistake to cut my hair?"

She smiled and tapped on the brakes as a deer's eyes glowed white near the side of the road before it bounded into the night. "Stop it right now. I keep telling you, it's gorgeous. And it makes your eyes look huge." She reached up to grab a hunk of her blond hair. "Mine feels like straw lately—how do you get yours so shiny?"

I flipped my short hair dramatically. "Thanks. It's probably from the Pie Hole. All that oil in the air—it's like pizza-scented deep conditioner."

Laura sighed loudly. "Another reason I should've taken summer semester off to get a job. I can't get over the idea that physical education is an *actual* college requirement. Are we not adults now? How am I being forced into running?"

I wound my cold hands into the soft underside of the halter top, keeping my gaze on the shoulder of the road to watch for more pairs of ghostly eyes. "Are you sure we took the right turnoff?"

I glanced at the Volvo's dash clock out of habit, even though I knew it would read 3:03 no matter how long we drove. This far into the hills, it felt like we'd been swallowed up by the night itself.

I didn't hear her response. As the dirt road crested a rise, we passed a skinny ATV trail ducking into the hills. A dark, hulking shape sat angled in the weeds like a black hole in the pale, dry grass.

A truck.

Everything is fine, I told myself firmly, channeling my inner Laura.

The moment we drove past, the truck's high beams blinked on, blazing into our rearview mirror as it roared to life and pulled behind us.

3

"It's the same car," I mumbled in disbelief.

"What? How can you tell?" Laura asked distractedly, navigating a pothole.

I squinted through the back windshield into the blinding headlights. "Same license plate: 2C GR275. I texted it to Tish earlier."

Laura shot me a look. "Liv, everything is okay. Even if it is the same car, it's fine. If they took this turnoff, they're definitely on their way to the bonfire. Maybe it's a couple that decided to mess around on the side of the road for a while." She grinned then cranked down the driver's side window, signaling for the other vehicle to pass us.

I stared at her in bewilderment as she calmly motioned out the window.

When the headlights in the rearview mirror didn't disappear after a few seconds, Laura slowed the Volvo to a crawl and motioned more dramatically, her pale skin illuminated in the foggy beams. "Go around, dumbass," she said in a soft singsong.

I quietly unzipped the travel pouch beneath my shorts and pulled out the flip phone with shaking hands. No service, as expected. And the battery had dipped to just five percent. Berating myself for not turning off roaming sooner, I quickly navigated to Settings then snapped the phone shut.

"Dick," Laura mumbled, her lips turned down in a frown. Her purple lipstick looked black in the darkness. "Why don't they turn off their brights, at least? They're blinding me. I'm going to find somewhere to pull over all the way. The road is super narrow here."

She hit the gas and brought the Volvo slowly back up to speed.

The other vehicle accelerated behind us.

"They could back off our ass a little," Laura grumbled, hunching in her seat so the glare of the headlights didn't hit her directly. "The good news is that if we get rear-ended, Tish's car won't be the one going in for repairs. It's probably been totaled for the past ten years."

The truck began flashing its brights on and off in rapid succession as if transmitting a message in Morse code.

"Give me a hot second," Laura exclaimed, tapping on the brakes as the road curved and emptied into another steep straightaway. The Volvo decelerated quickly, laboriously crawling up the incline.

"There should be—" I began as the other vehicle abruptly swerved left and pulled up alongside us on the narrow straightaway. It was so close to us that if Laura reached her hand out the window, she could have touched the passenger's side mirror.

"Who is it?" she asked, keeping her eyes glued to the road as we approached the next curve. "They're going to get plastered if they stay in the left lane and someone comes around that bend," she added lightly, as if that might be a favorable outcome.

I didn't answer right away as I stared into the darkness beyond Laura's open window. I had been secretly hoping to see someone we knew. Or at the very least, a car packed with random frat boys, their teeth flashing white as they laughed at our wide eyes. But as the truck came even with the Volvo for a brief moment, I could see the silhouettes of two men inside, facing forward. Each wore a dark-colored hoodie pulled up over his head, concealing all but the barest outline of his profile. Neither one turned to look at me.

I felt like I'd just been dunked in ice water, even though the cell phone in my hand was slippery with sweat. *This is bad,* my gut screamed. *Are you sure?* my brain fired back.

"Who is it?" Laura asked again as both vehicles crawled along in tandem. A hot trickle of adrenaline chipped away at the ice in my veins. "Do we know them or something? Maybe they recognize the Volvo. It's hard to miss."

"We don't know them," I whispered, clutching the seatbelt across my chest. Both men were still facing forward. Neither had even glanced in our direction. "Should … I call the police?" I asked shakily, hoping Laura would reassure me that the answer was *no.* That there was some reasonable and innocuous reason these men were toying with us. For all the times I'd repeated the catchphrases from my favorite bloggers—"Be vigilant, stay alive," "Screw politeness," "Stay safe, get weird," I knew deep down I'd only call 9-1-1 if I was actually in the process of being murdered.

I moved one finger to hover over the Emergency Call button, glancing between the glowing red text and the headlights. Still no service.

"I—I don't know. What do they look like?" Laura demanded. For the first time, she sounded rattled.

The truck stayed alongside us a moment longer. Then it roared ahead violently, the smell of dust and rubber filling the air as it darted past the Volvo, moved into our lane and disappeared around the approaching bend with mere inches to spare.

I shook my head, already second-guessing what I'd seen. "I—I couldn't tell very much, but I really think we should turn around. There's two guys. Neither one of them would look at me, and they were both wearing hoodies pulled all the way up over their—"

Laura gasped as we took the curve.

Red brake lights blazed just a few yards away.